BROTHERS AND SISTERS

Also by Ivy Compton-Burnett
and published by Allison & Busby

More Women Than Men
Elders and Betters
Men and Wives
Pastors and Masters

Books about Ivy Compton-Burnett
and published by Allison & Busby

Ivy and Stevie
Recollections and conversations with
Ivy Compton-Burnett and Stevie Smith
by
Kay Dick

Ivy When Young
The Early Life of I. Compton-Burnett 1884-1919
by
Hilary Spurling

BROTHERS AND SISTERS

by

IVY COMPTON-BURNETT

ALLISON & BUSBY

LONDON

First published in 1929
This edition published in 1984 by
Allison & Busby Ltd
6a Noel Street
London W1V 3RB

Copyright © 1929 by Ivy Compton-Burnett
Published by arrangement with Victor Gollancz Ltd

British Library Cataloguing in Publication Data
Compton-Burnett, I.
    Brothers and sisters
    I. Title
    823'.912[F]   PR6005.03895

ISBN 0 85031 578 6

Printed and bound in Great Britain by
Richard Clay (The Chaucer Press) Ltd, Bungay, Suffolk

CHAPTER I

ANDREW STACE WAS accustomed to say, that no man had ever despised him, and no man had ever broken him in. The omission of woman from his statement was due to his omission of her from his conception of executive life. No one disputed his assertions, though the truth of the latter had afforded satisfaction to few besides himself. He was of the class of men and women, though he would hardly have assigned himself to a class, even less a mixed one, who consider hastiness a sign of a generous heart. It was true that no man had despised him, though he would hardly have denied that he had despised many, not to say most of the men he had met, which perhaps puts the generosity of heart on the other side. Women he carefully did not despise, regarding the precaution as becoming to an Englishman and a gentleman, and not considering whether it implied a higher opinion of women or himself. It was also true that no one had broken him in, if by this he meant that all had given up effort to improve him, few had loved him, and none were at ease in his presence.

He lived in the time when the claims of birth were open and unassailed, and saw his pedigree of farming squires a ground for a feeling that vitalised his daily experience. One of the religious movements had swept him away in his youth; and a stern and simple Protestantism had mingled with his pride of race, had leavened his mind and his outlook, had given him a passionate zest for purity of life, and an eager satisfaction in the acknowledged rectitude of his own. When Andrew read prayers to his household, his spirit was that in which he surveyed his lands, of humility and authority, of arrogance and gratitude, of conviction of the worthiness of what he said and was and had. When he

5

spoke of his Maker, he spoke simply of the being who had made him—and perhaps been pleased in this case to execute one of his outstanding pieces of work. The capital letter was on his lips and in his heart. What was made was good. Andrew's native village of Moreton Edge lay at the gates of the manor house that was his home; and around lay the lands of the manor of Moreton Edge that was his heritage.

The manor house built of mellow, plum-coloured brick had its forecourt severed by a dwarf wall and black-painted iron railings from the village street. The pediment covering the front of the house was pierced by a circular window like a watching eye; as it might be the eye of Andrew brooding over his world. On the keystone of the arched doorway was cut a date in the reign of Anne, and above it the letters A. M. S., the initials of the builder of the house and his wife, Andrew and Mary Stace. Andrew sat at the head of his table, with his adopted son and his daughter, some time in the latter half of the nineteenth century, a fine old man over eighty, massive in the bone, with a high, arched nose, and full blue eyes set under a heavy brow, now passing from a late vigour into the feebleness of the last days.

"Fetch another glass, and don't fill it over the brim," he said to his servant, frowning with no less bitterness against old age, that he had taken every care to attain it. "I didn't hire you for you only to go to church and behave like a decent man. I beg you will use your eyes as well."

The second glass met the misfortune of the first, and Andrew set it hard on the table, as if to punish fate by making it overreach.

"Ah, I am a wretched old creature, spilling and shaking as if I were just out of my cradle or my grave. Just out of my grave! That is what is the matter, though I stood as steady as either of you a year ago. I don't wonder that you look at each other. I remember getting in my glance over my father, when he was younger than I am, but seeing himself go out as a burden in the same way. It has to happen at the end of a life, if the life runs to its end. It is a rough

6

time the end, rough just when we need it to be easy."

"We most of us wish to reach it," said his adopted son. "I learn that day by day. I can hardly remember your not getting what you wanted, in the twenty years I have lived with you."

"Well, it is clear now that I have it, if this is what I wanted. But twenty years, is it, you have lived with me, Christian? I shouldn't have managed that, if I hadn't lasted to be old. I have had what I wanted there. I meant to have it. I can't live only with women."

It was true that Andrew Stace had this inability; as a disability he hardly saw it; and he had discovered it to his second wife twenty years earlier, when it was clear that their daughter Sophia, a girl of five, would be her mother's only child. He had known the boy he adopted, in his orphan infancy; he had been his godfather and guardian; had named him in his own mood of the moment, thus doing what a real father does in the naming of his child; had arranged for his taking his surname; and had in all things allowed him to satisfy his longing for a son. By his first marriage he had no surviving child. On the death of his second wife he had not remarried; and his household consisted of Christian, Sophia and himself.

Christian Stace was a large, dark man of thirty, looking and seeming more, with a wide face and head, deep-set eyes, and the touch of sameness in gesture and voice to the Staces by blood, that grows from a long common life. He had a slow, strong brain and a personality felt as a support, a religious temper and no beliefs, a gentle opinion of others and a high one of himself. As a physician and a man he was becoming much beloved, a fact that called for no surprise, and from him had none.

Sophia was described as a feminine edition of her father, and Andrew would have been startled to recognise the unessential in the words. There was little need to add the feminine. His qualities had not lost in their descent. The high, arched nose, and high, arched brow, the full blue eye and short but finished build had gained; and in their feminine form made for beauty in his daughter's womanhood. Christian's eyes would have shown that this did not escape them, if Andrew had not on another matter been equal to a real parent, some bluntness of perception in family life. Other things there were in Sophia that she knew in herself; for Andrew had waived his belief in birth in his choice of his life companion and the continuer of his line. Andrew did many things in common with the men, among whom he walked, a lonely man. If he thought that qualities would hardly descend except through a male, anyhow when that male was himself, his daughter's appearance bore him out.

"Well, I must beg to differ from you," he was saying, "to differ from my children, at the age of eighty! I do not put it in another way. I say I beg to. I do not judge if there is a conclusion of the business."

"Yes, I think you do," said Christian, smiling. "You find that it is settled."

"Oh, I have dared to settle something, have I, a man of eighty choosing his words in his own house? Now no man has greater respect than I have for the work of women. I despise a man who does not respect it. He is dependent upon it. And I have much concern for the woman who has come to ease my old age for me. Some one must ease it. I need to be fussed over by women now. And all attention shall be hers while she is under my roof. Whose if not hers, when the roof is mine? And I hope she will not leave it until I am carried out from under it. But to think of her spending her spare time with us, a haberdasher's daughter, whatever it is!—useful people, useful people; we couldn't do without them—it shows a want of understanding, my dears, of what makes comfort for her and for us. Ah, I wish I could teach you all I know before I die. You won't know it until you are as old as I am, and it isn't any good to you."

Sophia leaned forward and took her father's hand. She certainly had no comfort to spare in the family group that

8

included him. Their natures collided and found no complement in each other, and she took the method of gaining his esteem, of suppression of her character, and assumption of a sprightliness not her own. Perhaps he unconsciously called for both. He never suspected her of a personality so like to his, never actually suspected her of one at all.

"Of course you are teaching us all you know," she said. "Dear Father! We love to learn it from you."

"Ah, you hoodwink me and bamboozle me, and make me out ten times as old as I am. That is what you do. And then you go behind my back, and put your heads together about all you will put through when I am gone. I remember doing it with my father. I shall soon be gone now. You will soon have your day, very soon."

Andrew had this remembrance, but he did not really suspect the same thing in his children, though he had no higher opinion of them than of himself. Perhaps he had a higher opinion of himself than of his father.

"I don't know if you are ashamed of yourself," said Sophia. "But we are ashamed of you for such a naughty speech. You know that Christian and I can't think of our lives without you."

"No, no, that may very well be. Always guided by me as you have been," said Andrew, with no thought that he might be in error. "Poor boy and girl! Poor boy and girl! You are a good girl, my dear, and good to look at too. That is a happy thing. You may well miss your father. But Christian will have an eye to you. He will be a brother to you, and see you are some proper fellow's fancy. He'll not leave you to be picked up by any sorry man, with the Stace looks as you have, and the Stace women's lively ways. You are your father's daughter, and you might do worse."

"Why, I shall get quite vain if I hear such things," said Sophia, looking away from her father, whose praise excited her.

"Well, you've more right to be vain than some poor

people," said Andrew. "You will see that the fellow who gets her takes account of it, Christian?"

"Yes, I will, sir," said Christian, raising his eyes to Sophia's.

"Ah, boy, you see what I see," said Andrew. "She is a girl to put your eyes on. Now, my dear, we have looked at you long enough. Run away and sit awhile with good Miss Patmore. No harm in that, no harm in that. She is doing her best to keep your old father for you. I am good for nothing but to make work for a woman now. Run away to the other woman. I don't always want women about."

"You don't always know when you are fortunate," said Sophia as she left the room.

"Well, I know you will have a care to her, Christian," said the old man. "The Stace looks come out best in the women. And she is not without money of her own. She will have seven hundred a year. And you will have the place, and the rest of what there is. Not that the whole is what it ought to be. The old place takes all it gives. But the old place, Christian, that has been the home of the Staces for hundreds of years! It will make a real Stace of you. This doctor's business brings you along, though I don't get to take to it much. You may leave it all safer for the one who comes next. I want him to stay on the land, Christian. I want that for your eldest son, though I shall never see him. I should like to see you married, boy, if I could bear my last days without you; but I was never one of those who don't know their own strength, which means their lack of it; that is why they don't know it. I have made my will as I chose, for all I am old, and people dictate to me as if I were young instead. I told that lawyer fellow to get straight to his business. I have done what I had to do. My time is ended; my sheaves are gathered. I go soon to stand before my Maker."

Andrew seemed to have no doubt of the quality of his sheaves, and the fitness of including his dealings with his advisers in them.

Christian was too attached to him to break his mood. "Father, I need not speak of my gratitude. That could hardly be put into words for dealings such as yours with me. It would become an ordinary thing. But I am no blood relation of yours. Your house and land must go to Sophia. What is yours is hers."

"No, it is not," said Andrew. "What is it to do with her? Moreton Edge is not for a woman. The girl will have what will keep her in comfort if she doesn't marry, and make her husband respect her if she does. What more does a woman want? What more can she do with for herself or her family? What is the use of making a woman not a woman? I have never seen it work. I will leave the place and the money to my son. I don't care what blood you are. You are the son of my life."

"But you must take into account that I am not your son by blood. You have never told me who I am, and I shall never ask you again. But I know you well enough, to be sure I am not that. What you have should pass to your own child. The world will say so, and say so justly. Sophia's husband might take your name. You could make it a condition in your will."

"I will not make it a condition in my will," said Andrew. "I will not be dictated to and told of conditions, because I am old. You forget yourself, boy. I will do things as I choose. I will have you for a son. I feel to you as a son. Never told you who you are! I have told you that you are the son of a gentleman and a woman he wanted and respected. Any man who asks for more than that is no man. I have not done so little for you, Christian, that you should hint for this other thing from me, when I have told you it is best for you and for others that you should not know. Now I look to you not to worry and wear me any longer."

"Well, you will have it as you will," said Christian. "I will leave the matter for the moment, as you wish it."

"Leave it for the moment, as I wish it! I will have it as I will, will I? Well, know that I will. Christian, I will have

II

no more of your moments, and your tutor's ways. It is enough for me that you are at the beck of any man with an ache or pain. I have not brought you up to be a parson and an usher as well. Be my son, boy; I have tried to be your father. I am not a child, if I am old, fifty years less of a child than you are. You may never gain fifty years on me. You can't come of a longer living stock. And why do you prick up your ears, when I have told you, and I tell you again, that it is right, and not only for you, that you should hear no more?"

"You said you had not done so little for me, that I should ask you for anything further. You said the words that should be mine. It is enough for me that I am your adopted son."

"Ah, you are a good boy, a good boy, a boy worth making a son of. I have made a man as well. What you have been to me! I can't live always with women. But you will look to the girl, Christian, my daughter, my only child; and see that she goes to some straight man whom you know the inside of, and who has left the things not fit for his wife behind him. You will do your best as my son, and look to my girl? Those two things I would have of you."

"Then those two things you will have from me," said Christian, "and anything else you ask. And those I can do in one, and with greater content to myself than if I had to deal with them apart. I have not spoken, for the thing is too near to my heart. But in being your son I shall do no wrong to Sophia. She is more than a sister to me. What will be mine will be hers, if she will have it so; and I find that she will."

"What, what, what?" said Andrew, sitting up and gazing at Christian. "What, boy? What do you say? Stupid, stupid boy! What do you plan for yourself? To be tied up to some one you have spent your life with, the only woman you have ever met, the only girl you have clapped your eyes on, to all purposes your own sister! So that is the life you would have for yourself and for her! I will not have it for her, my only child. I will not have her pent up in the

12

same place and the same life that have been hers from her cradle. I will have a new place for her, a new man, as is natural for a woman. I don't mean I don't think of her, because I give you the place in my will. So that is how you understand me! I make a man my heir because it is not a woman's place to do a man's business. If I wanted the girl to have the place and the land, I could leave them to her, couldn't I? Couldn't I?"

"It seemed to me natural that you should," said Christian. "But as you wished to leave them to me, I meant that I could fall in with your wish, and yet not take from Sophia what is her own, and possibly give you grandsons in your house of your own blood. But do not mistake me. My own need for Sophia came first. I were hardly the husband for her, if it did not."

"You will not marry Sophia, boy," said Andrew. "I have taught you to think well of yourself, and you have learnt the lesson. Now learn something else from me. You will not marry my daughter. When I take you for my son, I do not mean you are my fancy for all the world. Let there be an end of this between us. If there is anything in your blood that I do not want for her, there is something I will not have. I want change for both of you, for her as well as for you. You say I am used to have what I want. Then remember what you say. As for family blood, with every marriage the family blood is halved. There is no such thing as a family stock but in the pretence of fools. Family is a thing of name and place and affections. You are my son by name, and by my affections you are my son. Christian, I ask you not to harass the old age of a man who has loved you as a father, dealt with you as a son. I have done much for you, boy, though I have not said it, and would not say it, if you would let me leave it unsaid. I ask one thing of you."

"You make it hard for me, Father," said Christian. "But I should be less of your son than I am, more unworthy of your trust and your training, if I were not honest with you, loyal to Sophia, fair to myself. What I said I meant to do, I mean to do."

"You are a man, boy," muttered Andrew under his breath. But the words his son heard, were carried on a flood of wrath.

"Oh, get back to your physicking. Get back to your consulting-rooms—consulting-rooms! So people consult you, do they, and you would have me do the same?—and your stuffy leather, and your sick women, and your men who are worse. Get back to your professional pettiness, that makes you want to coop up yourself and my daughter in the atmosphere you breathed in your cradles. Get back to the rooms that I took for you, and the tables and chairs I bought for you, and the practice that came from the training I gave you, apothecary that you are! And leave me my girl. So there is something else you would take from me? And that is what was in your head, when you preached to me that I should leave all I had to Sophia, and that her husband should take my name! You wanted it both ways, did you? You want too much. Now you may sit there and drink my wine, and think of my dealings with you, while I go to fall exhausted on my bed. And tomorrow before I see you, leave my house, and without seeing Sophia; and return to it when I send for you. I have not brought you up to be unworthy of trust, and so far I will trust you."

Andrew staggered out of the room, disregarding Christian's hand, and enhancing his tendency to stumble. He did not go to fall on his bed, but walked with a firmer step to the room where Sophia was sitting with Miss Patmore. Miss Patmore was a spare young woman of Sophia's age, with a thin, sallow face, a narrow, long nose, and large, kind eyes. Her chief qualities, almost her only ones, for she was built on simple lines, were a great faithfulness, a great kindness, and a great curiosity. She looked from father to daughter with all of these.

"Well, this is a hash of a sorry business, girl," said Andrew, his tone for the problem of his daughter simply

14

petulant and tired. "You are a silly slave of a girl, to make up your mind to go and marry a man who is to all intents your brother. Go and marry! Stay and marry! Don't you want any stir-up then? Don't you want courting and house-finding and furbishing like any other woman? I have no use for a woman who isn't a woman. She can never be anything else. Whatever is the sense in it all?"

"It is Christian you must go to with that question, Father," said Sophia. "I suppose he sees the sense in it. I don't know what put it into his head."

"It was you who put it into his head. You know that better than I do. Some sight of you or some look of you, or something that wasn't either. Now see to it, that having done one thing, you do the other. See that you put it out. Because I will not have it, Sophia, and I will not say my words again. I want change for both of you, and I will have what I want. Do you take in what I say?"

"Well, I could hardly fail to, Father, or I should have even less power of comprehension than I have. But I am not the mover in the matter."

"Oh, well, well, you know that. But if you are not the mover, you can easily go on being what you are. So see to it. And as for Christian, I have had some words with him, plain enough for him to know his business. Oh, so you make big eyes, do you, Sophia? You didn't intend to pay attention to what I said? You meant to go on letting me preach, and wear myself out, old man as I am, and then to do things as if I had not spoken? Well, I know you now. I will see to it that the choice isn't yours, since you will have it that way. I am an old man, and worn out with all this coming when I am not fit for it. But I will be too much for the folly of both of you, though I have no spare strength, and you give no thought to me, and go on only thinking of the future that I shall not see. I will go to bed, Miss Patmore. With your help I will go to bed. I cannot go to bed without your help. Well, Sophia, I will worry you no more tonight."

15

"Father, stay and say good night to me," said Sophia. "Don't go and leave me like that. How can I understand you? We thought you would be glad to have our marriages making no difference for you, when they might have taken both of us out of your life. We had no idea you would see it in this spirit. Whatever did Christian say to you? We don't want a change from living here with you. We have been too happy. We had no idea that you wanted to get rid of us."

"Ah, you are a good girl," said Andrew. "Yes, kiss me, my dear, and think kindly of your father, who is wearing himself out in doing what is best for you. But I will do what I have to do. I will do it tomorrow. And I thought it was all over and done with. I thought it was. An old man doesn't often live his last days for himself."

"Now I ask you, Miss Patmore," said Sophia as the nurse returned, "what I can do more than make a simple sacrifice of myself to my father? What could any one dream he could desire, more than to have Christian, who is his world, spending his life here with him? If he thinks another woman would be a slave in his house instead of mistress in her own, he makes a mistake. 'Didn't I want a change?' Of course I want it. I am human, and I have never had it. 'Didn't I want what other women want?' What else could I think of, and be a woman? And if he is not careful, I will use my power to clutch it. Why should I wish my husband to give his attention away from me? It would be a strange eagerness. And he wants it less. When he works so hard—my father does not know what it is to work, and never thinks of the strain he puts on him—he cannot be anxious to come home and sacrifice the shred of time he has for his own life. And though my father has done all he has for him, he has got as much and more. What did it cost him to spend money on him, that he didn't have to earn, that he really took from me? And what has it meant to Christian to live with him as his son? Instead of harping on our debts to him, we should have thought of our duty to each other. My father is sparing a thought for himself, in some way of his own. That is clear. Miss Patmore, I hope you will stay with me? You won't leave me alone with my father? It sounds a strange appeal, but you can't live here and not understand it. Say that you will not forsake me."

Sophia looked very like her father as she made use of his gift of fluent speech.

"No, I will not forsake you," said Miss Patmore, her eyes on Sophia's beautiful face, and the seeds of her great faithfulness springing in her heart. "I will never desert you while you want me."

"Then you will always be with me," said Sophia, hardly guessing that she spoke the truth. "Hark! There is Christian on the stairs! I have been waiting for him to come up."

She opened the door and stood on the landing, as Christian reached it and passed her on her level. He raised his eyes and gave her a smile, but walked on, putting his hand on his lips.

"So that is how it is," said Sophia. "We must not speak to each other. I would not stoop to use absolute power like that. It shows how degrading absolute power can be." Miss Patmore in later years recalled these words of Sophia's. "I am sure I hope my father will have a good night, so that he will torment us all less tomorrow."

"Oh, I think he will," said Miss Patmore, beginning her life of service to Sophia at the cost of what happened to be indicated; in this case the truth. "He put some papers and pens by his bed, and the thought of them seemed to comfort him and help him to settle to sleep."

This thought kept Andrew awake until the hour of the morning when he summoned his daughter to his bedside. She found him propped up on pillows, his eyes very sunk and bright, and his hands dealing with the papers, feebly but without fumbling. The victory in the eyes angered Sophia, while the age in them went to her heart.

"Here, come here, girl. No, don't kiss me. We can say good morning later when our day begins. This is no good morning matter. Now I beg you will attend to me. Here is my will, a different will to any I have made. The last one that is in the lawyer's hands, leaves seven hundred a year to you, and the place and all the rest to Christian. I have made no secret of it; I will do as I will with my own. You know I don't make a man of a woman. I have taught you as much as that. This one does the same; except that it puts the whole on trust, and adds the provision: 'as long as you are not married to each other.' If you marry, you are both penniless. I need not tell you where the money goes. It need not go unless you wish it. But you know now; and I see by your face that you understand. I am giving you every chance to do well by yourself and by Christian. I don't know how much you want to do well by him. Now fetch me a couple of people to witness it."

Sophia obeyed; and her father signed the will with a shaking hand, but seeing that his writing was his own. His daughter had another pang of anger and pity as she watched him.

"Thank you, my good woman. Thank you, my good fellow. That will do very well. No, let the woman go out first. Men make way for women. And don't go chattering about what you have done up here. I had you up for my own purposes, not for yours. I know you have enough to wag your tongues over. On that point you don't need my care. Now, Sophia, take the will; yes, and glance at the main clauses of it. You have a good eye, girl, straight to the root of things as it matters to you. You are no mean woman. Now put it in that desk, and lock the desk again, and give the key into my hand. See, the key is the smallest on my chain. Now, if I die before the lawyer comes, here is the key, and there is the desk, and in it is my last will, dated and signed! I shall tell other people the same. Don't look so scared, girl. I shan't die this moment; and if I did, your head would soon be running on other things. It is, I dare say, as I am talking. So don't make a mountain out of what is a molehill to you. Not but what it is just so much. You are a decent girl. Run away, and don't carry a face as peaked as that, or you will have to find a fellow without eyes in his head to take to you."

The old man sank on his pillows, but seemed at once to be back in thought. After a time he sat up, and reached for pencil and paper. He made a draft of a letter, read it and altered it, and put it aside, and rang for Miss Patmore. He was silent and absent while he dressed, hurried his nurse, and when all was done ordered her to leave him.

He carried the letter to the table, and copied it in ink, and directed and sealed the cover. He found the key of the desk on his chain, took the will from the desk and replaced it by the letter, and sat for a moment holding the will in his hands, his head drooping forward as if his resolve or his strength were ebbing. Then he suddenly shut and locked the desk, strode to the fire and set the will on the flames, and holding it down with the poker, watched it blaze.

When Miss Patmore returned, alarmed by the smell of burning, she found him lying back in his chair.

"What, woman, what? A smell of burning? Can't a man burn a piece of paper in his own house? If a bird as much as flapped its wing, a woman would come in to know why. What is a fire for if not to destroy things? A lot would be pieced together if it were not for a fire. Take me down, girl. No, your arm is all I want. I don't want a woman to carry me. Thank you, my dear. Now send the other girl to me. I must have the paper read. As long as I am in this world I will know what is going on. It is the best preparation for the next. How I miss the boy! I did not do what I have done for my own sake. This is his day at home. But he will come back, and it will all be the same again. I can't go on long, living here only with women."

He could not go on long. He died in the early morning in his sleep, some photographs by his bed, and one of Christian in boyhood in his hand.

Christian reached home in the afternoon of the day, and Sophia ran into his arms and wept.

"Christian, I keep thinking of him, lying alone, and

19

perhaps knowing he was leaving us, and feeling that I was not good to him. I believe he was changed the last time I read the paper. He seemed too feeble to hear or speak. How I shall always remember that last time! He was so old and lonely. He was, poor old man! I keep wishing I had been kinder to him."

"We all wish that about any one who dies. But it is our life with people that counts, not our feelings when they are dead. They are to do with ourselves. You were as good a daughter to him as he was a father to you, and why should more be required of you? He did not perhaps give you the very best; but I am sure he asked no more than he gave. He was a man who never did that. And he had had fifty-five years that you have not. Time to think what he is missing when you have caught him up. May you and I do as well. Miss Patmore, come and tell my future wife, that she will be my actual one before she can think better of it."

"Oh, I have been hoping and hoping to hear that," said Miss Patmore, her face lighting up with kindness and joy in full knowledge. "And I am sure Mr. Stace would be glad if he could know it now. He was looking at the photographs of you both last night, as if he thought of you together."

"Miss Patmore has promised to stay with me," said Sophia. "We shall need some one now that Father is gone. And I want to have Miss Patmore, who was so good to Father, and who knows us all."

"Then Miss Patmore is very kind to us," said Christian, who had caught Miss Patmore's look at Sophia. "And we will do our best to be kind to her. And the longer she will stay with us, the better we shall think of her, and the more deserving we will try to be. Did you come to tell us anything, Miss Patmore?"

Miss Patmore had come to usher in a guest, who entered the room without waiting for the office. He was a thick-set, fair young man about Christian's age, a cousin of the

Staces and the doctor of the neighbourhood. He had attended old Mr. Stace in Christian's absences, and had been called in that morning on the discovery of his death. He had light eyes that seemed to serve for seeing and nothing else, a flat, vaguely-featured face with a very good-tempered expression, and a general air of a country gentleman that was encouraged by his dress. His name, Peter Bateman, seemed to fit him.

"Well, how are you, my dear Sophia? And Christian, my thoughts have been with you. I have been meaning to come in, but things prevented it. And I had planned to bring some of my roses, but I came away without them. Do you agree with me about the causes of death, Christian? Ah, we won't trouble Sophia with that. He had no pain, Sophia: he just went deeper asleep while he was sleeping. Ah, don't cry. You comfort her, Christian. She is more used to you."

"She will be further on that road by the time she has done with me," said Christian. "Why shouldn't this be the time to tell you? Can you guess how she and I are to manage to go on here together?"

"Well, now, it's strange I never thought of that," said Peter, stepping back, and seeming to try to make his eyes express surprise. "It astonishes me that it never came into my head, because it never did. But now I think of it, it seems to me an out-and-out suitable thing. It strikes me in that light. Because there won't have to be any change, and we shall have you both here amongst us as we always have. And if any two people are accustomed to each other, and have gone through trying times together—I don't mean that. You know what is in my mind, that I have nothing in it. But if any two people have, it is you two. But he was a splendid old man. I was downright proud of him as my cousin. But what I am saying, is that I am glad for you. I shall go on my way the happier. And it is a pity the poor old man couldn't live to hear it, and be cheered up by it at the last. But I dare say he did. I expect you told him, and he was the better for it."

Peter left without settling this question, and omitting the object of his visit, which had been to discuss his patient.

"I was glad you did not tell him that Father was against our marrying," said Sophia. "He would let it out all over the place, for people to cry out that we were crossing Father's wishes after his death; and there would never be an end of it. We can't help the fancies of his old age. He could not help them himself."

"No, you are right, Sophia. It is a small thing, but better not told. I shan't have to do much to help your judgment. I wonder what your father would have thought of you, if he had known you. And he had no right to impose his wishes on us. We were a good son and daughter to him. Even I who took so much from him, served him to the end of my powers."

"Shall we have to have business with lawyers and things of that sort, Christian? It seems somehow dreadful so soon after any one is dead."

"You will not have to trouble about it. We shall have the usual things to go through; but I am executor, and it won't be much. You know the will leaves Moreton Edge and most of the money to me, and seven hundred a year to you. That was not right; but I could not make your father see it, and it makes no difference. Now, Sophia, I am going to your father's room, but I will ask you not to come with me. Your life with him is at an end."

"I will do as you think best," said Sophia, walking with her arm in his to the door. "Give me dear Father's watch and chain, Christian. They are on the table by his bed. I want to take his seal from his chain and put it on yours. He would have wanted that."

Sophia stood on the landing, with her father's chain in her hand, and her other hand on his bunch of keys she had put into her dress.

She took them, and made a step towards the door, but checked herself, and went downstairs. In the library she summoned Miss Patmore.

"Miss Patmore, did you see any sign in my father's room of that document he wanted witnessed, a will or whatever it was? Because I can't remember seeing it, when we were called to him. I was too upset to notice much, but there was that smell of burning, and he never put things of that sort away."

"Oh, that is what it was!" said Miss Patmore, in a tone of relief in wonder allayed. "That is what he was burning! Because there was such a smell, that I ran to his room, and found he had been destroying papers. How he did what he wanted to do until the last! Well, I am glad to think he did. So that is what it was. I hope it doesn't matter?"

"It makes no difference," said Sophia. "His will was made a few weeks ago, in the same terms. He must have forgotten and remembered again, and wanted to cover up his lapse of memory. Poor, dear old man! Are you sure it is nowhere in the room? He might have been burning other papers."

"I am sure it was something he really wanted to burn. And the will is not among his clothes or in any of the cupboards," said Miss Patmore, unconsciously throwing light on her own character. "The desk is locked, and I have never seen a key to it. Mr. Stace never used his keys upstairs. I am glad no harm is done."

"There is no key to the desk," said Sophia. "It was not the shape for him to use, and the key somehow disappeared. Well, will you tell the servants who were witnesses, and any one else, how it all is; and ask them not to chatter? Because my father could never reconcile himself to getting uncertain and old, and we must be fair to the memory he wished to leave behind him. The lawyer has the other will, that is the same. And now you must go and rest."

Sophia remained in the library, her father's keys in her hand, and the image of the locked desk in her mind, the desk that her hand had locked, or his had locked again. At the sound of Christian's step on the stairs, she took up

23

her bunch of household keys, and linked the two rings together; and putting them into a drawer, turned to meet him.

"Well," said Christian, "the whole of our duty to your father is to take up our lives, and go forward with them, and show by putting our hearts into all of it, our faith in his real understanding. It is all we can do for him now."

Andrew Stace would not have desired it more. Five months after he was buried in the family vault, Christian and Sophia showed faith in his real understanding sufficient to do as he had forbidden them, and married and settled down at the Manor at Moreton Edge.

CHAPTER II

Sophia sat in her father's seat at the head of his table, a place where he would have been baffled to see his only child. The seat was symbolic of Sophia's position in the household. Neither in outward nor inward things had the place of the head been Christian's. From old Mr. Stace's death it had simply been Sophia's. Many things were simply Sophia's at Moreton Edge.

Sophia was a woman a year or two over fifty, like what she had been as a girl, with a deeper line between her eyebrows, and a stronger, quicker action of her limbs. A sidelong movement that was the result of a hunting fall, simply made her gait more individual, and imposed a tacit and indisputable claim. The whole of her, even her beauty, seemed intensified rather than changed.

Christian, heavy and old for five years more, sat on his wife's right hand, with a look of being contented under her guidance. He had been shaken by an illness in his middle years, and worked to the end of his strength, and was happy that his wife should be the ruling spirit of his home. He knew her little, and she knew him well, the relation between herself and her father, that seemed to her natural.

Their daughter, Christiana; Dinah, as she had come by some forgotten family process to be called, had her place at her father's side. The two chairs opposite awaited his sons. Dinah was as like her father as her mother had been to hers, with a touch of extra comeliness owed to Sophia, and more than a touch of humour that was her own. Her broad, young face, with its nervous features and deep-set eyes, was older than its age in repose. Sophia made life easy only for her husband. Sophia was a woman to whom one man was her life. For her children her love demanded more than it gave.

"Dinah, run up and call to the boys. It is tiresome of them not to be in time. I have taken the trouble to be down. I am sure I might be later than two young men. It is not for their mother and father to be waiting for them. It ought to be the other way round. And you should not be leaving your breakfast to chase about after them. No, sit down, Christian; it won't hurt Dinah to go."

Young Andrew sped out of his room, and downstairs in front of his sister, his glance of understanding, alarm, and greeting showing their relation. He was a tall young man, with eyes darker than his sister's and less deep-set, and a face that moved in a way that made a likeness between them.

"Well, I come to claim the concessions due to middle age! Late, as I ought to be. No more respect for seniors for me. I am one of them."

"Dear boy, don't be so absurd," said Sophia, lifting her face to the eldest and dearest of her children. "Twenty-five years ago today you were a tiny baby boy. I have been vexed about your letting your breakfast spoil, when I had ordered it for your birthday. And you should not keep your father and mother waiting. Dinah, just see if Robin is coming. I can't go on having to call and implore my children to come and eat the breakfast that is ready for them. It is because it is all done for them without any trouble for themselves. It would do them good to have to get it. Now, don't look harassed, Christian. There is nothing the matter really. There is Robin on the stairs. Is that Robin, Dinah? Then pass his plate, my dear, and don't sit there as if your wits were wool-gathering. You haven't had time to get sleepy yet."

Sophia had thrown herself into her father's ambition to restore the estate, and her long service to economy had given her its ways and words. Christian turned smiling eyes on his daughter, who held the same place in his life as

26

Andrew in Sophia's. His third child and second son strolled into the room, with his usual appearance of being the only member of his family at ease.

Robin Stace did not hold the first place with any one in the house, as son or brother, but his own place with each. He was a short, slight youth of twenty-two, with blue eyes and a small, sardonic face with a look of Sophia.

"Well, so it is a day of celebration," he said. "We are glad that another year of Andrew's life is gone. We go on rejoicing year by year until there is an end of Andrew. With luck I shall be in at the feast then. You have forgotten my coffee, Mother. I shan't make merry over my brother better for being thirsty. He was late too; I heard him. I hope I shall know better at his age."

"You are a silly boy," said Sophia, handing the cup, with a smile that showed that she both loved and judged this child the least.

"How would you like to be fifty-seven, my son?" said Christian.

"Well, since you ask me, not at all," said Robin. "It would be too much for me altogether."

"Oh, no, no. Hush. It is Father's age," said Sophia, as though reproving a child. "An age when people have had experience, and are not quite in the dark about things. You will find a great difference when you get there."

"I don't doubt it," said Robin. "And every shedding of light has been a shock to me so far."

"Experience is too much to the good of others," said Dinah.

"There is truth," said Christian.

"Oh, you should not talk in that way, with Father's example before you," said Sophia.

"It is the precedent of Father that makes us," said Dinah. "We have a respect for Father, though I don't think he profits too much by his experience. It is so wise of him. Experience is so misleading. It must be, as it leads to the good of others."

"You can hardly know, my dear," said Sophia. "You have not had a great deal of it."

"Dinah does not need it," said Andrew. "She is one of those people born with all knowledge."

"She must be a very wonderful person, then," said Sophia. "But my family could hardly escape intelligence, with their parents what they are."

"You think we have dodged some of our parents' qualities," said Robin.

"Well, you have, my boy," said Sophia. "If you ask me, I believe you have escaped a good many. As you get older you may see it."

"Experience seems to get worse and worse," said Dinah.

"I don't see why, my child," said Sophia. "Why should you object to realising that you are not equal to your mother? It is nothing to be surprised at."

"It needs rare people not to object to that sort of thing," said Andrew.

"And people do not exist who are not surprised at it," said Dinah.

"You ought to be more thankful for your children, Mother," said Robin.

"I don't know that I have so much cause for gratitude," said Sophia. "They think a good deal more of themselves than of me, I believe."

"Well, with your experience, that can hardly astonish you," said Dinah.

"I don't know, my dear. Many sons and daughters are different. And you three are a little too ready with your account of everything. Mere glibness does not take us far over emptiness and ignorance."

"It is true that our life is an empty one," said Dinah. "But more knowledge comes into the void. It could not exist, competing with anything else."

"No, your life is not an empty one," said Sophia. "That is a most ungrateful way to talk. It is a most luxurious, sheltered life. You know it is."

"We have had a sidelight or two on you, Mother," said Robin. "That is an extension of our experience."

"Oh, you have not used your eyes much on me, my son," said Sophia. "I think there are sides of me that you wouldn't even guess at. At least no one of you but Andrew. He understands his mother, I think."

"This seems at last a fitting way to single me out on my birthday," said Andrew. "I was thinking no difference was to be made for me at all."

"Dear boy!" said Sophia. "There is no need to make a difference for you. The difference is in you."

"Now, Sophia, flatter the young man after I am gone," said Christian. "My carriage is at the door."

"Don't hurry, dear. You have plenty of time," said Sophia, going with her uneven rustling to the hall. "Dinah, come and brush this dust off Father's coat. Don't do it as if you had no strength in your arms. I am afraid I am letting you grow up lazy. Give it to me; I will do it; I have to do most things, it seems to me. Boys, come and help Father on with his coat. We are not tall enough, we poor women. No, not you, Robin. You have not finished your breakfast. You, Andrew. Hurry up, dear boy. You are such slow children. Now, all go back to the dining-room, and let Father and me have a minute to ourselves."

Sophia had her minute, changed her bearing, and returned to the dining-room.

"My dears, I have something to say to you, that I must say for your own sakes and mine. I don't think it right of you, or fair to me, for you all to join forces and argue with me as if I were one of yourselves. Here am I with everything on me, all the strain of the house, and the anxiety about Father, who I know is working harder than he ought; and here are you, with nothing on your minds but your own concerns, banding together and baiting me as if I were just a person to be put right about everything! I didn't say this before Father, for fear of upsetting his work for the day. And I don't think I ought to have to say it to you, grown up people, with every opportunity to know what is right and wrong. Now, will you see that nothing of that kind happens again?"

They were silent.

"Well, you are not dumb, all of you," said Sophia.

"No, we are not so unlike you as that," said Robin.

"And you grant us more experience than you did," said Dinah.

"Now, there is no need to talk in that way," said Sophia; "to be silly and self-important because your mother tells you something for your own good. You don't want to be allowed to grow up with no knowledge of what is done and not done, do you, so that you make yourselves look foolish everywhere? Because you all contrived to appear so at breakfast this morning. Or is that what you all want?"

"Well, put in other words, I am not sure it isn't," said Dinah.

"Now, go upstairs, all of you," said Sophia, half laughing, "and keep out of the way for the morning, because you would be of no help. And mind that you get a walk before lunch. You are not to mope over your work after twelve. Dinah, you remember to remind the boys. Do you hear me, my dear? You stand there as if you couldn't comprehend. Now run upstairs, all three of you."

The three of them ran upstairs. Their occupations were established. Andrew, as a matter of his parents' filial duty rather than his own desire, had followed his grandfather's wish and stayed on the land; that is, remained at home at the command of his mother, supposedly engaged on writing of his own, to save him from the stigma of idleness. The contrast between his lot and his father's was too dubiously accepted, for his life to be one of ease.

Dinah lived under the same conditions, except that she was not held to share the duties on the land, which were shadowy and performed by either Christian or Sophia. Her freedom from domestic claims as opposed to her mother's service to them took the place of Andrew's leisure as against his father's toil, and gave them, as she said, all things in common.

Robin, who was granted the need for a livelihood, was about to leave Oxford for a government office routine, and was to have the compensation of a London life for the sacrifice of any talents that might be his. The reason why Andrew and Dinah were supposed to have literary gifts was among the things that their parents had not sought, unless they found it in the Stace fluency in words.

The household had little but formal intercourse with the country houses round. Sophia planned all matters for her family and herself; and Sophia had her life in her husband, and her interest in her father's ambition to reclaim his lands. These things that were enough for her, were to suffice her children. The few conventional social duties were their dissipations and her own. Their daily society was bounded by the people who dwelt at their gates. It hardly came to their mother's mind that difference in age and outlook demanded other difference. Seeing them, as she honestly saw them, as free of the constraint that had hampered her own youth, she held them fortunate. It was an outcome of her own enclosed experience, that she assumed that human lives must simply mark their own course.

The brothers and sister paused on the first half-landing out of their mother's sight, and Andrew surveyed a portrait of his grandfather.

The portrait was hung in the light, and had gained the dignity of the defacement of sun-cracked paint. It was executed by a hand unknown, though the artist had himself considered his initials, put in certainly with a distinguishing boldness, an adequate identification. It had the moving and menacing likeness, that is given especially by successful portraits that are worthless as works of art. From his own eyes did the elder Andrew look down on these descendants, who bore the signs of his blood.

"Well, old man," said Andrew, "so your choice of a

subject was yourself! There would have been better stuff for the painter in Sophia."

The three referred to their mother as Sophia, when not in her hearing.

"And enough of the same stuff," said Dinah. "He was perpetuated enough. Don't ask me to look at him."

"I am not asking it," said Andrew. "There are some sights not fit for a woman."

"Then the sight is not fit for either of you," said Robin. "To hear you use your tongue, Andrew! You are less of a man than Sophia."

"But quite enough of a man," said Dinah.

"Dinah and I are of the stuff that martyrs are made of," said Andrew.

"You are more than that. You are martyrs," said Robin. "The weak part of martyrdom is, that it is so bad for other people."

"I admit it brings out all that is worst in Sophia," said Dinah.

"And I bring out the best in her. You must notice that," said Robin.

"Yes," said Dinah. "It needs a very low person to bring out the best in others. I never thought martyrs were useful."

"The highest things seldom are," said Andrew. "You would not have us as low as Robin?"

"No, but perhaps a little lower," said Dinah. "We are very high."

"What passes me is, how Father has never got to know Sophia," said Robin. "Day after day, year after year it goes on under his eyes, and he never sees it."

"Not under his eyes, just away from them," said Dinah. "Don't you see how Sophia is on her guard?"

"Yes. Her cunning is on the scale of the rest of her," said Andrew.

"I always have doubts about Sophia's scale," said Robin. "I think she is rather a small, weak person in many ways. It is known that I am a little like her. Now Father is on a more considerable scale, though I often think his simplicity is the most appreciable thing about him."

"You give way to thought," said Dinah. "There is Sophia, calling to us not to lag and loaf and chatter. Three unlawful things is a large proportion for so early in the day. Sophia is reasonably struck by it."

On the second landing they turned with one accord to a half-open door. Miss Patmore had been their nurse and nearly their mother in childhood, and they had for her much of the feeling that might have been Sophia's. She was sewing by the window, a spare little, middle-aged woman, with her large, kind eyes and questioning nose much as they had been in her youth.

"Well, how is it all going today?"

"Not too well, Patty," said Andrew.

"There has been a coldness over our being late for breakfast," said Robin, "as if to be in time were the natural thing; a disturbance over Father's coat; and quite grave trouble about our banding together and baiting Sophia."

"Which we had the courage to do," said Dinah.

"And the usual extra touch of strife with me," said Robin. "Most of it hidden from Father, of course."

"And now judgment passed on our pausing to have a word together on the landing," said Dinah. "As though it were not a happy condition for a family to be on speaking terms!"

"Dear, dear, dear!" said Patty, her tone betraying how far her feeling had passed from Sophia to Sophia's children. "What about all that is to happen today?"

"Surely you know, Patty, that it is my birthday," said Andrew, "that twenty-five years ago today I was a tiny baby boy. I wish you would not be without heart. So Cousin Peter and Tilly and Latimer are coming to tea, and the Wakes and Drydens to dinner, to make my birthday a bright one."

"I suppose the Wakes and Drydens are supposed to feel it more," said Dinah; "though of course to him that hath

33

shall more be given. It shall by Sophia. And Cousin Peter really hath not enough."

"Father is hurrying home from the day's work I have never done," said Andrew. "I have been kept in idleness for twenty-five years, to have this heaped upon me."

"What a pity it all is!" said Patty. "You can't help any of it. Here is all this trouble and expense, and then, when you might have the pleasure, everything spoilt for you! I don't suppose you remember a birthday you enjoyed. But we must not talk like this."

"Indeed we must," said Dinah. "It must be the manner of our morning chat."

"Let us drop these echoes from the days before Sophia had overstepped the bound," said Robin.

"No. Everything is due to Patty," said Andrew. "Don't bring out your standard for her, Robin."

"Robin has one great thing to be thankful for," said Dinah, "his standard."

"Well, it never used to be like this," said Patty. "Hark! Is that Mother calling? Stop fidgeting, Robin, so that I can listen. Yes, it is Mother. Ought you all to be in here? Yes, Mrs. Stace!"

She got to her feet as Sophia entered, with a rustling of her garments that boded ill.

"Well, really, Miss Patmore, here have I been calling on the stairs, until I felt I should faint, or catch cold with the draught! I believe I have got a chill, and in that case how vexed my husband will be! And I can't make a soul hear, any more than if I were on a desert island, instead of in a house run for every one with every luxury. I don't know what things are coming to, when I can't claim a little attention in my own house. How am I to get on with my work of organising everything, if I am to be left entirely without help? Whatever are you all doing, that no one can hear me when I stand and shout myself hoarse? I don't know what Father would say to it."

"We were having a talk with Patty. We came in to say

good morning to her," said Robin. "Father ought to say that you had better come upstairs, than faint or catch cold, or even shout yourself hoarse."

"Both as a man and a physician," said Dinah. "And you might ring a bell and send a message, in a house run with every luxury."

"Now, now, none of those answers," said Sophia; "I am getting tired of them. I shall have to make you ashamed by reminding you that I am not as able-bodied as you are. And anyhow it is not suitable for your mother to be running up and down after people. You know that, and you know that Father would say so. And as for ringing bells, I don't summon servants as readily as you do, it seems. I don't know where you get your ideas from. It would do you good to earn a little of the luxury you take for granted. And what are you all doing in here? It is very nice to come and see Patty: but there is no reason why you should spoil her morning, and spoil yours, is there?"

"No, Mother," said Andrew and Dinah, seeing that response would be waited for.

"Now, Miss Patmore," said Sophia, in a milder tone, "I want you to be downstairs today, just to be about, not to help with anything—you can take your needlework—while I go and get a little ready for the afternoon. The servants work better when somebody is there. And you three, get to your study. How often am I to say it? Why should you waste a day because it is a birthday? Father is not doing that. No one else in the house is going to be idle."

Sophia and Patty went downstairs, discussing the questions of the day. In a way there was a close understanding between them. Patty had a trace of her old feeling for Sophia, and Sophia depended on Patty, and had never suspected in her a power of judging herself.

The three went into the room that had been their mother's nursery and their own, and had of late, as a study, been seen as a great advantage to them.

" 'Yes, Mother. Yes, Mother.' What an abuse of

the gift of speech! I should be ashamed," said Robin.

"You would," said Andrew. "Of your first victory over yourself."

"It may be a thing to be ashamed of," said Dinah.

"I hope it will never happen to me," said Robin.

"We see that rare thing, human hope on a solid basis," said Andrew.

"I hesitate to wound Robin," said Dinah, "but I admit that I admire his character."

"I am getting broken on the wheel here," said Robin. "I shall be thankful to get to London."

"We realise what a dreadful thing goodness must seem on the verge of London," said Dinah. "Of course it is a dreadful thing. Andrew and I know it."

"The problem is, whether Patty will stand things much longer," said Robin. "She has a home."

"Well, that is not always an allurement, as you find," said Dinah. "I can't think how you can put such things into words. It is a happy thing you have no religion; you would talk about it. I did not mean that your goodness would help you to understand a goodness of Patty's quality."

"Dinah and I are that greatest of all things, master of ourselves," said Andrew.

"Or slaves to Sophia," said Robin.

"Well, that is the greatest of all things," said Dinah.

"I am sure it is," said Robin.

"So am I," said Dinah. "There is Sophia! I am indeed sure of it."

"Let me get into my seat," said Andrew, "and not be idling away my morning. Am I master of myself or slave to Sophia?"

The three were sitting at the table when their mother appeared. Her toilet, a momentous matter to her household, had prospered. She looked bright and kind.

"Well, my three dear ones! Well, my birthday boy! Twenty-five years ago today, how proud I was of him, and how pleased Father was! And my Dinah is looking pale. She must not work too hard. You must not let her, boys. And my baby boy is rather spoilt sometimes. But babies are forgiven a great deal, aren't they?"

She passed her hand over her children's hair, and they looked up at her and smiled. It had not occurred to them or to her, that they might not adapt their moods to hers.

"Now, remember, all of you," she said at luncheon, "I don't want Cousin Peter and Tilly and Latimer to stay for dinner. They are coming to tea, and that is enough. The evening will be better with just the Wakes and the Drydens and you. You make a nice party, and Father will enjoy watching you. Tilly and Latimer bring in quite another atmosphere. It is no good pretending to be blind to it. And it is trying for Father to have to talk to Cousin Peter. Not that we are not fond of him; but he will be with us this afternoon." Sophia laughed as she caught the young eyes. "And we have to be sensible, and not think only of ourselves. So no one is to suggest their staying, because they always accept if they are asked."

"Abusing generosity in that way!" said Dinah. "It is safer to give up kindness. It only gets taken advantage of."

"The trouble will be to ask them to go," said Robin.

"We have been faced by this before," said Andrew. "Cousin Peter apparently part of his chair, and festivities ensuing, from which any fitness in things debars him!"

"You are silly children," said Sophia. "You can quite well say some little word that would be enough. It is easy for people to do these things, who know how to manage them. It depends on the quality of the person. You seem to me not to have any knowledge of anything."

"This is a difficult point in our training," said Dinah. "And it is the quality of Cousin Peter that is the matter. How does one say some little word? 'Go' would be that; but we have to think of what is due to ourselves as well as to Cousin Peter."

"Now, now, I don't mean you are to talk like this about people who are much older than you are, because

37

I take you into my confidence, and tell you I cannot manage more than a certain number at my table. I am afraid I told you other things that you are not advanced enough to understand, though I was quite up to them at your age. We are already a large party. There are people to be considered besides ourselves. You must not annoy your mother, when she is taking so much trouble for you. Do you see that I have no salad? You have all taken it a second time yourselves. Thank you, Dinah dear. Now remember that the Batemans are not to stay. They are coming at four; so they will have been here a long time if they go about seven."

The Batemans came at four, or more exactly at a few minutes before that hour.

Peter Bateman had no change to show for twenty-six years, except that he looked about twelve years older. In more intimate things, he had married, had a daughter and son, become a widower, and remained one for eleven years. His children had more to offer: themselves, two small, spare, open-eyed young people, aged twenty-two and nineteen, with a social vagueness over which the girl was unquestioning and the boy uneasy; and something stunted and strange about them, of which they and their father were alone unaware. The girl had been called Matilda after her mother, and the boy Latimer, because it was a family name, though no one knew in what way it was this, or wished to know.

Peter Bateman was a poor man, and happy in his poverty, had been able to afford his children little education, and seemed content with this too. Matilda, the elder, acted as his housekeeper; his little housekeeper he called her, to invest the routine with some rosiness for her; and Latimer was "going into business soon," a prospect for which he had no discovered talent, and no training, and at the moment no opportunity, but with which his father seemed also satisfied.

"Well, my dear Sophia!" said Peter. "So here you are,

standing here with your sons, in the room where you stood on your wedding-day! I remember it as if it were yesterday. Ah, she was a woman to be proud of, your mother, children, in the days before you knew her. And so she is now. That goes without saying. Well, I wish my children had their mother to look after them, and plan parties for them. Well now, Andrew, you are twenty-five today, and the eldest son and the hope of the house. And worthy to be it. We all agree that you are. Tilly and Latimer, come and say to your cousin that you congratulate him."

"We say to you that we congratulate you, Andrew," said Latimer, with the elfish grin that was not accounted for by his father any more than anything else about him.

"Yes, we do. I wish it was us who had a party," said Tilly, who was an almost startling example of failure to rise above a lack of advantages.

"Come and sit down, and have some tea, dear," said Sophia. "You are your father's little housekeeper, and no one wants you to be more than that."

"No, but I should like it for myself," said Tilly. "Nobody does ever wish for other people what they want for themselves, do they?"

"Yes, yes, Father does," said Peter, just articulating his words.

"Now, choose your places, all of you," said Sophia. "Come and be useful, my two great sons. Dinah, let the boys wait on you and Tilly. No, not you, Latimer. You are the guest. They must not let you do any work."

"No. I will have a rest before I go into business," said Latimer.

The young Staces laughed; Latimer looked out of the window; and Peter twirled his moustache with what was for him a touch of moodiness.

"Peter, do mind your cup," said Sophia. "You will have it over in a minute. There! I told you so."

"Oh, has it gone over? So it has. It has spilt itself all over the cushion! Well, there is quite a mess, but there is no harm done. Tilly, come and clear up for Father, there's a good girl."

"Dinah, dear, ring the bell," said Sophia.

"Cousin Sophia is very vexed, Father," said Tilly, keeping her eyes fixed in front of her to avoid Sophia's.

"Oh, no, no, she is not," said Peter. "No, no, she is not put out about a little thing like that, not Cousin Sophia. She has plenty of cushions."

Andrew and Dinah met each other's eyes, and Latimer, seeing this, grinned to himself. Sophia indicated the cushion to the man.

"Take that cushion to Miss Patmore, James. She will know what to do with it."

"Oh, yes, so she will," said Peter, lifting the cushion and handing it, as if with a great effort that he by no means grudged. "We will send it out to Miss Patmore, and put an end to any chance of damage. And how is she, our good friend!"

"She is very well," said Sophia. "She would be here for tea, except that she is getting things ready for Andrew's party. She would not let that suffer."

"Oh, well, we can't give parties," said Peter. "That is out of any scope of ours. We have to be satisfied with those at other people's." Tilly's glance at this swept Sophia's face. "And we are content. We ask no more than we have. And we have and receive a great deal. We know that."

"But he does ask more than he is to have," said Dinah to Andrew. "He is not to receive a great deal, only tea."

"I don't think we have a great deal," said Tilly, allowing her eyes to move from Sophia to her cousins.

"It is more blessed to give than to receive," said Latimer.

"Ha, ha! There is something in that," said Peter. "We have to have things before we can give them. Latimer had it there."

"There is always much in what Latimer says," said

Dinah, bringing to Latimer's face a distant adoration that hardly asked to come near.

"But the Bible doesn't have that meaning, Father," said Tilly.

"No, no, you are right, my Tilly," said Peter.

"But it was clever of Latimer," said Andrew. "And the Bible ought to mean it in that sense. It is subtler."

"The Bible is not subtle," said Sophia, gravely. "The Bible is simple, so that all of us, gentle and simple, rich and poor, can understand it."

"Yes, Tilly understood it," said Latimer.

"Yes, yes, she did," said Peter. "You speak the truth, Sophia."

"The Bible is too simple," said Robin. "It ignores the difference between cringingly submitting to favours, and generously appreciating them."

"Yes, yes, and we do appreciate them," said Peter, loudly. "We do appreciate them."

"Dinah, dear, run out and meet Father," said Sophia. "He is coming up the drive. He will be tired, and will want a rest at once."

The married pair did not modify their greeting for the eyes of the guests, and Latimer's face took on a look of doubt whether after all they represented what was highest.

"Well, Peter, old man," said Christian. "Well, Latimer, young man. Well, Tilly, little woman. So you have all come to help us deal with Andrew on his birthday. A person who has lived a quarter of a century will take some managing, won't he?"

"Oh, how nice you always are, Cousin Christian!" said Tilly, sighing.

"Do you all think how nice Father is, as Tilly does?" said Sophia. "I never hear any of you say so, as I do her."

"Well, we must be going," said Peter, his tone devoid of all expression, including purpose.

Tilly sat with her face equally uncharacterised.

"Yes, we must go," said Latimer, rising with the perception that any urge of self-respect would rest with him.

"No, no, you are staying to Andrew's feast," said Christian. "We have some more of his cronies coming to condole with us for twenty-five years of having him. Sit down, little Tilly."

There was a silence.

"Cousin Sophia doesn't want us to stay," said Tilly, her voice even with this utterance seeming better than nothing.

"Yes, yes, of course I want you," said Sophia. "I only thought you might all get tired of so much of our company, and find it dull to end up with a party of people you so often meet. And I depended on you for the afternoon, so that Andrew might enjoy the whole of his day. Your frock will do so nicely for the evening, Tilly dear."

"I'll be bound she put it on on purpose," said Peter, cheerful more with relief at not moving than with anticipation. "If you will excuse us, Sophia, I think Latimer and I won't go back to dress. You say that Tilly is all right, and it is the lady that matters."

"No, don't dream of troubling, Peter," said Sophia, as Peter ceased to dream of it.

"Father always looks nice," said Tilly. "And Latimer hasn't had a grown-up evening suit yet."

"And I couldn't wear an Eton suit at nineteen," said Latimer, covering with these light words the depths of him beneath.

"Oh, I'll be bound you could, you little Tom Thumb," said his father. "Ah, he will have one soon, the dear boy! So he will."

"Dinah, you must run and dress," said Sophia. "Patty will help you. And then you can entertain our guests while the boys follow your example. They won't take so long."

"Will Patty help the boys?" said Latimer.

"Let one of the boys not change to keep Latimer in

countenance," Peter suggested in simple thought for his son.

"Oh, they are such great things, they could not carry it off," said Sophia, bringing Latimer no comfort. "Christian, we must make ourselves fit to be seen. We don't want Andrew to be ashamed of his parents. You will forgive us, Tilly dear?"

"Cousin Sophia had planned for us to go after tea. She was awfully nice about our staying," said Tilly, easy and grateful in being entertained under these conditions.

"Oh, she doesn't have to plan things beforehand to the letter. She has a rein," said Peter. "You heard her say she was afraid we should find it too much."

"Perhaps she would have insisted on having us, if I had come in my Eton suit," said Latimer, in the belief that the prevalent preoccupation was his outfit.

"Oh, your suit has to be one thing or another," said Peter, a yawn behind his hand not preventing his giving reliable information to his son.

Tilly looked up at her cousins in their evening clothes with simple veneration. Peter let his eyes rest lightly on the clothes, and summoned a vague look of welcome.

"You do look so nice, Dinah," said Tilly, in a yearning and ungrudging tone.

"What? What is this?" said Sophia, rustling in. "Are you making Dinah vain? Are they, my child?"

"Well, we shan't any of us be vain, with you here, Sophia," said Peter, with grim satisfaction in the general levelling. "It doesn't matter what any one else wears or doesn't wear with you in the room. For you put the whole lot of them into the shade. Right into the back of it without a question. We needn't trouble about what we have on, need we, Latimer?"

"No, Father," said Latimer, his eyes on the spectacle.

Tilly looked at Sophia as if her appearance almost transcended the bounds of the reasonable, and so lacked interest.

43

"There is the bell," said Peter, with so open a modification of his deportment that it seemed a duty.

"It is the Drydens," said Tilly, in a tone of expectation being duly fulfilled.

The Drydens were a pale, tall brother and sister at the end of their twenties, both with auburn hair and wide hazel eyes, and a look of coming of a stock that had become worn out without ever being much. The brother was the rector of the parish. He had an old worldness that allowed him the church as a provision for his sister and himself. The sister had a name for being intellectual, and as a consequence content with a single life.

"How do you do?" she said. "I don't know that we ought to be here. We have been to several festive things since Andrew and Dinah came to a drab, economical, rectory one. It is a most undignified position. We do nothing but take."

"Oh, we must be able to take, Judith," said her brother. "It must never do for us to have diffidence about that. We must be glad we have the chance to accept the good things of life."

"Well, accepting is very nice," said Tilly.

"Yes, so it is, Tilly. So it is," said Edward and Peter in one breath.

"We have been talking about this giving and taking," went on Peter; "and we came to the conclusion that it all worked out the same, whoever gave or took."

"I protest that it is humbling to be giving a party," said Robin. "You must all be generous and make it easy for Andrew."

"In a way it is very humbling," said Judith.

"Well, I wish the other two magnanimous ones would condescend to arrive," said Sophia, in a pleasant tone, but with a light in her eyes. "It is needlessly humiliating for us to give our friends food they cannot eat. They would need to be generous."

"Ha, ha! So they would," said Peter, not quenching the light.

"Dinah, my guests are late," said Andrew; "and I know what a bad sign this brilliance is."

"Your hour has come," said Robin. "We will watch with you."

"The dinner hour has come too," said Dinah; "and we are all to watch with Sophia."

"There is the bell. There are the tardy ones," said Sophia. "It is all right, Christian. "Why, Sarah, we had almost given you up."

Sarah and Julian Wake were another brother and sister some years under thirty. They had long limbs, colourless hair and faces, and spare features that seemed to move as their expression changed. They were very like and unlike. They shared a cottage in the village street, and a flat in London, and were reputed to be very devoted and very well off, and enjoyed even more prosperity and mutual affection than was said.

"I don't know how to be sorry enough," said Sarah. "The pony went lame and had to be taken back, and we came the rest of the way on foot."

"You surely had not almost given us up, Mrs. Stace," said Julian. "You might have known we should not miss a party. We have been hurrying along, very upset because we were giving a wrong impression of ourselves; of our manners, which is a serious thing. Sarah was worried as well because of her shoes. And I was unselfishly disturbed about the pony. I did not give a thought to my shoes. I am so distraught when dumb animals suffer."

"Yes, yes, so am I," said Sophia, her eyes on Andrew pairing off his guests.

"Mrs. Stace and I understand what a credit it is to animals to be dumb," said Julian, giving his hostess his arm. "It is not every one who could appreciate that. And now we go into dinner after all the rest, as if we could afford to do it. It is so satisfying not to have to wait, and know other people have done it. But then they are not dumb. I am afraid they were not."

45

The party moved forward: Christian and Sarah, Andrew and Judith, Robin and Tilly, and Edward and Dinah. As Julian and Sophia advanced in the rear, Latimer suddenly came into being, to hover between them and the moving line, his expression somehow drawing attention to his garments.

"Why, Latimer, it is generally a girl left over at the end," said Sophia, who was blameless in consistently wounding Latimer, it never having occurred to her that he had a point in view.

"Why, my dear boy!" said a voice from the sofa, as Peter strode forward to join his son. "My dear boy, I will go in with you. I will indeed. We will walk in together, arm-in-arm, I and my Latimer. I declare I hadn't noticed anything was going on."

"There is no need to declare it," said Dinah, gently.

"Why, Peter, if you forget all of us, you see we shall forget you," said Sophia.

"He sees it," said Julian. "I don't like having him in front of us as well as a lady, Mrs. Stace. Which is the lady, he or Latimer?"

Latimer's face showed that he had no doubt which character would be assigned to himself, and that his feelings reached thereby their ultimate stage.

"Now, what shall we talk about?" said Julian, as they took their seats. "Talking any more about the pony would seem like being absorbed in our own affairs, such a nasty, unnatural thing to seem to be. Let us talk about the birthday Andrew. I don't mean he is not our affair, and that we are not absorbed in him. I only mean that he would pass even as an absorption."

"Now, what can we all say about Andrew?" said Peter, speaking in a strong voice. "I say about him that he is my very dear nephew; I mean my cousin, but I always think of him as my nephew. And Tilly says she will never like any one as much as him, even though she marries somebody else. And Latimer says the same, don't you, Latimer?"

"Well, not quite the same, Father," said Latimer.

46

"No, Latimer does not carry his character of lady as far as that," said Edward.

"It is absurd to say that prayer is answered," said Dinah, as the young people talked apart.

"What do you mean, Dinah?" said Edward.

"Well, Latimer was not struck down dead as he was going in to dinner," said Dinah.

"And none of the rest of us were," said Andrew; "not even Sophia, and she deserved it."

"And no extra woman fell from heaven," said Dinah. "You must have noticed that, Edward."

"Yes, God deserted his child, Latimer," said Robin.

"I don't know," said Edward, with easy good humour. "His father came to his relief as if by direct intervention."

"Sarah is silent," said Julian. "I feel it so strong of her not to be ashamed of her religion. I have much less, and yet I am so often put to the test by the little I have. Sarah is really helped by it. She promised I should tell our piece of news. The Black Lodge is let; the house a little way from your gates, just before the real village begins, with the ragged garden and the piece of old black timber. Now the place is tidy, and there is an elderly lady and a daughter and son."

"That is another brother and sister we shall be," said Tilly, in a dubious tone.

"And you would like some of them to pair off, wouldn't you, Tilly?" said Peter. "Well I am with you."

"We will hope they won't pair off with any of us," said Judith. "Living with the same people from the beginning makes for so much more understanding."

"Yes, there is truth in that, Miss Dryden," said Peter. "But marriage, you know, it is a great change, a great uplift, at the time. Of course it doesn't last. At least, of course it does last, beyond death and everything. We all know that." Peter recalled his widowed state. "But it was at the time I meant, because that is when we seem to think about it most."

"Robin," said Sophia, "can't you manage so that Cousin Peter does not monopolise the talk? And say a word yourself, dear boy, and let Andrew and Dinah. Any one might be in the party but you three."

"No, I can't remodel every one. I am not the Creator," said Robin.

"No, my dear. That is not what I meant at all," said Sophia.

"It was unkind of Mrs. Stace not to mean that, Robin," said Julian. "Bateman, you and I are monopolising the talk. Isn't it dreadful; not for other people; for us? I am going to be small about it. I am going to be silent until I am pressed to speak."

"What? What is that?" said Peter. "Monopolising the talk! Oh, have I? Tilly, why didn't you tell me? Ha, ha! Why, I don't think I have been chattering so much. You are not used to hearing me; that is it. I am one for the enjoyment of other people's conversation."

Peter sank into the state he chose thus to describe.

"I wish you would all sympathise with me about the Black Lodge," said Julian; "and there being a mother and a son and daughter, nearly everything there can be. It seems we ought to sympathise about a fatherless household."

"I paid a pastoral call," said Edward. "The mother is quite an old lady, though she does not look it at first. She is a Frenchwoman. The son and daughter are about our ages and rather good-looking. Gilbert and Caroline I think they were."

"Fancy not telling us that before!" said Dinah. "But it was your duty to call, and you would not take any interest in it."

"How nice for Caroline and Gilbert to be good-looking!" said Julian. "Both of them too! Sarah and I try to remember that personality is everything. Our old nurse says it is a mercy we are both tall, and even our mother said it was a great thing."

"I never know why people think so much about looks," said Judith, looking about her with her large eyes.

"You would not say that, if you and Edward were plain," said Sarah.

"Yes, but, Sarah, remember we are both tall," said Julian. "We ought to remember what our mother said."

"It doesn't follow that people have personality because they are plain," said Sarah.

"Or that they haven't it because they are good-looking," said Judith. "The two things are quite apart."

"Not quite," said Latimer, looking at the ground after he spoke.

Sophia was rising from the table, and Edward looked at her for a sign to him to say grace, a ceremony he found it congenial to perform at the tables of his friends. But Sophia, who daily insisted on it, made a point of omitting it with guests, and moved from her board almost with an air of ignoring it.

"It is clever of Sophia to give us the drawing-room, and really not be in it herself," said Robin. "We might almost think she had real understanding."

"You may speak as a son of the house," said Sarah.

"No, do not give him the permission, Sarah," said Andrew. "We have too much of Robin speaking in that character."

"I never talk in any other," said Robin. "I have no other at home."

"If Father had gone on talking, we should not have got here at all," said Latimer, again mistaken as to the general trend of thought.

"I do not admire people for not loving their parents," said Julian. "I would not be modern for anything. I have an ancestor in a portrait, whom I am like."

"Poor Father, in the library with Cousin Christian and Cousin Sophia!" said Tilly. "But we couldn't have him in here."

"Oh, the three will talk contentedly of the days we did not see," said Andrew.

"Every one we always discuss, is here," said Dinah.

"Can we speak without seeming to contradict ourselves to some one?"

"Sarah and I will offer ourselves," said Julian. "We know that the sort of something about us melts away when we are known, and that this devotion to each other will end in our not marrying. And that it is sad to see a young man frittering away his time in a life only fit for a woman. I wonder why people will despise women? I do the little I can to prevent it. It isn't as if a few little talents amounted to anything. It isn't, and I mind that. Because it is not that I once thought I had them. I still think it. Will any one else be sacrificed? I would not ask, except for seeming to feel that Sarah and I can afford to be better than others."

"Well, you can," said Robin. "Leading the life of babes at the age of men, and being too good and loyal to say a word, is worse than a few little talents."

"Perhaps it needs great ones," said Sarah.

"That is the part that Robin minds, the good and loyal," said Latimer, feeling at once that he had gone too far, but unable to cringe before Robin's eyes, as they were not turned upon him.

"What about being an out-of-date parson?" said Edward.

"Or his out-of-date elder sister, a blue-stocking and a confirmed and contented spinster?" said Judith.

"Or without an evening suit?" said Latimer, resignedly bidding for safety.

"Now, Tilly, up to your work," said Robin. "There is nothing worse for you than being a little housekeeper."

"No, but I don't much like it," said Tilly. "I think doing that is worse than most of what other people have."

"Well, you are a very staid company," said Sophia, coming in later. "Now don't you all want to be starting some game?"

These words somehow broke the party.

"Good-bye, Mrs. Stace," said Julian. "We will never be late again. I don't mean we think you will ask us again.

I mean we know you will, and that we will be in time. And thank you so much for not letting our being late throw a shadow over the party. Being the cause of a shadow prevents me from being at my best. Not that I have entirely done myself justice tonight. I hope you won't think I have quite."

"Good-bye, Cousin Sophia. Thank you," said Tilly, with such a world of feeling in her tone that Sophia found nothing amiss.

"Good-bye, Mrs. Stace, good-bye," said Edward, shaking hands with open affection. "You must all come to us soon, you yourself as well, if we can persuade you."

"Good-bye, Cousin Sophia. Thanks," said Latimer, inopportunely choosing this moment for reaching manhood.

"Good-bye, all," said Peter, turning to the steps.

"Well, that is a short good-bye, Peter, after your day with us," said Sophia.

"Oh, a short good-bye, is it?" said Peter, pausing with head thrown back. "Well, I will make it a longer one. It has been a beautiful evening, Sophia, a festive day for us all. For Tilly and Latimer, for the three of us. It has. We shall all remember Andrew's coming of age."

"Andrew is twenty-five, Father," said Latimer.

"Yes, yes, so he is. Twenty-five. So we shall all remember it," said Peter, again on his way.

"We have none of us said good-bye to Cousin Christian," said Tilly, pausing over this incredible omission to veil her loathness to depart.

"Good-bye, little Tilly," said Sophia, shutting her front door.

The guests went their ways; and the Wakes were the first to reach their home, an ancient cottage in the village street, derelict to the unversed eye, and choice to the discerning.

"Well, we are back from the party," said Julian to his old nurse, his glance going round his sitting-room, with its carefully cottage-like furnishing, that he had himself

51

carried out under his sister's silence and smiling eye. "You must have been anxious when you heard about the pony. You did not send to inquire if we were all right. I did not think of myself at all. Sarah will tell you how safe she felt with me. And you will do something about her shoes."

"That was not the most dangerous part of the evening," said Sarah.

"No. There were moments that were a real test," said Julian. "I stood them well."

"You did," said Sarah. "I hope you are as good a man as you are a guest."

"Thank you," said Julian. "You understand me, and know I don't like being a good man as well as a good guest. It is not such a distinguished thing to be, and deserves less credit, and gets much less."

"I can believe there were some moments," said the old woman. "I hear that things are not of the easiest up at the Manor."

"You misunderstand me," said Julian. "I mean you show you do not, which is not what I intended. I do not openly imply things after being had to a party. Now I am going to bed, to cry myself to sleep."

"Why to cry yourself to sleep?" said his sister.

"Thinking of Latimer," said Julian.

"Oh, yes, of course," said Sarah.

"Sarah, you follow me so quickly," said Julian. "How can I be much above the average, if your wits are always equal to mine? But I have more feeling than you, because I nearly cry when I think of Tilly. Not quite, because her capacity for suffering is less. But most people laugh at the thought of either, and I am so afraid it is not the laughter that is akin to tears."

"Do you laugh or cry when you think of Andrew and Dinah?" said Sarah.

"I do neither. I am very highly organised. To me Andrew and Dinah are Andrew and Dinah."

"They are," said Sarah. "And Robin is Robin."

"No, Robin is not quite so much," said Julian. "You are so levelling, Sarah. You should not exaggerate people's advantages as if they needed it. It is not really praising them, and you should always really praise people."

At this moment Matilda Bateman was sitting on her sofa in her drawing-room, a room whose purpose was much overlaid by the appurtenances of her men, which in Latimer's case she would have felt it unkindness, and in her father's almost sacrilege, to remove.

"Oh, wasn't it lovely?" she said, looking from her father to her brother.

"Yes, it was. Indeed it was!" said Peter, leaning back. "And I am downright glad you had it, little Tilly. It quite gives my spirits a turn. You are not more perked up about it than I am. Latimer, dear boy, bring Father's pipe."

Latimer did so, his expression deprecating the form of the request.

"Latimer did behave beautifully," said Tilly, with a sigh.

"So he did," said Peter, filling the pipe. "He was a credit to us, the dear boy! I declare I was prouder of him without an evening suit than I could have been of any other lad with one."

He strode off to bed.

"Don't you love Dinah, Latimer?" said Tilly.

"Yes," said Latimer, swinging his foot.

"Cousin Sophia does hate Father," went on Tilly. "I wonder why."

"I don't wonder why," said Latimer.

"Latimer! You don't hate Father?" said Tilly.

"No. I am too kind to hate people, and it would not be right to hate one's father," said Latimer.

"You did say that like Julian," said Tilly, and Latimer flushed; for he had intended to do this as an equal rather than an imitator.

In the rectory, the rector and his sister were exchanging their last word, seated in a room that was typical of their home. The pastoral income had the common discrepancy

53

with the dwelling to be maintained, and Judith and her brother had taken their own way to overcome it. Through their house, simplicity took the place of taste; and absence of ugliness, and indeed of anything else, the place of beauty; and economy was exposed and almost glorified.

"Well, Mrs. Stace looked very lovely tonight," said Edward. "And Dinah and Sarah both have a great deal of charm. And dear little Tilly looked very well for her. I am very glad they had the Batemans. I hoped they would. They are very nice in those ways."

"Did you think Sarah or Dinah the best-looking woman?" said Judith. "Young woman I mean. I suppose the best-looking of all was Mrs. Stace."

"Yes, I suppose so," said Edward. "She is a very beautiful person. But you were the most in accord with my own taste, unless it is that I like our family type. But Mrs. Stace has a wonderful appearance. And Sarah is very attractive along her own line. And Dinah is always herself, quite different from other people."

"Do you like women better than men?" said Judith.

"Oh, no, I don't know that I do," said Edward. "But one thinks of them in a different spirit. I had some very enjoyable talk with Andrew and Robin. Intelligent fellows both of them. I think I made certain things clearer to them. I always enjoy a passage at words with them. We are very well matched."

"Do you like Julian?" said Judith.

"Oh—well, Julian is the sort of man who is always thinking of the effect of what he says. But he is not a bad fellow. He is really a good-hearted man. We are fortunate in the people in the village. I should not like to leave it."

"Well, we are neither of us likely to leave it," said Judith.

"Well, I might get promotion, and you might marry," said Edward, putting contingencies in the order they came to his mind. "These things happen as they may."

"Or do not happen at all, if it can be managed," said his sister.

"Oh, I should not be averse to giving your hand to a suitable man, if he came to me and asked me for it," said Edward, allowing his drama to unfold itself before him.

Sophia shut her door on her guests, and smiled at her husband, but spoke to her children.

"Well, did you enjoy it? Did you like it as much as you thought you would? Did you have a happy time by yourselves? Did your friends think it was a success?"

"Yes, yes, quite as much. It was a most satisfying party. The best we have ever had. A great success. The guests could hardly tear themselves away. I doubted if Tilly would accomplish it. We had the most perfect finish possible by ourselves, a real orgy of inexperience. To think of that was a stroke of genius. I feel quite comforted for having got through a quarter of a century of life."

Andrew and Dinah supported each other, and Robin stood aside with a smile.

"Well, have not you liked it, then, Robin?" said Sophia. "You have been about, taking part in everything. There was nothing you left out that I saw. Wasn't there anything that you appreciated, then?"

"Oh, yes, there were several things," said Robin. "Having Sarah and Julian, and the food and drink. There was nothing I neglected, except talking to Cousin Peter and Edward. I came near to passing that over."

"Dear boy!" said Sophia. "You mean just the same as the others, don't you? Now all of you run up to bed. Dinah, your beauty sleep! We must think of it, mustn't we, boys? Mustn't we, stolid brothers?" She turned to her husband as they went upstairs. "She is so unusual in everything she says and does. I saw how the young men watched her. I noticed it all the evening."

Christian's eyes went after his daughter in ready belief.

"Is that you? Is that all of you coming up?" called Patty's voice. "Just let me hear a word about it. Was everything all right? There was nothing wrong, was there?"

55

"Nothing at all, Patty," said Andrew, leading the way into Patty's room. "Not a thing has been wanting to make my birthday perfect."

"Who wore the gold dress and who the black?" said Patty. "I couldn't quite see over the stairs."

"Sarah wore black," said Andrew, "and Judith yellow. I wore black and white. It is my birthday, and I will tell you what I wore."

"Latimer wore brown," said Dinah.

"Poor boy!" said Patty. "They all stayed then, Cousin Peter and all of them. We had everything ready. I knew they would."

"Of course you did," said Robin. "It was astonishing, Sophia's faith and hope. She has her own way so much that she can believe in nothing else."

"Oh, yes, they all stayed," said Dinah. "Cousin Peter did not do anything else. He forgot to go in to dinner, and had to be told to say good-bye. And after all did not keep to the safer side. He monopolised the conversation. There was over-reaching, for any one staying so long!"

"Really spending the day," said Andrew.

"Spending the day," said Dinah. "We were fearing him at luncheon, entertaining him at tea and dinner. Spending the day! Sophia told him of it. She always tells Cousin Peter of his faults, and spending the day was a bad one."

"Children, children!" called Sophia. "What are you doing up there, hanging about and gossiping? I told you to go to bed. What is the meaning of it?"

"We are telling Patty about the party," called Dinah.

"Oh, that is what you are doing?" said Sophia. "Well, don't be too long. You can tell her all about it tomorrow."

"They are telling Patty about the party," she said to her husband.

"Dinah, you have been too engaging," said Andrew. "They are coming up."

Christian and Sophia smiled in the doorway, arm-in-arm.

"Telling Patty about the party?" said Christian, his

voice holding appreciation of Patty and his children, and the benefits they all enjoyed.

"Well, it was a lovely party to tell about, wasn't it?" said Sophia. "You must go to bed now. Patty can hear about it in the morning. Good news can wait, can't it? And all the talk about it will last us for several days. I think you had better all have breakfast in here with Patty."

"We can't begin too soon to expiate our evening's pleasure," said Dinah. "Breakfast the next day is the time. We ought to be thankful we don't have especially hard beds to sleep on. But why should Sophia suffer, and be deprived of our company? Surely she has not enjoyed our party as well as organised it."

"Did they enjoy it, Miss Patmore?" said Sophia.

"Oh, yes, indeed they did. They have never been so excited about a party before. They are full of it," said Patty with energy, all indeed that remained to her after her share in the day.

"Well, good night, Patty," said Christian. "I have a day's work before and behind me."

"Good night, Dr. Stace," said Patty, who might truthfully have added the same.

CHAPTER III

"Dinah, I want you to come with me, to call on the new people this afternoon," said Sophia. "Be dressed by four, so that I don't work myself into a heat, shouting about the house. Absolutely ready to start at four."

"The new people?" said Dinah.

"Yes, that is what I said, my dear. Didn't you hear when I spoke? Why want to be told everything twice?"

"I need to be assured of this many times," said Andrew. "It is the first time fresh human beings have been approached in my life. I can't take it as a matter of course."

"I expect Dinah will take it as exactly that," said Sophia. "Now, Dinah, don't behave as if nothing in the world was anything to you. It is time you got beyond that stage. I want this family to see the best of you. So be yourself, and make a good impression."

"You have just suggested myself, and you hardly find that is what it makes," said Dinah, "even with maternal prejudices. Unless they are at the bottom of your misgivings."

"No, it does not always, my dear. I think I sometimes need a mother's partiality. But I am not so biassed that I can't speak a word to you for your own good. Simply make the most of what you have. You none of you have too much."

"Oh, surely we have," said Dinah. "That may be the explanation of Andrew and me, that we are over-endowed. Something in us seems to have got off the line, and to call for an account."

"Well, try to keep your endowments in hand this afternoon," said Sophia, leaving the room.

"The daughter of this new house may be an example for you, Dinah," said Robin.

"The son will be for you," said Andrew. "He is a rising

barrister, anyhow risen above you. It is on you that the real brunt of him will fall."

"My heart is with you, Robin, though Sophia hopes it is with him," said Dinah.

"I don't see how he can continue his advancing, if he settles here," said Robin.

"Latimer and I might as well take to bettering ourselves," said Andrew.

"He goes to London," said Dinah, "and progresses there, and comes to a standstill here at the end of the week. Patty told me about them."

"What is their income?" said Andrew. "I trust Patty has not failed us."

"They are not poor, for living quietly in a small house," said Dinah. "Nothing they have to keep dark. Those were Patty's words. It is such a pity they have nothing of that kind, because they would not keep it from Patty, and that would be so satisfying for Patty and for us, for every one but them. And I can't think they matter in comparison. Sophia is right about my attitude to them."

"I did not have the carriage for going this little way to people who are not well off," said Sophia, as they set off. "I thought it seemed better just to walk simply. One should be careful in those things. Now, would you have thought of that?"

"No, I don't think so," said Dinah. "Using carriages on that principle would come to having them for every one, to avoid accusing people of poverty."

"Oh, that is the way with you and Andrew," said Sophia. "You always give things some unworkable turn of your own. That is how you make an impression of not being anything at all. Now Robin will get more out of life than you. He does already. Well, I think a carriage would look very foolish going up this little drive."

"It could not be got up," said Dinah. "As a drive it fails of its purpose. It supports your view that the means of approach should be adapted to the visited."

59

But in spite of the suitable approach, the visit was not an easy one. The house was one of those muddled little buildings of many dates, that have been added to from time to time as need has arisen. Conformity of plan had vanished, and the windows had become simply windows, and the doors doors, and the whole seemed to serve the purpose of a dwelling and nothing more, and thus invoked as much disapproval as anything can that fulfils its real function. The garden did not even do as well, unless the purpose of a garden is to accommodate a moderate quantity of potsherds, and a considerable one of properties the neighbourhood finds dispensable.

The inmates of the house accepted it with a smile as it stood, as they accepted foreign blood and simple living without a claim on anything beyond. These were not the things which urged Sophia to her best. Mrs. Lang was a tall, old woman, some years over seventy, upright and hardly looking old; with a pale, intellectual face, hair in arresting streaks of black and white, and a sudden sympathetic smile. The son was a vigorous man of thirty, with bright brown eyes, and a touch of foreign charm; and his sister very like him, with a face at once more English and more alive.

"Oh, now we shall have some friends!" said the son, with an unconscious gesture of his hands. "Some real friends, who don't mind our mother's being French, and our not taking enough interest in the house, even to make the best of it."

"Or anyhow who have conquered themselves and called," said his sister.

"I will not think it needed a victory," said Gilbert. "Why should they not call, when Mother is a personality, and was one even when her hair was black? We shall have a houseful of friends, because I know there are some more at home. And I can hardly bear coming down from London, and finding only my family."

"That is hardly a word we need, my son," said Mrs. Lang.

"I am not telling you. I am explaining it to my new friends," said Gilbert. "And you will not have to suffer having only me; and you make it clear that it is beyond your powers."

"You must come very soon and see my two sons," said Sophia. "They will like new friends as much as you will."

"I knew you had two sons," said Gilbert. "I have been going prying and probing about the village. But how nice that you have brought your daughter, and not her two brothers, as you did not bring all three!"

He sat down by Dinah, and looked into her face, with eyes that recognised that she was hampered by her mother's presence. It was his habit just to show what he felt. He was a versatile, simply endowed man, who prospered through directness and ease.

His sister was less simple and more silent, with gray, observant eyes.

"Won't you all come and spend the evening with us?" said Sophia.

"Oh, yes. Do you mean this very evening?" said Gilbert. "That is the one I choose."

"You see they would like it. And I should like it for them," said their mother. "But for myself, I am an old woman, and weak even for my age. I will not come today, nor in the evening any day. But I should find it a pleasure to see more of you in an easy way, as time goes on."

"Mrs. Lang is a beautiful old woman," said Dinah, as she went home with her mother.

"Beautiful?" said Sophia, in astonishment at this tribute to looks so different from her own, and at a young woman's being struck by beauty in an old one. "What an odd child you are! Here are you, just come from a young man who admired you very much—I could see he did— and the first word you find to say, is about the allurement of his aged mother! You are as different from what I was at your age, as one woman could be from another. I didn't think about old women or women at all. I only

61

had eyes for your father. Of course she may have been good-looking once. But I should not think so very."

"Not when she was young," said Dinah. "Not until her hair had changed and her face had got its experience. I wonder what Andrew will think of her."

"Well, I hope you will have your own experience," said Sophia. "And I hope Andrew hopes so. You are such an odd pair that one hardly knows what to expect of you. Mrs. Lang is a very old mother for those young people. They can't be more than thirty and twenty-nine. She must have married very late."

"There are Sarah and Julian with Andrew and Robin on the lawn," said Dinah. "And Tilly and Latimer and Cousin Peter. I wonder why they are all there in a body."

"We may trust Cousin Peter and Tilly and Latimer to be there in that way, if they are there at all," said Sophia. "They only seem to come when we have people. There seems to be a fate about it. I suppose, like most fates, it has a human form."

"Oh, Cousin Sophia, how nice you look!" said Tilly with instant and eager amends for her presence.

"What else can any of us say?" said Sarah.

"What else indeed?" said Peter, knocking out ashes from his pipe on a tree, his eyes on his employment.

"Mrs. Stace, we must explain our seeming intrusion," said Julian. "Of course we could not be really intruding. This semblance is explained by our hearing that you had gone to call at the Black Lodge. Neighbourly interest and not curiosity overcame us."

"And Tilly saw the party through the gates, and come in she would," said Peter in a loud voice, tapping. "I couldn't prevent her. It was quite beyond what I could do. How are you, Sophia?"

"Oh, Father, it isn't true?" said Tilly, with tears in her voice.

"Yes, we have been to do our duty to our new neighbours," said Sophia. "And the son and daughter are following us back for dinner. Dinah quite took to them, and they to Dinah; that last wasn't hard to guess. So, Tilly dear, I think we are rather too many of the same family, for strangers to encounter. They would be overwhelmed by us. We must put off seeing them all together to another day."

"Yes, Cousin Sophia," said Tilly, turning with docility and compunction to go, followed by Latimer with a courageously humorous glance behind, and Peter in simple acquiescence in the move.

"Mrs. Stace can't tell us to go as we are not relations," said Julian to his sister. "I heard her tell Tilly. I saw her. No, I think I felt her. Suppose we should begin to feel something. It would be too much for me. I have never felt anything. We must hope to meet the two from the Black Lodge on our way. I think we might smile at them, being in the country and near neighbours. I think they would remember my first smile."

The guests, fresh from this sight, which Julian was right was remembered, were shown to their new friends' study.

"This is the kind of room I hoped for, when we came right upstairs," said Gilbert. "It is a schoolroom; no, it is a nursery."

"And the lettered atmosphere has come later," said his sister. "And what a deal there is!"

"Was that your nurse looking out of that door?" said Gilbert. "And are there old toys in that cupboard?"

"Yes, we have never sent them to a hospital," said Dinah. "Nothing is given away here. I expect it was our nurse taking a cursory survey. It is a thing she does."

"You are right that we are to be seen as people of letters," said Andrew. "That was a hard and forced choice for us. You don't do anything so unnatural to you. We heard you were rising."

"Yes, I am now. For a time I could not rise," said Gilbert.

"We were lettered all in a moment," said Dinah.

"This room only tried to be called the schoolroom," said Robin. "We had a nursery until we were twenty. Now it is called the children's study. You see it is such a great thing for us to have it. Why should children have a study? Having one must take its place among the great things. You would never guess how many things here are great. I don't see what could put you on the track."

"I could tell when I saw your sister, that she came from where she was one of the children," said Gilbert. "Carrie and I are having to stop being the children. It means we no longer have a real home."

"Our mother is getting old, and we can't afford a nurse," said Caroline. "We are uncared for and might as well live for others. And I do not try to be a second mother to Gilbert, though I ought, as I am only two years younger."

"She says I am ambitious and that I don't read, and other contemptuous things," said Gilbert.

"Those are the worst," said his sister; "and they are necessary to rising."

"Our mother is in her prime. I can hardly tell you how utterly she is in it," said Robin.

"We live for ourselves," said Dinah, "and our parents live for others; no, for us. We bear that burden."

"Do you love your nurse better than any one in the world?" said Gilbert.

"Yes. You have got hold of us," said Andrew.

There were no reservations based on habit and reticences born in childhood here. The truth on which intimacy feeds came out. Andrew and Dinah had reached a point where their courage failed them to go further. The others were uprooted, and waiting for break and change. The soil was ready and the time was ripe. Sophia had added to her functions that of prophetess; and the thing she had foreseen was soon abroad.

"Well, Sarah," said Julian, coming one day into his parlour, "you and I must face the truth together, and go hand in hand along the path of life."

"What do you mean?" said Sarah.

"We can't go as I said, if you have not the understanding that does without words," said Julian. "It is no good calling life a path without that; and I find it a little comfort. Of course I have never proposed to Dinah; but not doing a thing does not make me think it more natural that any one else should do it. And Andrew has never proposed to you—because you do not keep things from me, do you?—but that does not prepare me for his offering himself to Caroline. And you and I do not want to marry; but that can hardly help us to sympathise with people who do want to."

"No, we must manage without help," said Sarah.

"It takes more generosity than I possess," said Julian. "I must leave a dead self behind, though it seems rather a pity, in the path. Now you and I cannot marry, because I could not give you to any one but Andrew, and you could not give me to any one but Dinah. You would not let Tilly have me, would you, Sarah?"

"Well, Tilly would make a dear little wife," said Sarah.

Julian suddenly knew what no one else was ever to know, that Sarah would have married Andrew. He hardly made a pause.

"Sarah, don't be too much for me. I should give way so easily today over anything like Tilly's being a spinster."

"I don't think that is Tilly's danger," said Sarah.

"There is something about her that puts the notion into my head," said Julian. "Ideas are so real to me. I don't mean that it could come true."

"Now are we to go on to Latimer?" said Sarah.

"No, we are not," said Julian. "You make me peevish by implying that my talk goes according to rule. Latimer would not make a dear little husband. At least he would, and that would be very uncongenial to him; and it is nicer not to talk of what is uncongenial and inevitable to any one."

Latimer was sitting, swinging his foot with a moody

65

expression; and Tilly wore a look of resignation that gave an older touch to her face.

"A penny for your thoughts, my Tilly!" said Peter from behind his paper, drawn by a mental current unusual about him. "For what is simmering in your small head, my Tilly."

"I was wondering about something. I was not thinking about anything," said Tilly.

"Oh, yes, yes, you were," said Peter, adjusting a page. "Tell Father."

"I was realising," said Tilly, her voice giving full weight to the fitness of the advanced word, "that we shall not be all brothers and sisters together here much longer."

"Not brothers and sisters!" said Peter, raising his eyes. "Have you and Latimer been quarrelling? Then make it up like my good boy and girl. Say to me that you are friends again."

"No, we have had no disagreement," said Latimer, dropping as if from a height an aloof word.

"Then what is it?" said Peter, addressing himself to paternal interest. "What have you on your minds?"

"I believe that Andrew and Dinah and Gilbert and Caroline are going to be married," said Tilly. "I know everybody thinks so. To each other. I mean Andrew to Caroline and Dinah to Gilbert. So that there will be two less of each of us for the rest of us here."

"Andrew marry Caroline and Dinah Gilbert!" said Peter, slapping his paper on his knee. "Well, and I never thought of that. What a bat I am! Because it has been going on under our eyes. I am a mole, and no mistake. Well, I am right down glad of it. I like to see young people getting things for themselves. And these are dear boys and girls, and deserve to get free; will appreciate a little happiness. It is a good piece of news."

He returned to his paper.

"Well, but things will be so different, Father," said Tilly.

"Will they?" said Peter, in a withdrawn tone. "Will they, my little Tilly? No, I don't think they will. Not for you, you know. Why should they be? It won't make any change for you. Because they wouldn't either of them have married you, wouldn't have been the kind for you."

"I know they wouldn't," said Tilly.

"Well then, what difference does it make?" said Peter, from out of a crackling sound. "What is the trouble, Tilly?"

"Latimer knows it will make a difference," said Tilly, looking despairingly at her brother.

"Does he?" said Peter with genuine question, his eyes looking over the paper's rim. "Does Latimer know it will make a difference? Why, what odds can it make to Latimer? Latimer didn't think he could marry either of those two girls, did he? Dinah or Caroline? Latimer! Ha, ha!"

Peter crossed his knees, and Tilly acted on her knowledge that glancing at her brother would be going too far.

CHAPTER IV

"WELL, so I know whom you are both to marry before I die," said Mrs. Lang; "and am spared a mother's anxiety and a woman's curiosity. I am glad you are to marry Dinah, my son, because she is better than you; and one of a pair must tend to be superior, and I am glad my child is to have the best. And Andrew contrives not to seem to be above or below your sister. So it will be easy for her. She does not look up to people or down on them. And I am happy that she is to have things smooth. I say nothing for a training in rigours. I want nothing hard for my daughter."

"You are overdoing your content, Mother," said Carrie. "We shall think you have some quarrel with life."

"No, my dear. Only that it has to end. And that is certainly not a quarrel. And that I have in some ways made bad use of it. Now you may leave me. Your dear boy and girl are in the road; and Miss Patmore is coming to me again this morning. That is a kindness of Mrs. Stace's, that I can so easily accept. I was never of those who do not welcome kindness. I hope you both will always have enough of it."

"Mrs. Stace does not like my being older than Andrew," said Caroline, as she reached the gate. "I ought not to blame her, as I would not choose it myself."

"But you do blame her," said Dinah. "You must get into the way of condemning Sophia, before you join our family."

"I like it," said Andrew. "I love experience. Even four years more of it excites me."

"So does seven years me," said Dinah. "Four and seven years are so much better than the twenty to thirty extra

68

years of Sophia, which have never stirred our blood, except in other ways."

"Patty's extra years are the best of all," said Gilbert. "There is Patty, going in to visit Mother! I am so looking forward to belonging to Patty, and enjoying her wisdom."

"Yes. I have seen the depths in Patty's eyes," said Carrie; "a great accumulation of other people's experience."

"You are one who perceives, Caroline," said Andrew.

"Yes. Patty would be baffled by any development of her own history," said Dinah.

Patty was continuing to prosecute her dealings with other people's.

"Well, so you are very nice, and are waiting for me, Mrs. Lang. I don't like people to look as if they were surprised to see me. Mrs. Stace picked these flowers for you herself. And I have brought you a book of old photographs to amuse you. There are all sorts of odd things in it. There is Andrew as a little boy, and another of him older! And here are Dinah and Robin; Robin quite a baby then! He has altered the most of the three. And Dinah by herself, such a funny little girl! Her eyes used to twinkle when she was ten months old. Her father was so fond of her. She has never got really different. These are of Dr. and Mrs. Stace, taken together when they were married. Isn't Mrs. Stace beautiful? And on the next page some of her and Dr. Stace as children. How odd these old photographs are! Fancy dressing children in those clothes! This is Dr. Stace as a little boy, before he came to the Manor. Old Mr. Stace had some photographs of him. Do you feel tired, Mrs. Lang? Let me hold the book, if it is heavy."

"Oh, no, no. I am not at all tired. The book was a little too much for me. It is only my heart; I am doing what Dr. Stace tells me for it. It was just a moment. Was not Dr. Stace his father's own son, then? Was he not born at the Manor? Is this a photograph of Dr. Stace as a child?"

"Yes, that is one of the earlier ones. He was not at the Manor as young as that. These were taken later when he was there. Mr. Stace adopted him as a young boy, and gave him his name. Some are of him and Mrs. Stace together. They were brought up as brother and sister. How little he alters, doesn't he?"

"Yes, he has altered very little," said Mrs. Lang, as if this might have struck her. "Was Mrs. Stace another adopted child?"

"Here he is, as an older boy!" went on Patty. "One nearly grown up, you see. Dinah is the most like him of the children. His father was proud of him, his adopted father, prouder than he was of his daughter, though he made a great deal of her looks. She was his own child, the only one he had. And you know he left the property to him, though people thought he ought not, as he had a daughter. But it didn't matter, as they were to marry each other."

"His own child! Was she? You are sure? Yes, she is like him. I knew . . . I have seen his portrait. Did Mr. Stace like the idea of their marrying?"

"Oh, no, no, he did not," said Patty, as though overcome by a flood of recollection. "There was such trouble. I shall never forget it. I had just come to take care of him. He would not have his daughter marrying some one she had lived with all her life. That is what he seemed to take so hard. He would have a change for her. He seemed to be thinking more of her than of Dr. Christian, though it wasn't his habit."

"And what did Dr. Christian do?" said Mrs. Lang, her tone faint on the baptismal name.

"They were wonderful about it, both of them," said Patty. "I was a great deal with Miss Stace at the time. Miss Stace she was then, you see. They didn't know how long it would be before they could marry. Mr. Stace sent his son out of the house, and forbade him to see his sister. And then he died in his sleep, the poor old man! I was

70

so upset that I was not with him; but they said he did not suffer. And I stayed on in the house; and they were married in a few months, and have been so happy with each other. He little knew what a beautiful thing he was against. And I never thought, when I came to his house, how much of my life I should spend in it. It was all like a book to watch."

"Yes, it is very like a book," said Mrs. Lang. "Thank you, dear Patty, for telling me. Will you leave me the photographs to look at? I will give them to Dr. Stace, when he comes to me tomorrow evening."

Christian came at the appointed time.

"Well, you must have a guilty conscience, Mrs. Lang. I commanded you to rest, and you have been hard at work. What have you been busy with? You have been at it day and night."

"Yes, it is true that I have," said Mrs. Lang, keeping her eyes on his. "You will not wonder at it, when you hear what I have to say to you. I don't know what it may mean to you. I have not tried to guess."

"Well, say it, and never mind," said Christian, expecting some confession common to his ear. "Whatever it is, say the whole of it simply, and bid it good-bye. You would never guess how many of us do the impossible thing. Most of us can rise to it, given the cause. If you think you can startle me, you are wrong."

"No, I fear I am not," the old woman said, just smiling. "You will find it will be a shock. But it may not be so much of a thing for you to hear. It is bad for both of us, for me to delay it. Now you will see that I can startle you."

"No. You make a mistake," said Christian.

"I think you are my son," said Mrs. Lang. "Now you see that I have startled you."

"Tell me," said Christian, coming near to her chair.

"I have been thinking for many hours how to tell you. You were right that I had been busy with something day and night. I was a young girl, foreign as you know, and

71

nursery governess at an English country house. I am eighteen years older than you. You are fifty-seven. You can't know that for certain, but I know it. My father was good, but we had come to be poor. Your father was a guest in the house. He was the only person who could speak French. We came together in many ways; and when I found I was to have a child, I wrote to him, and found he was going to be married. It was true: there was nothing for you to be ashamed of in your father. He put me in the farmhouse where you were brought up. My parents thought I was still at my post. It was hard to keep them deceived. When you were born, I went back to them, because I had to go. You must see how it must have been. And your father kept you at the farm. Now you know more of your life than I know. I am your mother, but I know nothing of you until you are fifty-seven."

"How do you know now that I am your son?"

"You see this book of photographs? You recognise it. It comes from your home. These photographs in it are of you as a child and boy. I have had some by me for fifty years, that were taken and sent to me, by your father's thought, as you grew out of babyhood. They are the same. Look, and see that they are the same."

"I see they are," said Christian. "I remember having some of them taken. Do I see that I am like you?"

"Yes, you are like me," said Mrs. Lang. "More like than my own—than my other children. And your daughter is like me."

"How did you come to this place where I am? How did you lose sight of me for all these years?"

"I lost sight of you on purpose. I will tell you the truth. The letters from your father made trouble. I could not use the money he sent. Nothing was supposed to be kept to ourselves in our family life. I never went away to stay: we had no friends in England. When you were eight years old, you were ill. A letter came with the news, referring to you as a pupil. I see you remember my coming to you. I found you cared for and recovering; brought up as a child of gentle birth by worthy people whom you loved as kindly servants. You turned from me, and called for the woman who was your nurse. It is strange to say it, but that was an easing of my mind. I thought the deception had better cease. I agreed with your father, that we should be silent, unless things were not well on either side. I never heard. I lived with my parents in their old age, and I married when I was forty-four. My husband made me promise to take no steps to hear of you. To be honest, you were getting to seem far away to me then; and I knew you would have a fair lot in life. I had some contented married years, and a son and daughter, Gilbert and Caroline. I was left a widow years ago, and lately we have had to give up our home. Then I had a longing, unreal to you perhaps, as I had put you behind me for so much of my time, to see my eldest son before I died; to see the son who was almost near to me in age, to hear how it had fared with him. I did not know even that you were alive. I had seen many years ago the notice of your father's death. Your father had known Andrew Stace, had known him well. I knew no other of your father's friends. I thought his family might know of you; and I have found that he took you for his son."

"He came to see me when I was a child," said Christian. "I never to my knowledge saw my real father. I looked on myself as belonging to him; and when I was ten, I was taken to his house, and taught to call him Father; and my name was changed to Christian. I had never been told my surname. He was in all things a father to me, but on the question of my parentage would be always silent. Did my real father arrange for my adoption? Are you now going to tell me who my father was? It seems to me just, that I should know now."

"Yes, it is just," said his mother. "But I will not tell you today. I will tell you this. Your father was a man who never failed any one to whom he owed anything of any kind. His word to me was, that I should hear if things were not well with you. You see they were well. So much Andrew Stace may have told you."

"Yes, he told me so much," said Christian. "And what more there is for me to know, I think you will tell me. And now I have something to say to you. After all these years, as a man of nearly sixty, I am glad that I have known my mother."

Mrs. Lang's face only trembled for a second.

"I will not answer that I am glad to know my son. What is there in my feelings that matters to you? There is the trouble coming of it. You do not see it yet. Our children, yours and mine, have come together in a way they must not come. The pity of it, that we should meet to fear this!"

"What do you mean?" said Christian.

"You are my son," said Mrs. Lang. "You are Gilbert and Caroline's half-brother. They are by half-blood uncle and aunt to your children. What is to be done?"

There was a silence.

"I will go and tell my wife," said Christian. "I will tell her what you have told me, and leave her children to her. It is the most I can do for them. I have been a busy man, and know them too little. I can serve them in no other way now."

"It is strange of me," his mother said, "but I had not given a thought to your wife. After not having seen you for forty-nine years, I suddenly thought you were all mine; come to me across that gulf, to help me in the trouble fallen on us with each other. But I am a strange old woman to you, risen from the past as something out of it you had better not have known. And indeed you had better not. I will do all I can to help you and your wife. What will you tell her about me? What shall we any of us say to any one?"

"Simply what will spare our children, yours and ours, all that we can, in this that has come upon their innocence. It may be of no good to my sons to know what you have told me of my birth. In that case they shall not know. It may do harm to yours, to hear what you have told me of your youth. In that case he shall not hear. But I am glad that I have heard, glad that I know who I am on my mother's side, glad that you and I have met. Shall I call you——?"

"No, do not call me anything. I am no longer Mrs. Lang to you, and I am not your mother. Speak to me without giving me a name, as if you were uncertain what to call me, as you are. But I will call you Christian, because I find that to me you are my son."

"I am happy that you find that. As far as you will have it so, I will be a son to you. Now a difficult thing done well is a strain even for you. You must spare yourself. What shall you tell your children?"

"The truth," said Mrs. Lang; "as I have told it to you, my eldest child. They have never had anything but the truth from me. Part of my life has not been revealed to them; but they must know that. They shall have the truth from me now. What we tell the world, will not be for us to judge. My children are not young, and they will help me. You need not think of me as without support. What you tell your children, my grandchildren, though you do not think of them as that, you will explain to us, and we will follow what you say. We will not say good-bye; we do not know how to say it, and it is not worth while to learn. I am here, to say anything or do anything that may be of use to you or yours. Tell your wife that as my message. You and she may depend on me."

"We shall do that," said Christian. "I am getting to know my mother. I will go home now, to tell my wife what I have learnt of her."

Sophia was waiting for her husband in the hall.

"Well, my dear, how late you are! Is anything wrong? Is anything the matter, Christian? Is it Mrs. Lang? She must get worse some time. That is nothing to wear that troubled face about. What is it, Christian? Tell me what it is."

"You will never guess it, Sophia," said Christian. "I have been to see Mrs. Lang this evening. Yes, of course you know that; but let me tell it as it comes to my head, or I shall never get it into words. She had been looking at that book of photographs that Patty took to her. There were some pictures in it of me, as a child and boy. Some of her own, that she had had for many years, were the same. So it came out who I was. Don't let me startle you, Sophia. It is nothing to be afraid of. It came out that Mrs. Lang is my mother."

"Mrs. Lang your mother?" said Sophia. "Your mother? Mrs. Lang! Well, what is there to be startled about in that? We have always known you must be scme one's son. It doesn't matter if she is your mother. What difference can it make? What is the problem about it? Is there anything that has to be hidden? Who was your father? So that is what you have been doing! Talking to her, and finding out that she is your mother! And having to make a sort of scene over her, I suppose. Poor darling! It must have been trying for you. And I don't see that a few photographs can prove so much. Anything might seem to come out of them. Whatever is it to give you so much distress? You might have had some great sorrow. If she is your mother, then she is your mother, my dear; and we will treat her as your mother; and I shall like her better for being your mother. Of course I shall. But why think of it as a trouble? Whatever the story is, it can't have so much effect on us."

"It is not a trouble in itself, Sophia. I am glad to know my mother. Had things been otherwise, I should have been grateful for that knowledge of an ordinary man. I hope soon to hear of my father, though he is dead. Let me give you the account, as she gave it to me."

"Well, I don't see that it has much importance," said Sophia when he made an end. "You could not help the way you were brought into the world. We have always known it must be something of this kind, or Father would not have made such a secret of it. I can't follow now why he did amongst ourselves. I am not going to harass you by saying it is not true. I know you feel it is. And you may be like Mrs. Lang: I don't say you are not. I see you are like her. And Dinah is like her too. Dear little Dinah was so attracted by her face when she first saw her. It may have reminded her of you without her knowing it. And Mrs. Lang was only a child when it happened, and away from home. And your father seems to have done his best with his mistakes. It doesn't do to make a tragedy of these things. After all they are natural. Let us forget about it, and go on as we always do. I have you; and I am glad I am your wife, whoever you are."

"Sophia, that is the way I hoped you would look at it, your own way. But there is something else. Don't you see? Mrs. Lang is my mother. Her children are my brother and sister on the mother's side. They cannot marry our children. Apart from the truth's coming out and swamping their lives, it brings other dangers. What are we to do, Sophia?"

"You sit down, my dear. We will think of something. It is a shame that you should come home after a week's work, and be worried and worn with all this. Mrs. Lang should have told me first. Then you need only have been brought into it at the end. But she must have it all out with you, of course. But we will find some way out together."

"There is no royal road, Sophia," said Christian, almost laughing. "You can't impose your own will here. Though I wish you could for all our sakes. It has to be prevented, this that is going on."

"It is very hard on them," broke out Sophia. "Here they have been so dutiful in their home, and had very little to fill their youth! And now just this they were about to reach, snatched from them! I have always felt it for them, their not having much. I know how I resented the same thing for myself. This crashing down on them, as if there

77

were no justice in the world! My poor, good boy and girl! Well, they have their mother and father. They shan't want for anything their mother can do."

"Sophia," said Christian, "I shan't be at ease until this is done. I shan't know peace—and I am needing peace—until I know this harm is not going on. For we must see it as harm. It might turn out as such for them. Mrs. Lang is to tell her children the truth. What shall we tell ours? I think the truth. It is so likely to come out from one of us, and they are past childhood. What we are to tell the world we can decide together."

"Leave it to me," said Sophia. "We will do our best to shield them. They are too young in themselves. They have encountered too little of life. Their parents must protect them. It will be better for them not to know. I will try and manage it for them."

A message was sent, and the three young people came.

"Oh, you have all come!" said Sophia, with an awkwardness that went to her husband's heart. "Well, Robin always hears about things, doesn't he? Come in to us, my darlings. Father and I have something to say to you, something that may seem hard. We would help it for you, if we could. We would smooth out everything for you, if we could. You know that. We want you—we hope you will see a little less of Gilbert and Caroline. Not see quite so much of them. Will you do that for us?"

"Well, not unless we hear the reason," said Robin.

"I was not appealing to you, Robin," said Sophia. "I am talking to Andrew and Dinah."

"What is it all about?" said Andrew.

"Tell them, my dear. You will have to tell them," said Christian. "Let them have anyhow the main truth."

"This is what I am asking you, my children," said Sophia. "Simply not to see so much of the Langs. To meet them only when you must, and to trust your father and mother, that they are asking what is right for you. Will you do this for them?"

"No. It is expecting too much," said Andrew.

"It is wishing nothing for ourselves, Andrew," said Sophia.

"Tell them, Sophia. Or I will tell them," said Christian. "We can't hope they will take it from us, except as thinking beings."

"We might hope they would take something from us," said Sophia. "We have done a great deal for them."

Christian turned to his children.

"My son and daughter, I have discovered something today, that must prevent your marriage. You know I did not know who my parents were. I have found out today that Mrs. Lang is my mother. You will ask me how I know, and I will tell you. You may ask me anything more, and I will answer you. Anything you wish explained, I will seek for you. Everything I can do, I will do for you. Your mother will help you to the end of her power. We would have given a great deal to save you this."

There was a silence.

"Does it make any difference?" said Andrew. "I don't question what you say. I know you are sure, or you would not say it. But why can't we go on as we are doing? Of course we are related, but not closely. Nobody would know of it. A great many things must happen like that."

"Yes, you see, my son," said Christian.

"We can't give them up," said Dinah, looking at her mother. "They have become too much of our lives. We have too little without them. You must see so far."

"My child, we do see it," said Sophia. "We have been talking about it, Father and I. We will do all we can to make up to you."

"You have no power there," said Dinah. "You have nothing to give that will do it. And why should you try? It is not your fault that this has happened."

"Oh, isn't it, my child? I should have thought from your tone and Andrew's, that it was," said Sophia.

"No, no, Sophia. That does no good," said Christian.

"My dears, is there anything at all in which either of us can serve you?"

"You can make it easy for us to go on seeing them," said Andrew, raising his head. "If we cannot marry, we can spend our time with each other. It is all that is left to us. People must know in what way we are related; and we can be together as the relations that we are."

"But, my boy—" began Sophia.

"I suppose Mrs. Lang and Father's father were not married," said Andrew. "Do we know who Father's father was? Of course we always realised it must be something like this. How much better if Grandfather had told us! How much wiser a course, we see now. Don't let us have any more secrets. Let the relationship be known for what it is. We are none of us to blame. It is pitiful that we are not. There will be other complications in the future, if it is not disclosed. Who was Father's father?"

"I do not know yet, my son. When I do I will tell you," said Christian.

"My boy!" said Sophia, holding out her arms to Andrew.

Andrew moved to her as if he hardly saw her.

"I will not have it all known everywhere," Sophia broke out. "You don't ask me what I want. You go on thinking of yourselves— And of course, it is a very hard time for you. I know it is, darlings. Your mother feels it to the bottom of her heart. But you must think of me a little; I am not no one. I don't even want it known that Mrs. Lang is Father's mother. I don't care for it for him, somehow. And as for the whole thing's being spread about all over the county, I won't have it, for all your sakes. I know the world better than you do. You must listen to your mother."

"So this is what has been hushed up for half a century!" said Robin. "Mrs. Lang as a grandmother, whom two of us chose for a mother-in-law! The county has made less of it than I did, if it hasn't made more of it than that. Though of course the danger is the unrevealed grandfather."

"Dear boy!" said Christian, seeing the feeling under Robin's words.

"Darling, you think of Father, don't you?" said Sophia. "Mother knows what you mean. And any one who is Father's mother, is Father's mother, isn't she? But the world is not what you fancy it is, dear boy; not kind and compassionate for helpless trouble, as you think now you are young and generous. Poor children!"

"We had better say that Mrs. Lang and my father were married," said Christian, who had been in thought, "whoever he turns out to be. We will tell the truth, except for that, and for anything else that may prove to be better untold. We must decide what is to be said, and say it. We could say that my mother was left a widow so young, that she returned to her parents, and gave up her child for its own sake. It is known that Andrew Stace watched over my life from my infancy, and that he was set on bringing up a boy. We may not be justified in bringing what the whole truth might bring, upon those who have not the power of choice. We are probably not justified. Patty must be simply given the account when it is settled."

"Patty must be told the whole truth," said Andrew. "Dinah and I will want to talk to her about it."

Sophia looked at her son, and was silent.

"Well, people will have to accept what we say to our faces," said Robin.

"Robin, I think you must not deal with the matter, as if you were Father or me," said Sophia. "You don't know about these things yet, my boy."

"We never have much practice in things like this," said Dinah, trying to speak like herself.

"Well the truth is a safeguard against anything's going on, that must not," said Christian, in a weary tone. "I am talking about you as if you were not here, my dears. Why should I say anything behind your backs? As one of you said, we see the harm that comes of secrets."

"Andrew and I will go upstairs now," said Dinah to her

mother. "If Father will tell Robin all there is to know, he can tell us later."

"Yes, go, my darling. You do just what you like," said Sophia. "Robin will hear it all, and come and tell you. You and Andrew go and be together. You have each other, haven't you? Now, Christian, put the whole thing out of your mind. It is not such a tragedy. Just explain it once to Robin, and let that help you. They are young, and will easily put it behind. They don't feel what you imagine they are feeling. They will soon be themselves again. Now I am going to ask Patty to have her eyes on them, and not to let a word escape until she hears what is to be said."

Christian had hardly ended his story to his son, when a message was brought, that Mrs. Lang was worse. Sophia came downstairs to find him leaving the house.

"Yes, go, my dear. Of course you must go," she said. "You will find me waiting for you when you come back."

She smiled at him as he went, but turned to Robin, weeping.

"I hope it will be the end this time. How can I help praying for it? Father will be worn out if all this goes on. What has he done, helpful and hardworking as he is, that he should be hunted and dragged about like this? He has not the strength for it. I see he has not. He looks so old and weary for his age. It is not his fault if Mrs. Lang is his mother. It is not any one's fault. I wonder why Grandfather wanted to keep it a secret. It only made every one guess worse things than the truth. I know it did me. It would have been much better to make up a definite story."

"It would indeed," said Robin. "But contriving stories wasn't in his puritan line. There was his simple, immortal soul to be considered. And he did not choose for it to be known that Father's parents were not married. So he took the way to make the whole truth occur to every one, with a lot a deal worse; unless the unknown grandfather can't be worse."

"Oh, hush, dear," said Sophia. "He has been dead many years. Mrs. Lang told Father so. And anyhow he was

Father's father. Now go and explain what you know to the others, and make them think it will be nearly as good to know Gilbert and Caroline as friends. Uncle and aunt is absurd of course. We might call them cousins. Run and do that, my helpful boy."

Christian found his mother lying in bed, with Peter, who acted as his deputy, in the room. She turned her head towards him as he entered, as if she had just the strength.

"Well, you have come to say good-bye to me. It is not long between our meeting and our parting, is it, as what we are? It is easier for us that way. My children, you will find an elder brother to you here; and all three of you—I can say all three before I die—will tell each other that I have been helpless in what I have done for you. You may all find something coming out of what you have lost."

"She is wandering," said Peter.

"No. Hush. She is not," said Christian.

"No, I am not wandering," said Mrs. Lang with a smile. "But I don't wonder that you think so."

"She is my mother," said Christian to Peter in a low, clear voice. "It has been found out today."

Peter gazed at him in silence.

"Yes, today," said Mrs. Lang. "It is not long that we have had to know it. But it was yesterday that I found it out. I have had two days to be with it. You will all be able to remember that." She could just be heard. "To remember that I had two days with what I wanted, the last thing I needed in my life."

"She is sinking," said Peter, even his whisper having a penetrating tone.

"Hush!" said Gilbert.

A smile again crossed the old woman's face, and seemed to mingle with its last quiver. Her children always liked to recall the last expression they had seen on it.

"She hears nothing now," said Peter, and his words were true, or she would have heard them.

"Well, you know it all, my dears," said Christian. "This

has been too much of a day for you. I can't think I can do anything for you now. I will leave you to each other, as I have just left the two more my own. You know how hearts are with you in my house. And as the days go by, I hope we may come together in the way she wished."

"I hope we may," said Gilbert.

"Talk everything over," said Christian. "And if you have no chance to sleep, sit up together."

"Yes, yes, you give yourselves to doing all you can for each other," said Peter. "You talk it out, and get it off your minds, whatever it all is. It has been a great deal to come on you in one day, enough to crush all the spirit out of you, what with losing your mother on the top of it, as well. I shouldn't like my son and daughter——"

"Come, Peter," said Christian, "you have things to arrange for them. You and I will set off. There is no good in wishing there was a use for us here. I hope there may be a slight one later."

Sophia met her husband at his door.

"Well, it is all over, Sophia. You have guessed that it was the end. The two young people are rather on my mind, my brother and sister. But I must have a moment to breathe. I don't know who my father was. The moment for knowing did not come. The feeling I have always had against ferreting out what your father hid, must still stand me in good stead."

"We will turn our faces to the future," said Sophia, laying her hands on his arms, "and live in the present, and let the dead past bury its dead. If we ever know more of the truth, we will meet it with a strong front. But perhaps it was meant that we should not know. It seems as if it was. Now, settle down, Christian. We will do something about the boy and girl."

Christian obeyed as if the relief were great; and Sophia, on her way again to Patty's room, came upon Robin.

"What are you doing here, my dear? Where are the others?"

"In with Patty," said Robin, raising his eyes to the floor above. "They have been talking in there for some time. I don't think things will ever be so bad for them again."

"Dear boy!" said Sophia, passing him. "What a good, understanding boy you are! But don't talk to your mother with your hands in your pockets."

Robin took them out, and stood with his head thrown back, and after a moment followed her.

Dinah and Andrew were sitting together at the table, with Patty standing over them.

"Well, my dears, sitting for a little while with Patty?" said Sophia. "We all like to be with Patty sometimes, don't we? Miss Patmore, you have heard about it all? Well, we have to know now, that Mrs. Lang has passed away." Sophia never used the word death. She seemed to feel a threat in it. "She was suddenly worse, and my husband was sent for just in time. It all seems one thing coming on another. We can't feel to the last about everything. Christian looks exhausted as it is. You know all the rest from these poor children."

"Mrs. Lang dead now, is she?" said Patty, in the tone of one almost sated with excess of happening. "Well now, is she? Well! Did she say anything more before she died?"

"No, nothing more. We do not know who my husband's father was," said Sophia, yielding to Patty's need. "The end came before she could tell him. We have no clue to how it all may be. But we don't want to come upon anything more. We cannot stand any fresh disclosures just yet."

"Well, you would think she would tell him that first of all, wouldn't you?" said Patty, her eyes wide.

"I don't know. I have not thought about it," said Sophia, repressive in time.

"I suppose she meant not to tell him," said Andrew. "There must be reasons for keeping him a mystery."

"Well, we can't help them," said Sophia. "We have done nothing wrong. Now I must go back to Father. He is worried about Gilbert and Caroline. He does not give a thought to himself, though all this is really his trouble. Miss Patmore, go and bring them here for the night. That will set his mind at rest. People will have to know how they are related to us. It had better come out at once, if it has to come. Unless you would rather not, my dears? You would have to remember—"

"Yes, we should bear in mind that we must be on a different footing," said Andrew. "We should like them to come. We have been wanting to see them. It will be easier to have the first meeting while the shock is new, and while they are fresh from their other trouble. It will disguise the new relationship and be a help. For it is a great adjustment."

Sophia was wrought upon both by the pathos and the egotism of youthful grief.

"Well, if your first encounter is such a great thing, the sooner you get it over, the better for you and other people. I did not know that mattered so much, just the meeting. But if that is so, it will take your attention off the other things. I am all worked up, and hardly know what I am saying. Well, go, Miss Patmore, and fetch them, and bring them straight up here. My husband must not be harrowed again tonight. I will come out and say a word to them in the hall. And you must remember, all of you, that Father has had two great shocks, and that he is not as young as you are, and works hard for us all. You must try not to show him dreary faces. We can't only think of young, strong people and their troubles, can we?"

Andrew and Dinah looked at her, as if they hardly heard, and Robin stood with his eyelids drooping over his eyes.

"Do take your hands out of your pockets, Robin," said Sophia. "I told you that just now. Can't you find something to occupy them? Or must you stand about all the evening because other people are in trouble?"

"Yes, of course I must be about at people's service, when things are amiss, and they might have a use for me," said Robin. "I hope you will do the same when you get down to Father. To do you justice, I believe you will. And I discover something to employ my hands in opening the door for you. You are doing harm up here."

Sophia went out, without looking at and almost without thinking of her son. When voices came in the hall, she made a restraining sign to her husband.

"Well, my children, I couldn't have you alone tonight. It went to my heart to think of you. Why, Caroline, you are our little sister; and we can't have you crying the first time you come to our house as one of us. Yes, we thought you would come to it as one of the family in another way. And you miss your mother in your first set-back in life. I know how glad I feel that my boy and girl have theirs. But that has to be over; and we must make the most of you as we are allowed. And what we are going to say about your mother, is just that she was married a first time. We think you will like that best; and we like it best, too. And we think it is what she would choose for you. So we need never talk of that again. The others will tell you just what the words are to be. Now go up to them, and all make the most of each other in your new way. That is better than no way at all. It isn't as if you had lost each other."

"Sophia, I couldn't have done it better if I had rehearsed it for a week," said Christian.

"Ah, you will never get to the end of finding what I can do," said Sophia with a flash of her eyes. "You will always go on discovering that. I sometimes find myself marvelling at the gulf between the average person and myself."

"There must be worse kinds of loneliness," said Christian.

The young people greeted each other as their custom was, and Dinah broke the silence.

"Well, if we are equal to this occasion, no other in our lives can find us at a loss. We may look forward to all emergencies without misgiving."

"You may," said Caroline. "To speak at this moment and in that spirit! It is a great word and a great deed!"

87

"Did you compose it in your mind before?" said Robin.

"As Caroline and Gilbert came up the stairs," said Dinah.

"Then the act was immense," said Robin. "To say what you planned before, when the time for it came! Has any one ever done that? Can anything in life get the upper hand of you?"

"No, I said it could not," said Dinah.

"The circumstances are perhaps an unusual stimulus," said Andrew. "Not that I seem to find them so myself."

"We shall be able to talk in a natural way in a moment," said Caroline.

"Let us achieve it at once," said Andrew. "Let us put it all into words, and save ourselves a future of things that are never said. The future is enough for us without that. You have lost your mother. That is one thing."

"And what a normal and uncompromising thing!" said Dinah. "The next is our gaining and losing a grandmother in one day."

"And the next your all losing your future husbands and wives," said Robin. "Let us say it; then it is done."

"And our gaining an elder brother, and a niece and nephews! And your finding an uncle and aunt," said Gilbert. "Let us say it; then it is done."

"Well, it is done now, isn't it?" said Dinah. "We needn't mention obtaining the public eye, and losing hope, and keeping Sophia, and not coming upon our paternal grandfather. Those things will attend to themselves."

"If he is ever gained, he will end our story about Mother's first marriage," said Gilbert.

"Surely he will remain in darkness," said Andrew, "as through long lives and on death-beds he has held to it."

"Your mother was so kind to us, when we came in," said Caroline.

"We didn't mention your gain of a sister-in-law," said Robin. "I wonder if that is the word."

"We shall never change our feelings to each other," said

Gilbert, knowing himself the one with the power of speech. "I could never feel to Dinah except as I have felt. We shall not lose each other. We shall just have to live for what is left to us. It is not nothing."

"We shall not lose each other," said Caroline. "But some loss will come. It is coming. Let us say it; then it is done."

Patty came in with a tray, without warning; knowing that her entrance would not be felt an intrusion.

"Now, here is something hot for all of you to drink. And then you must all go to bed. Mrs. Stace wanted you not to stay up."

"Well, we have gained a nurse!" said Gilbert. "That is our real gain. But we should have had it anyhow."

"Patty, we are so haunted by our paternal grandfather," said Dinah, leaning against Patty as she stood behind her.

"Oh, I should not worry about him," said Patty in a voice too light for truth.

"Patty, you know you would worry about him," said Dinah. "You know he is clouding your mind and complicating your every thought. It is not just death and tragedy, all comfortably found out, that is making you look as you do."

"We shall all get dark feelings for him," said Gilbert. "I am already jealous of his knowing Mother when she was seventeen."

"Well, you do feel that you want to know a thing, when you know it must have been somehow, don't you?" said Patty with candour. "But I dare say it is better for us not to know."

"I don't doubt it is for us," said Dinah. "Though I am not so sure. The other grandfather can't be worse than we have imagined; so he is probably better than other people have; and the sooner he comes to light, the worse for them and the better for us. But I don't think we will be selfish about it."

"No, don't let us think of it," said Patty. "Thinking can't do any good anyhow."

"I am afraid not, Patty, not by itself," said Dinah.

"Well, we should keep it to ourselves if we did know," said Patty. "Hark! There is Mother coming."

Sophia's rustle sounded on the stairs as if she meant it to be heard.

"Well, here is a good, sensible group of dear people! Here is a dear party of brothers and sisters. Because that is what you must be, isn't it? We know that Gilbert and Caroline are a funny sort of brother and sister to Father really. But that is not what we want. So we will have you all brothers and sisters together. And now you must all go to bed. You have had such a wearing day in your different ways, poor children! Dinah, my dear one, you look worn out. How have they both been, Robin? How are they really, Miss Patmore? Promise Mother that you will try to sleep."

CHAPTER V

"I AM DOING the thing I am most ashamed of, of all I have ever done," said Julian. "I don't mean those things in a young man's life that he does not speak of to his sister, though if you look at me with eyes of unbelief, Sarah, I shall feel obliged to mention them. I mean little, innocent, degrading things, like asking acquaintances to tea to gossip about friends. And such examples of each as the Drydens and the Staces! It is the sort of thing I have always had done for me; and to be able to find no one to do it makes me feel I must be losing the way I had. But we can't put gossip off until we return from London. It has a frail hold on life like all precious things. I did hint to Tilly; but I know now about hinting about a tea-party to Tilly."

"Dear little Tilly!" said Sarah. "Is she an acquaintance or a friend? A friend of course."

"Yes, of course," said Julian. "I am so glad that she and her father and brother are coming this afternoon. Of course."

"You are just in time to put them all off, if you really want to," said Sarah. "I can be ill if you like."

"Do you think I would stoop to deceit," said Julian, "and about a matter so near to me as my sister's health, to save myself a little loss of self-respect? You don't think I shall lose the respect of others, do you? And you know I do not really want to put them off. That is what I have just explained to you with shame."

"I could not bear to," said Sarah. "And I don't feel shame. Why should we think we are above the average?"

"Well, I can hardly say why," said Julian, bringing in a vase of flowers. "That is the kind of thing one does not say; but surely there are some reasons. Look at my compunction this afternoon. I really think we must be a little above. Even a very little is quite a rare enough thing to be. Now suppose no one should bring up the subject?"

"Well, you will have to," said Sarah.

"I could not," said Julian, "for fear it might be thought that I was giving the tea-party for my true reason. I owe it to my guests to show them my best side. I have just shown you my worst, and you see it is not fit for guests."

"Only for your sister?" said Sarah.

"Yes, only that," said Julian.

"I don't know why it is your party," said Sarah. "People will think it is as much mine."

"I am afraid they will not," said Julian. "If they would look on me just as a young man happening to join a group of his sister's friends, I could broach the subject. But they know I am not that kind of personality. I believe they do think about my personality a little."

"Well, I will sacrifice myself," said Sarah. "I am sure they don't think about mine, even a little."

"Well, sacrifice is known to be a thing that women are better at than men," said Julian. "Men, I know, are hopeless at it. That is why I have such a respect for womanhood. It is such a sure ground, and that is suitable for that class of feeling. But I don't think it matters making an exception of Judith. She and Edward will sit and not say a word about the subject, and feel that keeping off it is exalting. And sitting, doing that seems worse than just doing it. It seems to imply a breach of the rules of hospitality. And I find keeping off it lowering. I find I have less and less in common with Edward."

"Oh, do you indeed?" said Edward's voice. "Well, it is good to know how we stand. But, my dear Julian, I feel that I have more and more in common with you."

"Well, I have been fearing that you and Judith feel yourselves above gossip," said Julian: "and that is out of sympathy with me today. I find myself on a level with it, and even Sarah finds herself tolerably placed. So I hardly know how we are to talk."

"Why should we talk about it?" said Edward, revealing that he knew what the matter was.

"It is not a particularly interesting thing to talk about," said Judith.

"I think that is just what it is," said Sarah.

"Do you, Sarah?" said Edward. "I should have thought you would feel it better not to discuss the affairs of our friends, when they are painful for them, and nothing to do with us."

"I am susceptible to that appeal, Edward. But the affairs of our friends are surely something to do with us," said Sarah.

"Sarah, how clever and cunning you are!" said Julian. "I see now that it is our duty to discuss them."

"I don't see what people get out of threshing out things like this," said Edward.

"Have you really had the chance to draw conclusions?" said Sarah.

"Do you mean it is actually not apparent to you?" said Julian. "And you a man conversant with the needs of the human soul! And 'things like this,' as if it were a common kind of a thing! I knew a parson's life was rich in human secrets, but I didn't know it was as good as it is. I wish I had been a parson and given up my life to others. It is always others who have things come upon them. I see that virtue is its own reward."

"Well, a parson has done something if he makes you see that," said Edward.

"Edward, persistent good humour is really an attack on the sly," said Julian.

"Oh, but gossiping about people, and gloating over their difficulties, and indulging in a sort of offensive pity is such an average sort of thing," said Judith.

"I don't think it is at all. Most people are a long way above that," said Sarah.

Edward broke into laughter.

"Sarah, do make an end of pretending to be dense. You know what I mean," said Judith.

"Yes, yes, of course I do, my dear," said Sarah.

"Well, we couldn't any of us be average," said Julian. "I do agree with Judith there. Perhaps that is why she was trying to be below the average. But Cousin Peter is coming, and it does not matter if he is forced to the dead level."

"Poor Cousin Peter! Why should he be sacrificed?" said Edward.

"Because none of us will be, and he is left," said Julian.

"Well, what are you all so engrossed about?" said Peter, entering in front of his children, his tone showing he was aware of a theme that would lead to this state. "You are all in the thick of it, I can see. Well, I can tell you we had a time coming along. I am all in a heat and flurry. First a drove of cattle; and Tilly must get up on a gate! That was the thing for her, after spending the whole of her life in the country! And Latimer and I standing by her, for the creatures to lunge at as they passed, and all of us getting more of it that way! And then we passed Sophia and Christian Stace; and Tilly would not meet them; not after all that had happened, she said. She would get behind a haystack. And sheltering there, behind that haystack, feeling too broad to be hidden by it, I never felt so small in my life; felt so big; ha, ha! No, I will have some muffin, Tilly. Spying on me, for fear I am getting fatter! Staring at me, in case I am taking something to eat! You have your own tea, don't you? Would you wish your father to starve? How am I to go on working for you? I have been in the stress of things lately, too. And it's not such a thing to be such a pair of little skinnamajinks. It's nothing to be proud of. It would be a good thing if you and Latimer got a little size! How I can have had two such—"

"And were you hidden by the haystack?" said Julian.

"No. Well, yes. Yes, I think so. I don't think they saw me," said Peter, taking his cup.

"Cousin Sophia did," said Tilly, as if this was hardly of consequence, as contact had been avoided.

"I hope she appreciated our delicacy," said Latimer.

Julian laughed, and Latimer looked rewarded for what he had undergone on his way.

"What were you saying about coming along?" said Sarah, turning her chair to Peter.

"I was saying— Oh, I was saying, I was saying that we got delayed, yes, got delayed," said Peter, stirring his tea with a ruminative look.

"Some one will have to be average," said Julian. "I wish it were not a thing that I have such a distaste for. If some one else will be average, I will do the next thing that is really wrong. That is my kind of conceit, I am afraid the average kind."

"They are all expecting you to say something, Father," said Tilly, her little pale eyes going in a birdlike way from face to face.

"Expecting me to say something? Me? No, I don't think so. I didn't come with anything to say," said Peter, his voice low under the pressure of his thought.

"Those columbines are wonderful, Sarah," said Edward. "Did you grow them?"

"I grew them, and cut them, and put them in that pot," said Julian. "Every little womanly touch in this cottage is mine."

"Now, upon my word," broke out Peter, as if his reflections had gathered to a head and now burst forth; "this is an extraordinary thing, this that has come out about the Staces and the Langs! Upon my soul it is. This about their being related, and Mrs. Lang's being Christian's mother, and all of it! It is the most astounding combination of things I have come across in my experience. In all my years as a doctor, if you will believe me. It is indeed."

"We will believe you," said Latimer.

Peter gave his son a look that hardly took a definite character, and went on:

"I'll stake my life that I have never conceived of such a thing, as a man's not knowing his own mother, and then coming across her in a stranger on the verge of death. It gives you to think; it does. There must be a providence in these matters. To my mind it puts it beyond a doubt. Its coming out through those photographs in time to prevent those four young people from marrying! That gives you to stop and speak to yourself. For if it had come out after, it would have been a ghastly thing, an out-and-out horrible thing for all of us. We can't be too thankful we are spared that."

"We can't be. We could never have spoken about it at all," said Julian.

"Providence might have kept it back altogether, if it had kept it back as long as that," said Latimer.

"Is Providence 'it'?" said Tilly.

"Ah, we can't see behind these things," said Peter. "But I never thought to come across such a thing in my ordinary life; in my professional life it was, really; in my professional life."

"Truth is stranger than fiction," said Latimer.

"Yes, yes. There it is. You have it there," said Peter, causing his son's eyes to seek those of his friends.

"I don't think it really is," said Tilly.

"Well, upon anything you like," went on Peter, openly at the end of his resources of emphasis, "when I was standing there, thinking that Mrs. Lang was wandering, and it gradually dawned on me that she was herself; that she meant what she said, and that she was Christian's mother; well, you could have knocked me down with anything; you could indeed. I didn't know where I was. And when I saw Christian—"

"Oh, Father, don't go on," said Tilly.

"Not go on? Why not? I am just telling them about it. It isn't often one has a thing like this to describe. Why, I was there amongst them, actually in the room, as near to them as I am to any of you, watching it all come out before my eyes! It was a thing to mark, I can assure you. I was downright moved. When I saw—"

"Father, that will do," said Latimer.

"That will do! Oh, that is your opinion, is it? When will you learn how much of your voice will be enough, you piping morsel of a boy? When I am trying to entertain people, to tell them something for their pleasure—to—well, what are you all laughing at? First it is all so solemn, as if there were something wrong in what I was saying; though I can't help it; I don't know if you expect me to prevent what has been happening. And then you all begin to laugh, as if I were making—ha, ha!—some joke. Ha! Well, it does make one feel inclined to laugh in a way. It is because we are so worked up about it. That is what it is. Well, when I saw—"

"No, Father, don't," said Tilly.

"Don't? Why, what is the matter with all of you? Oh, you find it upsetting, do you? Well, it is enough to knock you all out; it is indeed. I am thoroughly out of spirits, myself. I can't bear to think of those poor boys and girls, all with their lives upside down. I was feeling it a relief to talk of it. But if you all find it is too much for you, if it affects you in that way, I can quite understand it. I can quite follow its taking people like that."

"But it was dreadful when it took him like that," said Julian. "We are being ungrateful, and failing as hosts, and making a guest feel awkward—though I don't believe we are—and behaving in a shameful way. What are we to do?"

"I don't see why we shouldn't talk of it," said Sarah, turning to Peter. "Everything is less depressing when it is talked of."

"Yes, yes, that is what I think. You are right, Miss Wake," said Peter. "That is how I judge, myself. Well, as I was saying, when I saw Mrs. Lang lying there, and heard what she said to Christian about his being an elder brother to her children—well, I won't be too much for you; but when I heard that, well, what struck me was not that the young folks wouldn't be able to marry; I never thought of that. What came into my head was: 'Well, what is coming out now? Who is Christian's father?' And then she died before she could get it out, passed away before she could tell it, poor old lady! Well, what is it? Ah, ha! What is it now?"

"Nothing that came out could make any difference to Cousin Christian," said Tilly.

"No, no, Tilly, it couldn't," said Peter. "I like to hear you say it, Tilly. Cousin Christian is a man whom anything that came out, or might come out, would leave simply as he was. I declare that he is. I say that about him."

"It goes without saying, doesn't it?" said Judith.

"I am glad it didn't have to this time," said Julian. "I can hardly bear that sort of thing to have to go without saying."

"Well, I do believe in saying plainly anything in that line," said Peter in a modest tone. "I am for coming right out with what one has to say in favour of a friend, when he happens to be in any kind of difficulty. That is what I believe."

"So do I," said Sarah.

"Sarah, we are falling short as hosts again," said Julian. "This time towards a lady, because Judith's hosts ought to regard her in that light. And it must be failing as a host to be glad that a guest has hardly spoken, and I find I feel that about Edward."

"I don't really much like Mrs. Lang to have been Cousin Christian's mother," said Tilly. "I mean, I like him to be how he has always been, just by himself."

"So do I, Tilly," said Julian.

"Yes, yes, I know what you mean," said Peter. "But as the truth has emerged, you know, I wish that it had all followed suit; that she had told him who his father was, while she was about it. In fact, if I had known what was in the air, I would have tried to bring it off, while I was in the room, and in a way in authority, you know. It would have saved a lot of talk. I almost wish I had."

"I quite wish it," said Julian. "But people can't do what they almost wish and quite wish, of course. They must do what they don't wish."

"Not even to save talk," said Latimer.

"Oh, you couldn't have, Father," said Tilly. "You weren't really in authority, with Cousin Christian coming."

"Well, we must be off. I see that Judith and Edward are," said Peter, with no rancour towards his daughter.

"Oh, don't talk about being off, as if you could hardly stay," said Julian. "It sounds so full of zest, being off. Wait while I go to the door with Judith and Edward. Look at them, being off, and think how humbling that is for us."

"I know where Edward and Judith are going," said Tilly, nodding her head.

"Where?" said Sarah.

"To the Manor," said Tilly.

"Well, why shouldn't they go to the Manor?" said Peter. "What of it?"

"I don't know," said Tilly.

"I do," said Julian, returning. "I do believe you are right, Tilly."

"Why, whatever is it?" said Peter. "Are they, because they are going to the Manor, to be thought to be courting the young Staces? Is that it? I follow you, you see. Why, surely people can pay a call without implying that. Though it would be a right down good thing. We can't but see it would, for those poor young things to have something else in their lives. But you can't take people up in that way for making a visit to a friend. Why, you often go to the Manor yourself, Tilly; and no one would say you wanted to marry Andrew, were likely to marry Andrew. Or you might want to marry Julian by being here, or Latimer might want to marry Sarah. Ha, ha!"

"Or you might want to marry her, Father," said Latimer, with fierce eyes.

"Oh, well, so I might. Well, I hadn't thought of that. I always think of myself as a married man, as a widower,

99

you know. But that shows how people can do things without meaning anything."

Julian escorted his guests into the garden, cut some flowers for Tilly, and opened the gate. Peter at once strode through it.

"You should not go out before Tilly, Father," said Latimer.

"Not go out before Tilly? Oh, what is this now? One can't go to that length in standing on ceremony with one's own family. What a thing to make a fuss over now! Tilly doesn't mind."

"No, do go first, Father. I think you ought to," said Tilly, carrying her flowers as if almost too much had come to her.

"Well now, you are a nice little thing," said Peter, linking his arm in hers. "You are the kind of little creature I like. Not always carping about everything. You and I will walk together."

They did so, and Latimer walked apart, bearing the flowers with an air of gallantry unrepressed.

"It has been a dreadful tea-party, Sarah," said Julian. "I must cheer myself by having a real tidy-up. No, don't put the saucers together on the top of the spoons. Leave it to me, Sarah. I must ask you not to attempt to be a help to me here. I need the support to my spirits of active usefulness. I think that is braver than having a good cry. My party—your party has been a most humiliating unsuccess. We have asked people to come and see us, and given them no pleasure."

"We have," said Sarah.

"Do you really think so," said Julian, "apart from showing your power to look clearly at your own failures? I see you have that. Do you think they really didn't enjoy being with us? Do you think my reputation as such a charming young man, that it hardly matters his doing nothing, is gone; and that people will expect me to do something now? And that we must leave the village, when the passage floor takes a polish, and people understand about this room's being called the parlour, and start again in those uphill ways in another place? If so, try to forget yourself, because men are so helpless in trouble. And you never did feel sincerely about the parlour; and you know that the one thing I mean I am not saying."

"Yes, I know," said Sarah. "I wonder why Tilly was so sure of it?"

"Tilly does know those things," said Julian. "She must by now. She knows that I don't want to marry her. I am too out of spirits to mind beginning with myself. You know, when I am in spirits, how sensitive I am about Tilly. And that Edward doesn't want to marry her, and that Andrew and Robin don't. She must know them from practice now. And we must admit that you and I are slow about them."

"We must," said Sarah.

"Do you think we haven't really anything much in us?" said Julian.

"I have often suspected it," said Sarah.

"Apart from being courageous and dispassionate, do you think so?" said Julian. "I agree you are both of those."

"About myself," said Sarah. "You have some little qualities."

"Well, I shouldn't expect you to admit a thing like that about yourself," said Julian.

Judith and Edward had paused at the gate of the Manor, where their own way turned aside.

"We might as well go in and see them," said Edward. "I think we may do so much."

"It would be the decent thing to do," said Judith.

They walked across the lawn, where they had seen, without speaking, the group of Dinah and Andrew and Gilbert and Caroline. Dinah was talking to Caroline, and the two young men together. Robin was strolling on the grass apart, calling contributions to the talk.

"Dinah, I hope you will let us come in," said Edward. "I don't suppose you care about seeing us, but we go on wanting to see you."

"And so we consider ourselves first," said Judith.

"We are eager to meet every one as soon as we can," said Dinah; "to get all our encounters over before time heals and our spirits return, and we are alive again to embarrassment, which will be very soon, our comforters say."

"We are glad to serve any purpose of yours," said Edward, "and that you care to see us for any reason. You are not letting anything get the better of you, I know."

"Things have done that without any slackness of ours," said Robin.

"Now we are seeing about other people's lives not being shadowed by our selfish troubles," said Dinah. "I wonder why other people's lives are always especially thought of, when certain ones are stricken. People have only to get into trouble for every one to be in a fever about other people. And why are troubles called selfish? We none of us compete for them, and they don't seem the things for selfish people."

"They are not, Dinah," said Edward. "I knew that nothing would be too much for you. I have been saying that to myself."

"I don't think anything else can be," said Dinah.

"I wish you would give me some praise," said Andrew. "I am behaving equally well with Dinah."

"Praise often means more when it is not said," said Judith.

"It is worse for Caroline and me because we have not such good characters to help us," said Gilbert, unconsciously setting forth the change in their lives.

"We are only imitating," said Caroline.

"We are all of us acting," said Dinah.

"That is often the bravest thing to do," said Edward.

Gilbert got up suddenly and took his leave.

His sister, walking at his side, saw that words on his trouble would be best for him. "Does anything ever take the place of a thing that is gone?" she said.

Gilbert suddenly smiled into her face, and took her arm.

"It is people who do, people who must," he said.

CHAPTER VI

"CHRISTIAN, YOU KNOW what I told you," said Sophia. "Come and look out of this window. Now do you often find me wrong? Just watch them, walking together, Dinah and Edward and Andrew and the girl! It is plain enough to you now? They feel that no one can see them so close to the house. They forget this window in the hall, poor children! Do you see now that I am right?"

"I see no proof that you are not, and signs that you may be. So we again contemplate losing them, and again rejoice?"

"We ought to be glad that they have got their spirits back. That should be more to their parents than losing them. I am sure it is to me. They have been so brave and good through all the confusion. I haven't been always very patient with them. It is such a relief to feel they are themselves and looking forward. Whether we want it to come to anything or not, it is a comfort to their mother to feel that."

"It is to us both," said Christian.

"Christian, what is the matter with you lately? You seem as if you couldn't take an interest in anything on earth. Don't you feel it concerns you, then, that your children may be shaping their future lives?"

"Yes, I do, Sophia. I am glad that the future can give as well as take."

"What is the matter, Christian? Do you mean something you are not saying? Oh, I do hate that habit of yours. Come into the study and tell me. I knew you had something on your spirits; I have tortured myself about it for weeks. Only I was afraid to speak of it. What is it?"

Sophia's voice rose towards a shriek.

"Sophia," said Christian, "I am going to ask more of

you than I have had need to yet. So you can guess it must be a great deal. You know I have something on my mind. I need not have thought you had not seen. I have only you to turn to."

"What is it? I will not fail you, dear one. You may trust me. Do I have to tell you? Have you done anything wrong? Has any one of our children? I will stand by any of you to the very last. You know I will. What is it?"

"Nothing of that kind, Sophia," said Christian, his voice shaken with pity for her, that she should clutch at these things to protect her from the truth. "Don't you guess what it is?"

"Yes, yes, I guess. I know what it is. You are not well. I have seen you are not. I have known it in my heart all the time lately. I have tried not to face it. Tell me, Christian. Whatever it is, you and I will meet it together."

"No, I am not well, Sophia. I have half felt you must know. I have promised you to keep nothing from you, and I will keep my promise. I have the same trouble of the heart that my mother had. It has come to me much earlier than to her. It is thought to be hereditary. I am doing my best with it, and hope to get the upper hand. If I do not, I may live for years. But I have told you, to put it all on to you. You see I still have the instincts of a healthy man. I am laying more on you than there has ever been on me, than there is on me now."

Sophia stood silent. This first moment in her life of placing restraint on herself was terrible to her. It was her instinct to burst into wild grief.

"My dear, sit down, and I will keep at your hand. Now tell me something, my husband. I must ask you that one thing. All my interest in life depends on it, all my will to live. I must say it once. What chance is there of your curing yourself?"

"All the chances," said Christian, his tone light with his relief that the truth was told. "I am as busy as can be with my precious self. So are one or two others of the trade. We all think I shan't be got out of the way so easily."

"You have taken other advice?" said Sophia, the significance of this working into her mind.

"My dear, I have done all there was to be done, of course. I know you have no use for a fool, and shouldn't have faced you with a fool's tale. But that only means there is something not right, as I have said, and that measures can be taken."

"Do they think they can do any good?" said Sophia.

"They think so, and I agree with them, and I have great faith in myself. The thing is to keep at peace and at work. You must not hinder me in either. You can see I am not feeling ill. I am shifting the whole on to your shoulders. I could see you expected that. You must treat me as a creature to be spoiled and saved; and no serious thing must be kept from me. That would trouble me in the worst way, and would have a wrong end at last. I shall be about much too long to make that sort of thing possible."

"How long do you think you will be here anyhow?" said Sophia.

"I think I shall live to be an old man, Sophia. I think I shall heal myself. But 'anyhow' is a big word. Anyhow, I shall live for a longer time than we can manage without settling into ways that work. Now I am going to smoke my pipe and read my book, and do the things I shall be doing for the next twenty years."

Sophia left him at once. He had seen that she could not control herself for another moment. He held himself back from entering into her grief. It was what he could do for her now, for her and for all of them, to spare himself. Both his native simplicity and the heaviness caused by his illness helped him.

Sophia went with a stumbling step up to Patty's room. Patty looked up with startled eyes as she saw her face. Her step had prepared her for something, Sophia's step, stumbling!

"Miss Patmore," said Sophia, pausing white and tense before her, "you have been with me through all my time of happiness. You were at my hand at the hour of my romance. You have watched my feeling for my husband grow with my growth, with every day of the twenty-seven years we have gone our way together. Now it is threatened, Miss Patmore, our love and our life with each other. It is not safe any longer. Christian is ill; his heart is not right. He is a sick man, my husband. He has told me as he promised he would. How thankful I am that I made him give me that word! It is the illness that Mrs. Lang had, his mother. There is this great cloud come over us!"

Sophia in her extreme moments, when she suffered more than most, never ceased to listen to herself.

Patty had sprung to her feet; and Sophia saw her face and fell into her arms, breaking into weeping loud enough to work on Patty, but not to reach the ears of her husband below.

"The children must be told," she said. "I must bring this shadow on them. I will tell them the whole before you, Miss Patmore, so as only to make the effort once. That will save me most. I shall need to spare myself. Where are they?"

Patty stood with uncertain eyes, stricken by the thought of the truth's being broken to Sophia's children by Sophia. But Sophia did not read faces easily, and had never thought to read Patty's at all.

"Are they in the house?" she said, standing up with the tears still on her face, and consciously not wiping them away.

"I am not sure where they are now," said Patty. "I will find them and tell them. But it is you we must think of, Mrs. Stace. You must come and lie down. Then I will look for them and break it to them."

"No, I will do it," said Sophia. "It is for their mother to tell them of this great darkness that has fallen over all our lives. Over yours too, I know, Miss Patmore. For them to hear of it from her lips. I must not shirk what is binding on myself. It is indeed not for me to get into the way of doing that. That is for any one but me."

She moved to the door.

"Andrew! Dinah!" she called, in a voice that took an imperious note, as the answer was not to the moment. "Andrew! Dinah! I want you both."

Andrew and Dinah appeared at the door of their study.

"Where is Robin?" said Sophia. "Is Robin there too? Tell him to come to me with you."

The three came and stood in Patty's room, their gaze on their mother. Patty turned her eyes from their faces.

"My children," said Sophia, "my boys and girl, I have a great anxiety to bring on you today. Dear Father is not well, dear ones, not well and strong as he used to be. There may come a time when we feel we may not have him with us much longer."

There was a silence.

"What is it all? Tell us about it," said Andrew.

"Yes, your mother will tell you, my son," said Sophia. "Your mother will say all the words that are so hard to be said. She will do what has to be done. She will indeed have to now. God grant that she may have strength and courage for it. For it will need both. You will have to help me, Andrew. For the spirit may indeed be willing, but the flesh weak."

She looked at her son with steady eyes.

"What is it?" said Robin. "We do not know yet."

"Yes, you know, my boy," said Sophia. "I have just told you."

"What illness is it?" said Dinah.

"A trouble of the heart, my daughter," said Sophia, "my daughter who has always loved her father, and always been a comfort to him. You will all have to be a help to him now. For he must not be troubled in any way, if we are to keep his presence in our home. He hopes to be able to cure himself; and we will all pray, indeed we will, that he may be given power. Truly it means everything to us. But we shall have to do our share; and that will be to think only of him, and to give our whole lives to planning how we can please him and save him in everything. Will you be able to do that, Robin?"

"Yes," said Robin, looking at her in the eyes.

"That is my darling boy," said Sophia, turning them away. "And my Andrew will be such a strength to his mother, such a solace and support. And my Dinah—you must not cry, Dinah dear. We have not to yield to our own needs just now. Now I tell you what, my children. I have told you the truth, because you are old enough to take your stand at my side, and it is not right that I should carry such burdens alone. I know you would be unhappy at the thought. But I think it will be best for Father not to understand that you realise how ill he is. Then you will be able to meet him as usual, and not show him any sad faces. I will just tell him that you know he must be taken care of. That will be enough. So that will be the first thing you have to do for him, to be your own bright selves, that he loves to have about him, and not let him see you are anxious, or that any trial has come to you at all. So you may run away now. We shall have some more talks together."

Sophia ended on a firm, bright note, and Patty's eyes recoiled before what she did unconsciously. As she went downstairs, the three came back to Patty's room.

"Patty, tell us all about it," said Dinah.

"I don't know anything more than you do, darling," said Patty, the endearment meaning much more on her lips than on Sophia's. "I only heard what you heard, and the same just before you came in. But I am sure and certain that he will get well. I never felt more convinced of anything in my life. He doesn't look at all as Mrs. Lang did, and Mother said her illness was the same. She was his mother, and she did not die of it until she was seventy-five. That shows he has plenty of time to cure himself. Oh, I know he will do it; I feel it with all my strength. He can do so much, that time is all he wants. And I believe Mother thinks so too. I can tell that she does."

"Yes, I gather that she does, too," said Robin.

"Patty, I believe it is spurious comfort," said Andrew. "But what a good thing your kind of falseness is!"

"Nothing that has happened, would be as bad as Father's being cut off at fifty-eight," said Dinah, turning to the door.

Andrew went after her.

"Well, Patty, you wouldn't have thought that our home life cried out for any extra burdens," said Robin. "I don't quite see the place for them myself. We couldn't have had worse news, unless it had been one of us, or you. Of course, I shall escape the stress of it by being in London. It sounds like myself, but Father hadn't had much time for me; for any of us, but least of all for me. The other two will have to pay dear for the difference."

"I am glad, I am sure, that one of you can escape some of it," said Patty. "The strain on the others will be dreadful; and they are so young, Dinah only twenty-four. To have to know it, and to seem as if they did not! There couldn't be anything harder. Mother does not think of what she is putting on them. It ought not to be like that. She could not take that on herself, and we should not wish her to. She is very brave in her way, and it is terrible for her. And Father as ill as that! Oh, I don't know what to do for all of you."

Patty wrung her hands, and looked imploringly at Robin, rather than with encouragement, as she would have at the other two. She felt that he needed her less, and had come to lean on him, when she felt she must lean on some one; and the two had many equal discussions together.

"Oh, yes, she has her own courage," said Robin. "She has no experience of what it is to be required to show some one else's. How could she have any? She has never done anything in any one else's way. But I am glad that Father has her. She will do well by him, unless she finds it too much. And it will have to be a good deal, to get the better of her. The worst of it is, that it is not a little. We shall see in the next few days."

They saw in the ensuing days that Sophia did well by her husband. This was not too much for her. But something was. She was unlike herself in her way of taking her trouble. She made strangely slight demands on Patty and her children, hardly spoke unless Christian was with her, and seemed as if something was holding her from giving herself to her grief. On the fourth day she came to Patty's room, looking wearied and desperate.

"Miss Patmore, I must talk to you. I can't go on a moment longer without a little human sympathy. I must ask you what you advise; I have no one else to ask. I cannot turn to my husband. I must not trouble him. I must do without the help I have had all my life. I have something on my mind; and I must share it with a human being. I don't mean about Christian; there is no need to say that that is ever present with me. It is something that nobody knows of, that I have been carrying alone. It seems that I have enough to struggle under, but it is not to suffice. In a way, this is wearing me more than my husband's state, because in that we are helpless. I feel that it may be causing his illness, that his health may have failed because of it. Do you remember the day before my father left us; and how he was busy with some papers early in the morning? The day before he passed away in the night."

"Yes, I remember," said Patty. "He was very taken up with them. Two of the servants were sent for to witness something; a will, I think; before he was up; the two who left a little later, when you got them a married post; and he would hardly finish dressing, he was in such an impatient mood. But he burnt them directly afterwards."

"Well, I think he may have put some of them in the desk in his room, that is my room now; and I believe he must have meant them to be examined after he was gone. It went out of my head at the time, with all I had on me. What a life it was, for a girl of my age! But it has been borne in upon me, that he meant some papers to be found and read. I have been living again all my time with my husband, and a strong sense has come to me that that was in his mind. I don't know why I never thought to do it. I suppose I was in a state of utter confusion from shock. The desk has always been locked, hasn't it?"

"Yes, always," said Patty. "I thought there was no key to it."

"Yes, I thought that too," said Sophia. "But I suppose there might be one somewhere. It might be on the ring that used to be my father's. There seems no reason why it should not be there. I don't know all the keys on that bunch. I have a feeling that we ought to open that desk, and read those papers; that there may be a sort of curse on us, until it is opened, and all has been done to put right its being forgotten before."

Sophia said what she said simply. She held unquestioned her parents' religious beliefs, and had a vein of superstition from her mother's touch of peasant blood. These were not the things on which she had turned her strong reason. Patty had freed herself from such trammels by her simple instinctive process of following what was new.

"Oh, no, I don't think it can be that," she said with a swift look at Sophia, uneasiness conquering the curiosity in her eyes. "I don't see it can make any difference now; I am sure it can't. Mr. Stace would have said, if he had wanted it opened. He always spoke so firmly about anything he wished, I should leave it alone, as it has been left— as nobody has thought of it for all these years. Things have quite another meaning after a long time. The papers couldn't bear on anything now."

"But it would be doing all we can do, to atone for our long neglect of it," said Sophia. "I have a feeling that there will be a kind of doom on the house, until I have faced what I should have faced all those years ago. That my husband is being sacrificed to my leaving it undone. I feel that, Miss Patmore. After all, it is nothing to do. Even if it were to turn out to be something like a will, leaving everything to other people, instead of to us, and we had to leave the place, it would not matter to me, compared with my husband's health. He has other money now, enough for us to manage. This trouble may have come from his working too hard. Not that I think it is anything of that kind. The thought only flashed across my brain. There may not be any papers there at all. He may have burnt all of them. But I have made up my mind that it must be done, Miss Patmore."

"Let me just go and see, and tell you if there is anything there," said Patty.

"No, no, Miss Patmore. It must be properly done," said Sophia, smiling.

"Well, then, I should tell Dr. Stace," said Patty, slowly, "and ask him if he agrees it ought to be done; just tell him easily, as if it were a thing you had just thought of." Patty betrayed her surmise that Sophia had not just thought of it, but Sophia cared little, almost too little to observe it, for a knowledge in Patty that would never be put into words. "Then he could say whether it would have any importance now, whatever it is. He would not make too much of a thing that perhaps should never have been done at all."

"He would do what was just," said Sophia. "That is what he must have the chance to do. I knew I was doing right in coming to you, Miss Patmore. We are never wrong in making that decision. I will tell him in a way that cannot disturb him, and get my mind at peace. He said that nothing was to be kept from him; and it is time that I had some peace. I feel cheered already, now that I have made my resolve. I feel as if his efforts to cure himself will be blessed, now that nothing is to be hidden. It hardly matters what it is, as long as we can face things all together, safe with him. Miss Patmore, you might go and say a word to cheer those poor children. I am afraid I depressed them more than I needed the other day. I might have given them a little more heart. And they have seen me going about since, as if there was such a tragedy over us. And indeed there is. They must not be heartened, so that they relax their efforts to consider their father. You must just say what you think best. I will go down now, to do what must be done."

Patty, uncertain how to fulfil her mission, remained where she was, and Sophia went down to her husband.

"Christian, I have something to say to you that has just come into my head, quite a little thing. You need not even stop reading if you would rather not. I dare say there is nothing in it, but it has got on my mind. It is being anxious about you. And you look better, my dear. You look more yourself even the last hour or so. I have been going over all the days we have had together, and something has come back to me. You remember when Father was ill, that he sent you away, to get us apart? How strange it seems! Apart from each other, you and I! And I was in the house alone with him and Miss Patmore. Well, he was arranging his papers on that last morning—I forget if I told you— and he put some of the papers, I believe he may have put them, in the desk in his room, that I took for my room later. And I think he locked it and took the key. He must have, because Miss Patmore says it has always been locked. And I have a feeling that he meant the desk to be opened, and the papers examined after his death. Of course, it may be a fancy. Miss Patmore says he burnt the papers, but we can't be sure he burnt them all. I thought we might look into the desk some time, in case there is something in it he wanted us to see."

"Oh, yes, my dear; yes, we will," said Christian. "Did your father say anything of it, that you recall?"

"I hardly remember if he did," said Sophia. "I had so much to cope with at the time that I hardly kept things separate. I may be wrong that there is anything there. But I have a feeling that, now that your dear health is not so certain for the moment, we must not leave anything un-done, that might make us deserve less that everything should go well with us."

"Oh, well, it is easily attended to," said Christian. "You are right that I am better, Sophia. I feel stronger; I have all day." Sophia turned and clenched her hands, and raised her eyes with a look of thanksgiving. "It is shifting everything off myself on to you. We will look at the desk some time. Is it locked, did you say?"

"I don't know. Yes, it is. Patty says it has been locked ever since she remembers. She didn't know there was a key to it; but there might be one on the bunch that Father used to carry. That is where it would be, if it exists. And there are one or two keys on that ring that I don't use. I will put them here; and if it isn't one of them, we can have the desk broken."

"Yes, put them there. And one of us will look before long," said Christian. "It may be something the old man wanted us to know, but it probably isn't much, as he was not more definite about it. But we will see."

Sophia left the room, and Christian read on, with the keys on the table at his side. The talk just past began to impress itself on his brain. Things he had noticed unconsciously, returned to him; Sophia's bright eyes and studied ease, her care to save him, her fluency, as if she had thought what to say! It all suggested she had something on her mind. He rose, to dispel uneasiness before it took a form, and taking the keys, went up to Sophia's room. Patty, her ears attuned to every sound in the house, ran out on to the landing above, and watched him enter.

He tried the keys in the desk, found one of them fit, and opened it. The desk was dusty and empty, save for a letter lying at the back. It was in Andrew Stace's hand, and addressed to himself, and bore the words: "To be opened after my death."

Christian, with a smile for the old man's simple drama, sat down to read it, half expecting a revelation of his parentage. He read it, holding it in both his hands, his elbows resting on the unfolded board. He read it again and again, and raised his head. A tremor went through him. He partly thew up his arms, and remained sitting, with his head falling forward, and his hands with the letter in one of them, sinking down on the open desk.

Patty, who had listened for his leaving the room, came in with a duster in her hand, as a pretext for entering. She looked at the figure at the desk, and stood still. She went up to it and put her hand on the shoulder, murmuring the words: "Are you not well, Dr. Stace?" She stood for a moment gazing at the face, felt the hand, and saw the letter falling from it. She snatched up the letter and read it, with her look of grief and terror conquered by a yearning as fierce. She remained with the letter in her hands, her eyes going round the room; made a movement to tear it, and glanced at the empty grate. Then she returned it to its cover, thrust it to the back of the desk, and turned the key, touching Christian tenderly when she could not help it; and with the key in her hand, rushed out of the room, and up to the young people's study. Patty was not of the character to take things further upon herself.

"Oh, I don't know what is the matter with Father," she said, her instinct telling her that sudden breaking was best. "He is sitting quite still at the desk in Mother's room. I don't know what it is. Some one must go for a doctor at once."

Andrew sprang to his feet, the truth in his face.

"Send some one for Cousin Peter this second," he said. "This instant, Patty! I will go and see him."

But Dinah had run out of the room in front of him. Patty clutched at them both as they passed her.

"No, don't go. You must not go," she said. But Robin was brushing by her, repeating Andrew's injunction as he went.

Dinah was standing by her father, looking into his face.

"Do people have heart attacks that leave them like this for a time, when they are ill like Father?" she said, as her brothers came to her, her young voice clutching at hope and losing it.

Andrew went up to his father, and touched his hands and his head.

"No, I fear not," he said.

Robin was standing near the door, white and trembling. Dinah went to him, and led him from the room. Andrew met her, and put his arm in hers, and the two stood, still and silent, until Peter's voice was heard with Patty's on the stairs.

"Mother will hear!" said Dinah; and at her words a flash came over them of their future life with Sophia. Andrew sprang and opened the door, and Peter came to the chair where Christian sat, and in a minute turned to Patty.

"No. It is all over," he said. "Who would have thought it? A strong man yesterday! A strong man this morning, apart from that trouble that might not have killed him for years. These poor children! And poor Sophia! Ah, poor Sophia! Who can tell her?"

But Sophia had heard the sounds on the stairs, and came into the room, the knowledge in her eyes.

"What is it? What is the matter?" she said. "What is wrong? Tell me what it is. Oh, what is it? Why was I not told the first of all? I am here, dear one. Sophia is here, here with you. You are ill, my love. I am here, close to you, holding you. Your wife is with you. What is it? What is it, Peter? Is he gone from me? He is gone from me! Why did you not fetch me? Did he ask for me? Was he in here alone? What was he in here for? Tell me. Why can't somebody tell me? Tell me."

Her voice reached a scream, and Andrew stooped to help her from the ground.

"It was over when we came to him," he said. "Patty found him here, sitting as he is now. He could not ask for you. We could do nothing. We simply sent for Cousin Peter, and waited."

"You should have fetched me," said Sophia, not rising. "I would have done something. I would not have waited. I would not have left him here to swoon alone. I would not simply have waited. Why did they not bring me to you, my husband?"

"Sophia," said Peter, bending to take her arm, "there would have been no good in sending for you. It was over when they saw him. Patty found him dead."

These words, unsoftened in Peter's way, struck home to Sophia, and she rose and listened.

"It must have been absolutely sudden, over in a moment. All in the twinkling of an eye! A most merciful death. And if any one deserved an easy end, it was he. Patty saw him go into this room an hour ago; and half an hour later, as he didn't come out, went in herself, and found him as he is now. She told these poor children, and sent for me; and I was here with all the haste I knew. It was the fastest journey I ever made. That is all I can say. He had been dead less than an hour when I saw him. That is about ten minutes ago, nine minutes by my watch. He must have died directly he came into this room. Sudden heart failure! What a thing it is!"

Sophia had turned to Patty.

"Tell me everything, Miss Patmore."

"It was just as Dr. Bateman said," said Patty. "I heard him go into this room; and in half an hour, when he did not come out, came in myself, for fear he should want anything. And I found him like this. I told Andrew and Dinah, and we sent for Dr. Bateman that second; and then you came in."

"And I have been so distraught and absent-minded with him the last few days," said Sophia, her first words coming as a surprise to her hearers. "My last few days with him! My last days! My husband!"

She sank on her knees by him again, and they stood round in silence, until she raised her head and saw Dinah's face.

"My poor children!" she said, getting up, and holding out her arms. "You should not have been in here alone. They should not have let you. Oh, I wish I had been about.

Here is a great tragedy come into your young lives! My dear ones, my only comfort now! All I have left. Did you come in here, and see him, darlings? Were you in here by yourselves? They ought to have fetched me to you. Were the two of you together? Oh, I am glad of that. My poor girl and boy! Where is Robin? Does Robin know?"

"Yes, he knows," said Dinah. "He went away. I think he was frightened."

"Frightened?" said Sophia. "Poor child! Of course he was. They should have called me to him. His mother should have been with him. I will tell him now. Where is he? Robin! Robin!"

She went to the door and called, more clearly, as no answer came, unconscious that she sent a shiver through her son and daughter, that was to return to them all their lives.

Robin came slowly from the doorway, and Sophia put her arms about him.

"Robin," she said, "don't you know, my darling? Haven't you heard?"

"Yes, Mother," said Robin. "I think I heard. I wasn't sure."

"You weren't sure, my boy?" said Sophia, raising her eyes.

"Leave him for a minute," said Dinah. "He has had a shock."

"Yes, he has, my child," said Sophia. "We have all had that. But he will have to realise it, with the rest of us."

Robin looked despairingly at Patty, and suddenly ran into her arms, crying like a child. Sophia turned gently from him, as if leaving a child to its simple comforter, and spoke to the others.

"Come with me, my dears. We three will go away and be together. We are at this solemn moment of our lives, a moment we shall always remember." At the note as of grave reproach in her voice, Robin gave a shudder on Patty's shoulder. "We will go apart, and try to meet together our great, great sorrow. Great for you all, but infinitely greater for me. You will have to remember that, in all your future dealings with me."

Andrew and Dinah followed her, Dinah too sunk in her own grief to listen, Andrew doing his best to begin his part as the man.

"We shall all love you more and more," he said, giving his mother his arm.

"Yes, my son," said Sophia, leaning her weight upon it. "And I shall need your love. For the light of my life has indeed gone out."

At the door of the drawing-room, Sophia turned aside and entered her husband's study.

"Come, we will go in here," she said. "We will go in here, where he was such a little while ago. Such a short hour. Sitting there in that chair, where I had my last word with him! Yes, that is where I saw him last. And he will never be here again. Never again, my husband!"

She sank on her knees by the chair, and broke into open weeping. Andrew and Dinah stood by, stunned and helpless. Sophia was just enough conscious of their presence to know that her laments were heard. Patty came in at last, her simple personal sorrow drowned in her eager service. Sophia looked up at her from the ground.

"Miss Patmore, you were with us all through our married life, through all our twenty-seven years together. You saw us and lived with us day by day. Did I do all I could for him? Was I a good wife to him? Can you think of anything I might have done, that I did not do?"

"Oh, no, no. Nothing, nothing," said Patty. "You were all it was possible to be to him. No wife could have been better. No one was ever more to any one. He would have said that. Now you must have some rest. You all must. He would have said that too, you know. They have carried him to the spare room. You know he would not wish you to grieve too much."

"I will go to him," said Sophia, rising, with a return to

her slow, solemn voice. "I will follow him where they have laid him, and have my last time alone with him there, my last time after twenty-seven years. Such a little while it seems to me. Don't come in to me, Miss Patmore. Don't let any one break in on us, on him and me. Let me have my hour alone. I will not stay too long. I promise I will not. As for you, my dears, you have seen him, and you know he looks peaceful and at rest. So you will just think of him as he always was, as you have known him all through your happy youth, made happy by him. Whatever comes to you in the future, you will never find that complete happiness again. There will always be the one thing wanting, something missing. Go with Patty, up to Robin, and comfort each other. As for me, there can be no help. I can go and be with him alone. I have that left to me, my last moment. For me there can be nothing more."

She left them, and they heard on the stairs the familiar rustling that seemed as if it should be different.

"Now, come with me," said Patty. "Come up to my room. Robin is there, and I can take care of you all together."

They followed, too intimate with Patty to show or restrain what they felt. Robin was sitting at her table, looking almost himself.

"Well, I have failed at the first test of life," he said. "I wonder if I shall always be able to spare myself."

"You could have done no good," said Dinah. "We have done nothing."

"Had you been standing all the while down there?" said Patty. "The whole time! I ought to have come down before. I might have known you were doing something like that, alone in there with Mother. Sit down, both of you, at once."

"Did you all stand all the time?" said Robin, fearing to guess the scene.

"No," said Andrew, with the truth of desperation. "Sophia knelt by Father's chair."

"Well, come now, and try to have something to eat," said Patty. "I must go down soon, and bring Mother up. She mustn't stay down there alone too long."

The cloud of their future fell on them, with Sophia over them, dependent on them.

"Where is she?" said Robin.

"In the spare room, where Father is," said Andrew.

"Patty, what if we had not got you," said Dinah.

Patty, weeping, went out of the room, to wait on the landing below, until Sophia answered her gentle call. The answer was not long in coming. Sophia's lifelong exercise of her own will had led her almost to expect response from the dead. She came in to her children, with the tears still on her face, and her smile seeming to force itself through them.

"Well, my darlings," she said. "Well, Robin, are you better, my boy? Is he all right, Dinah?"

Andrew made a movement as if to protect his sister, who met her mother's eyes in silence.

"Well, I have said good-bye to him," said Sophia. "I have said my farewell that is to last my life, my life that will never be a life to me again. Your dear father! My husband!"

She stooped her face, contorted again with weeping, over her teacup, and Robin's face showed a spasm of stricken nerves.

"What is the matter, my boy?" said Sophia, looking at him. "Is anything wrong?"

"No, nothing, above the main thing," said Robin.

"He must go to bed early," said Sophia to Patty. "He had better go directly after this. Andrew and Dinah can sit up for a little while with me."

"Oh, I think they all ought to go to bed," said Patty, her tone bringing a change to Sophia's face. "Dinah looks dreadfully shaken, and Andrew is very tired. And you ought to go to bed early too. You know you ought. You will be worn out."

"Well, I will go to bed, or I will sit up," said Sophia in

an aloof monotone. "Nothing that I do will make any difference to me now. Nothing will ever help me again. But I will go to bed, so that other people may go. So that they will not feel that they have to wait up with me, to watch with me one hour."

A sound as of hysteria came from Robin.

"Are you laughing, my son?" said Sophia, in a simply incredulous voice.

"No," said Robin.

"What is the matter with him, Dinah?" said Sophia.

"He has had a shock," said Dinah. "It has been too much for him. He won't be himself again today."

"Yes, he has had a shock," said Sophia, again in her tone of being apart. "I know he has. I can understand that. I can follow anybody's shock. But no one can enter into mine. No, no one will ever gauge it. I shall go on my way alone. Well, go to bed, my children. Go and try to rest. I will come to you before you go to sleep. Your mother will spend your last moment with you on this night of your lives."

She turned to Patty, as the door closed.

"Miss Patmore, what had he been doing at the desk? Had he unlocked it? He had not opened it, and shut it again, had he? If so, I must go to it, and see what is there."

"Oh, no, no, I am sure he had not," said Patty. "I know he had not unfastened it. I could see he had not. I could tell by the way he was sitting. Didn't you notice? There was the key lying on the floor, where it fell out of his hand, just as he was going to use it. Dr. Bateman said it was going up the stairs that put the strain on his heart. It is often a little thing like that, that is too much in the end. Oh, no, he had not opened it. I brought the key away, for fear it ought not to be left near the desk."

"Yes, that is the key," said Sophia, revealing that she knew it. "He had not used it, then? But how did he know which of the two keys was the right one? There were two keys."

"No, I am sure he had not used it. I could see he had not," said Patty, looking at the key as if she wished it back in her hands. "The other key was about somewhere. I saw it. I will fetch it some time. He must have been meaning to try them both. The keyhole was full of dust. When I pushed something in to see, it came out in a mass in my hand."

"Then," said Sophia, slowly, "if he left us, just as he was going to do what I thought ought to be done; if it failed, his heart, just when he was putting his hand to it, then it was not because of its being undone that his illness came. There was not the blight on us that I thought there might be. Then I think I need not distress myself about it. I shall have enough trouble in my empty life. I shall indeed."

"Yes, you will," said Patty. "I should not think of it for another moment. Unless the desk is just opened, in case there is anything there. I could go and do that some time, if you think Dr. Stace would say it was best."

But Sophia had put the key on her chain.

"My empty life!" she repeated. "My life drained of all hope! Miss Patmore, your life will be emptier too."

Patty was weary, and her own future lay before her, bereft of the safety of Christian's kindness. Sophia put her arms round her neck, and they wept together.

"I must go to my children," said Sophia, drawing herself apart. "I must not think of myself. I must say my word to them on this night of their youth, the last night of their real youth, I fear; the last night of my own prime."

She went to Andrew's room, and found him lying in bed, his eyes strained with the effort of combating his young exhaustion until she came.

"Well, my boy," she said, stroking his hair, "my eldest son, who will be my comfort now, we have to say good night, just as I have said it to Father for ever. No, not for ever; I must not say that; but for what seems very long to my poor mortal sight. Well, you have your mother in your

123

first great sorrow. You have her, and she has you. Though what she has, and what she may have, can make little difference to her now."

She left him, giving her smile at the door, and entered Dinah's room without knocking, as was her habit. Sophia never knocked, if she could help it, in her own house. Dinah was sitting on a chair, near to nothing else in the room, and looked up blindly at her mother.

"Darling," said Sophia, going quickly to her, "go to bed at once. Remember that your father's love will always be with you, always surrounding you through your life. You must go to sleep with that thought. And if it is this to you, what must it be to me? Think of that; and that will help you have courage. Dear one, you must listen when I speak, or you will make things even harder for me. That is the last thing you must do. Must I tell you that? I will send Patty to you very soon, and she will expect to find you in bed. Good night, my Christiana, my girl with Father's name and Father's face."

She went to the third door, where she had no answer to her knock. Robin was lying in the first deep sleep of shocked and wearied youth. Sophia went up to him, and gently moved him by the shoulder.

"Have you gone to sleep, my boy? Gone to sleep tonight, without saying good night to your mother? You knew I was coming to you; I thought to tell you that. Do you hear what I say, Robin?" Robin was looking at her with eyes that did not see. "Well, go to sleep then, go to sleep. I will not wake you; I will not try to force you to what you cannot bear. Go to sleep, then, my boy."

She went back to Patty.

"Robin had gone to sleep," she said. "He is not quite like the others. He does not feel as much as they do. I did not really wake him. I left him to sleep."

"He is so young," said Patty. "And he was so tired, poor boy!"

Patty's tone made Sophia look at her face.

"You must go to bed too, Miss Patmore. You are worn out. Will you have a look at Dinah before you go? And I must not stay up, to crush people to the ground with my sorrow. It is great enough to wear everybody out. But it must only do that for me. I must remember it. I must take it away, and be with it alone, until I carry it with me to my grave. And I can't help hoping that that won't be very long."

She left the room with a different smile; and Patty, after finding Robin asleep, went in to Dinah.

The next days passed as a continuation of the same day. Sophia's grief hung like a pall on the house, crushing its inmates with a load as if of guilt, that their sorrow was less great than hers. She sat with her children in Christian's study, a room that it became a sacrilege to leave; and begged with untiring eagerness for assurance of her virtues as a wife, that were given at first willingly, but by degrees with the last weariness. On the second day, at what hour nobody knew, Gilbert and Caroline came to the house, and their message was brought by Patty.

"No; tell them we are not equal to seeing any one today," said Sophia. "It is good of them to come. Tell them how kind we think it is, and that we will see them later, after the—after what has to be is over. But just at the moment we are fit for nothing. That is right, isn't it, my dears?"

"I think I should like to see them," said Robin. "We must speak a word to a human soul, and they have a share in our loss. We should not forget our relationship. We ought to see them. And Andrew and Dinah would be better for a moment's change."

"Oh, I didn't know you were ready for change, my boy," said Sophia. "I didn't realise that. Go and see them, by all means, if you feel you want to. I am only too glad to hear it. But I don't find you very easy to understand. What about you and Andrew, Dinah? Shall we send word that you would rather sit with me?"

"No. I think we will all go and see them," said Andrew.

"It will be a relief to talk to some one outside ourselves. There is no good in getting morbid."

"Oh, I didn't know you thought in that way of helping your mother, my son," said Sophia. "But go, if you wish to, of course. It is a relief that you feel inclined to, only a relief that I hardly expected. I ought to have told myself that you can't feel as I do. I should be the first to follow it. Only I should not have thought you would be prepared for change yet."

"We expected them to be ready for it after their mother's death," said Robin, "and to face another great break in their lives as well. We mustn't be too self-indulgent."

"Oh, no one would give that name to your grieving for your father, and comforting your mother, my boy," said Sophia, giving what she knew to be an odd little smile. "And I don't think that is what you quite mean. The pandering to self is what you are going to do now, isn't it? Not that there is any harm in being honest about it, my dear. But it is just that to you, then, is it? Gilbert and Caroline's mother, and your father! It is all the same. No notice taken of all his difference from other people, and all his wonderful ways with us all! He is just the same as every one else, just your father, as Mrs. Lang was their mother. Yes, well, go, then, and have your change."

She turned away, and rested her head on her hand. Patty regarded her in pity both for her and her children.

"Every one thinks their own people different," said Andrew, hesitating to leave the room. "Father is a greater loss than Mrs. Lang, or may seem so to many, and must to us; but we were not with him even as much as Gilbert and Carrie were with their mother. He was not enough with us, for us to miss him every hour of the day."

"No, he was away from you in London, working for you," said Sophia, in a musing tone. "That is how it is. The more people do, the less they are missed. That is the irony of things. Away from me too, securing our future for us all. No, I never had him with me, as many women have their husbands. But I miss him, I yearn for him every hour, every minute of the day, just because he is not in the same world with me; and my heart will cry out for him until I join him."

She turned from them, her mouth drooping again into lines of weeping, and fixed her eyes on the window. After another minute of looking at her, her children left the room.

"Let me sit with you for a little while," said Patty.

"No, no, Miss Patmore, I will not embitter and drag down people with my sorrow. I will keep it to myself. I see that that is what I shall have to do. I shouldn't have had him all my own, as I had him, if other people could grasp what this is to me. I must reckon with that. In a way, it is all I have left, that that should be so. But why do not you go and talk to Gilbert and Caroline, and have a change as well as the others? I do not see why they should take it all. You must need it as much as they."

Patty fetched a tray, and sat with Sophia while she took the food she needed. With bodily relief there came a reaction in her mood, and she went to the drawing-room, beginning to follow her children's craving for change, and to feel a rush of sympathy and compunction towards them. She settled her dress as she went, and touched her hair. No one must see Sophia except in beauty. She had a dim feeling that this was due to Christian from his wife.

The five were sitting apart in silence, their intimacy shown by nothing else. Sophia suddenly saw how much they had suffered before this second grief. She was too spent to shift her emotion from herself, and simply left them. She turned with drooping head and figure, and glanced towards them as she went. They none of them raised their eyes, or spoke to her. Their hour was dark.

The stir of the day of the burial seemed to challenge sorrow and threaten it with hope. Sophia had luncheon with her children in Patty's room, while Patty, foregoing luncheon by reason of its not occurring to her in relation to herself, organised a meal in the dining-room, where Peter presided. Andrew and Robin were to go to the funeral, and Dinah to remain with her mother. The brothers knew which was the heavier part; and Dinah, white-faced in the black that was rather too plainly poorer than her mother's, was sadder to them than Sophia.

Sophia seemed more like herself.

"Well, they will soon be going, leaving us," she said. "It is nearly time. You will know that Dinah and I are with you through every minute, my sons. We shall just think of you, and read the service to ourselves. You will not feel that we are away from you? Yes, it is almost the hour. Have they come out of the dining-room, Robin?"

"I have not heard them," said Robin.

"Just go out on to the landing, my boy, and see if they have come out," said Sophia.

"No, they have not," said Robin. "The door is shut, and talking is coming from it. I went part of the way downstairs."

Sophia was silent.

The truth was, that Peter was host, and true to himself in this character; and that Patty felt no authority to hurry the party, strong enough to conquer her interest in what they said.

"You will have to go down, Robin, and tell them that it is time to start, time to go," said Sophia. "Fancy my having to think of that, on this day in my life!"

Robin had a word with Patty in the hall, and the party assembled. Peter came up to say good-bye, and the three men embraced the women and left them. Dinah felt left to the unfaceable. The coffin was carried from the house by tenants; who had been prompted to the office by Edward; the functions of the great house not being definite enough at the Manor to make the duty spontaneous. Sophia drew Dinah to the window.

"There they go!" she said, her real voice gone again. "Good-bye, Father. Don't you want to look, my darling?

Well, life has to go on for us. Come, we will read the service together."

She read it in her beautiful, self-conscious voice, putting too much expression, and too much of her own choosing, and allowing her tones to break when she felt the need. When it was time to go down, she went at once, as if willing for some human intercourse, and found that the rooms were light.

"Who pulled up the blinds?" she said, her manner more her own than since her widowhood. "I don't like to see them drawn up directly everything is over, as if people were eager to get back to their lives at once, and put it all out of their minds. I cannot bear to have it here. They must be pulled down again. Who drew them up, Miss Patmore?"

"I did, in here," said Patty. "I knew it was the custom to have them up, before the people came back from the funeral, and I thought you would want it done. The maids are doing the others all over the house."

"Let them all be drawn down again," said Sophia in a deep tone. "I cannot endure this look of sweeping everything behind, directly it is out of sight. I do not mind about the custom. See that it is done, will you, Miss Patmore? I hope that no one has seen they were up."

Patty went out of the room, with a face of simple fear of the future, under Sophia's untempered sway.

The funeral party was shown into Christian's study, where the will was to be read. Sophia had found it fitting that her husband's will should be read from her husband's place. It seemed to her that in his own room it would be his own voice speaking! People who grieved but gently for him, should take the benefits coming from his death from his own hands. Of his own will he should give them, not forced by his death, not by giving up all himself! Thus Sophia dealt with the surge within her. It was well that her reason was sound. Andrew and Robin came in and went up to their mother. Peter followed them, settling his shoulders into his coat, and glancing at the darkened windows. Caroline and Gilbert followed with Latimer and Tilly, the effort at mourning made by the last not of a kind to escape attention. Those who were not related had gone straight away from the church.

"Well, Sophia, you look in better heart. I believe you do," said Peter. "Now do you feel more like yourself, Sophia?"

"I shall never feel that again, Peter," said Sophia, with a faint smile. "I fear that is gone, what used to be myself. But I am trying to learn to take up my duty, and I hope I shall be able."

"Yes, yes. Well, let me draw up the blinds for you," said Peter, his voice suggesting that this was a comforting office, and holding a note of anticipation.

"No, don't trouble, Peter," said Sophia. "There is no need for you to force your mind to such things. I must ask you to listen to me, Peter, and not to trouble. We don't want them up just yet."

"Don't you?" said Peter, turning round. "Why, there isn't much light, is there?" His eyes just rested on the lawyer. "It is usual to have them drawn up when the party —when the people come back from the funeral."

"Well, what is usual does not affect me much, I am afraid," said Sophia. "I am finding that I am not very usual, either in what I do or in what I feel."

"Mrs. Stace, the blinds will do very well as they are," said the lawyer, turning round from his bag. "I am just settling my papers, and shall be ready in a moment. There is quite enough light."

"Oh, well, I see," said Peter, leaning back, his fingers going towards his moustache, but drawing back as if of his courtesy.

"How did it all go off, Peter?" said Sophia, in a tone of being apart from what was happening. "Andrew and Robin, sit down, my dears. How are you both, my sons? You will tell me all about it presently."

"Oh, it went off all right, very well, Sophia. There was nothing amiss, I think. I was moved. I declare I was never so stirred in my life." Peter magnanimously warmed to his task, and put aside his own widowed experience. "Edward gave the service well. He read it with all its meaning. And when he spoke a few words, you know, I could have broken down; I don't disguise it. He couldn't have done it better, or said more, if he had been Christian's son. I wished you were there, Sophia. Of course it would have been too much for you. You wouldn't have been fit for it. But still, I couldn't help wishing it in a way. And Andrew and Robin bore up like men. They were beyond praise. I was proud of my nephews. I wished they were my sons, the two of them. Latimer didn't do quite so well, the dear boy! Well, I had all I could do not to follow him. And Tilly, she did break down, poor little woman! She couldn't help it."

"Come and sit near me, Tilly dear," said Sophia, who was inclined to regard breaking down as a sign of extra feeling. "I have not seen you since—since I was the person you used to know, have I? I shall never be that again. But I shall always be fond of little Tilly."

Tilly moved with a look of grateful awe at Sophia. The lawyer sat down, and the short, clear will was read. The terms were known to Sophia, who had arranged them with her husband. There were legacies to Gilbert and Caroline, to Peter, and to Patty. The house and estate were Andrew's, and his son's or brother's at his death. There were incomes from trust securities for Robin and Dinah. The bulk of the money was Sophia's, in trust for her children, in stipulated shares, when she died.

The estate was known to do little but pay its way. Robin's and Dinah's incomes were too small for independence. It was clear that Sophia would hold not only her former place, but her own and her husband's. Her children were little affected by the knowledge. They would hardly have been surprised if the whole had been their mother's.

They knew how well their father knew, and did not know Sophia; how equal and unequal Sophia was to her life.

The lawyer, leaving to catch a train, was attended to the hall by Peter, who continued his duties as host with an intensity and identification of himself with the household, that came from being benefited as a member. Peter ordered his life on a scale just above his means, which it was difficult for him not to do, as the scale was indicated by necessity. He was at this moment an out-of-place example of the truth, that relief is the keenest form of joy.

Sophia read his feelings, and was shaken by her own.

"Andrew dear, ought you not to see Mr. Conway out?"

Andrew looked up with a start, to see that Peter had forestalled him.

"Well, Mr. Conway," came the deputy's voice from the hall, "I am glad you have got everything done for us, and set off yourself in good time. I must thank you for the way you have acted for us today. I must acknowledge it for my cousin and her family. They are fit for very little this afternoon. I must take their place, and I do it with all my heart. Yes, I will let you hear from me. Good-bye."

Peter's voice dropped, and rose again; and he returned to the study with a striding step.

"Well, Sophia, you look more up to things," he said with truth. "Well, that is something to cheer us all. You don't want the blinds drawn up, do you? No, I see what you feel; I know what it is, Sophia. Well, I think everything has gone off well. I saw Mr. Conway out. I thought I had better do that. I escorted him to the door."

"Yes, Andrew was hardly equal to it," said Sophia.

"No, I thought he was not. I could see he was not. He has borne up well today. He has done all his best. And Dinah! She looks almost more knocked up than you, Sophia."

"Oh, we know better than that, don't we, Dinah?" said Sophia, taking Dinah's hand. "But she has been through a great deal, poor child! Her father was everything to her."

"Don't let me upset you, Dinah," said Peter. "Don't, I beg of you, my dear. Well, so your position won't be altered, Sophia. It won't be any different. You must be glad of that, relieved by that."

"My position won't be altered? I don't think you can be thinking what you are saying, Peter," said Sophia, drawing in her brows with a look of pain.

"No, no, to be sure," said Peter. "I didn't mean what I said. What I meant was, that there won't be any change for you in a practical way. I am happy to feel that for you. You must be glad of that."

"I don't think 'glad' is a word that can be used to describe my feelings just now," said Sophia, whose forehead had registered Peter's preceding words.

"Oh, well, no, of course not," said Peter, with the stubborn good temper of spirits. "But you know what I mean. But you are all shaken about, Sophia. I am the first person to understand it. You must be allowed to get some rest. We will leave you all to take care of each other. You can do it best for yourselves. And I have some letters I ought to write, as I can't do anything for any of you. Come, Tilly and Latimer. And, Sophia, I am at your service. Command me to anything, I beg of you. I ask that of you, Sophia."

"Good-bye, Peter. Thank you," said Sophia, with a weak voice and smile. "There isn't anything any one can do for us, except what we can do for each other, simply share our sorrow together. Andrew, go to the door with Cousin Peter and Tilly. You must do your duties as host, mustn't you, my son? Dear boy, you are not used to being host here, are you?"

"Oh, by the way, Sophia," said Peter, "I had a word with Edward and Judith after the service. And they were to come in tonight, unless they had a message before four. And I declare in listening to Mr. Conway, in being with you and Mr. Conway, I forgot about it. So they will be coming. But it will be good for Dinah and the boys to have a change, to get away from things a little, you know. They are young, Sophia."

"Well, they will have no choice, as the message has not been sent," said Sophia, her eyelids drooping. "They are not inclined for it; but they will have to see them for a few minutes, and I will sit alone."

"Well, Andrew, my boy, I hope things won't be too much for you," said Peter, as he buttoned his coat in the hall. "Because there will be a great deal for you to help along. I can see there will. I shouldn't like my boy and girl to have to shoulder what will be on you and Dinah. And all your own trouble into the bargain. For you miss your father; I can see you miss him. I feel the want of him myself already, all over the house. It isn't the same place without him. It seems more like a great empty shell than a home." Peter glanced up the staircase with a slight shiver. "And it isn't as if you were getting anything out of it, in a way, as some eldest sons—I mean, your life will hardly be altered, will it? I don't imply anything, Andrew."

"We should all do everything together, anyhow," said Andrew.

"Yes, yes, of course you would," said Peter. "You don't need to say that to me, Andrew. Good night, Andrew."

He set off with rapid steps, his children hurrying silently on his either hand.

"Well, I hope that Andrew will really plough his way," he said. "I wouldn't have the two of you put to face what confronts him and his sister. I said so to him."

"I know you did," said Latimer.

Peter, just glancing down at his son, continued.

"It isn't always the best off young people, who are the most happily placed. Not that we are in troubles of any kind. We are not. Cousin Christian was a fine man. He was a large-minded, open-handed man, the sort of man one looks up to. I saw him as a person above myself. I don't mind saying that I did. I shall always remember him in that spirit. And your Cousin Sophia is a great woman. I know she helped Cousin Christian in everything. I look up to her. Well, I am glad the Drydens are going in tonight. I don't like to think of those young people."

"Cousin Sophia despises you, Father," said Tilly, in an incidental tone.

"Oh, no, no, she doesn't," said Peter, striding along. "You mustn't say that, Tilly. She would not like to hear you. She is all worked up and down at heart today, poor Cousin Sophia! We must have sympathy with her. She has always shown me every consideration."

Sophia had at this moment dismissed him from her mind.

"Well, we have to take up our lives again," she was saying; "to start afresh, and try to look forward. That is all we have the power to do for Father. I must school myself for my life of empty endeavour. It will be enough for me just not to be always looking back. Don't fidget with the blind, Robin dear."

Patty came in to ask if dinner should be in the study.

"Miss Patmore, you stay and have dinner with us," said Sophia. "I want you. I feel I need you. We should all like to have you with us for a little while."

Patty's face acknowledged this ample repayment for her sufferance of the last days. She watched the setting of the table, and led Sophia to it.

"No, I won't have anything to eat," said Sophia, raising her eyes to Patty's face. "I will just try to drink a glass of wine."

The five sat silent, the young people at the end of their strength. Patty made a few attempts at talk, but when Sophia spoke, it was not to respond.

"I don't know whether you all like sitting there, having your dinner, with your mother eating nothing? On this day of all days! I don't know if you have thought of it."

"Oh, I understood that you wouldn't have anything," said Patty, rising and hurrying to her side with food. "I am sure I thought you said that."

"I may have said those words," said Sophia. "It is true that I do not want anything. I hardly could, could I? But I may need it. It may be all the more necessary for me, for that reason. I don't think I should be left without a little pressing today, sitting here, as I am, with my life emptied. I hardly feel you should let me depend quite on myself."

Her children's power of rising to such demand was spent. Patty pressed food with a simply remorseful face.

"No, I will not have anything," said Sophia, with her eyes on the things in a way that gave Dinah one of her glimpses of her mother as pathetic. "Nobody minds whether I do or not; and that would be the only thing that would persuade me, somebody's caring. I can't make the effort alone."

"Here, come, try some of this," said Dinah. "It is so light, you can get it down without noticing."

"And this, and this," said Andrew, coming forward with a dish in each hand, and an air of jest.

"Darlings!" said Sophia, taking something from Dinah. "Dear ones! Yes, I will try to eat a little to please you. Let me have something from you, my Andrew. I will do my best."

Robin sat with his eyes turned from the scene.

"You don't care whether your mother eats anything or not, Robin?" said Sophia.

"Oh, come, you are not a child," said Robin. "You said you didn't want anything."

"No, my son, I am not a child," said Sophia. "I am a grief-stricken old woman. That is what I am. But I should have thought that would make you the more concerned for your mother."

"You made a very fair luncheon," said Robin. "There is no need to be anxious about you in that way. You are eating better than Dinah."

Sophia was silent, rather appeased than otherwise by this observation of her.

"Dinah dear, try to brighten up a little, and take something to eat. We can't go on with these constant comments on you. We are all going through the same, you know. At least, all of you are. Think of what I am suffering. We can do a great deal for ourselves."

She got up, smiling to Dinah, to lighten her words; and went to her room to simplify her dress, to be able to give herself at ease to her emotions. She was never to be seen again, when they were alone, except with this difference.

"Make a good dinner, my dears. And when Edward and Judith come, be good companions for them."

The Drydens were shown upstairs, as the drawing-room fire was low, and the table in Christian's study had not been cleared.

"Dinah," said Andrew, as they went to them, "let us follow Sophia's advice, though she did not mean it. We shall have to protect ourselves; that is clear. Even Cousin Peter saw it. We can't live our lives as if they were not lives. We have not lost what Sophia has. We have never had it. We can't keep it up that we have."

"No. Let us never keep up anything again," said Dinah.

"Well, it is good of you to come," said Andrew, in a resolutely cheerful tone. "We hoped you would think of it."

"It is good of you to see us," said Edward. "It goes without saying that we thought of it."

"We were craving for a change from sorrow," said Robin. "I am the only one who can say that without giving a shock; and I may as well be put to the use I can be. I am not fond of sorrow."

"It sounds a natural taste," said Dinah, but could say no more.

"The thing I like least about it, is that it does not destroy the human instinct to judge," said Robin; "though it destroys so much else."

"Everything else in this house," said Dinah.

"Oh, no, no, not quite that," said Andrew.

"Is Mrs. Stace fairly herself?" said Edward.

"Entirely herself," said Robin, "through all the depths

of the last days. I told you what trouble did not destroy. And if any one is in trouble, Sophia is. And if in any one it is not destroyed, it is in Sophia."

"It is on the eldest of the young ones that the brunt of things falls," said Judith, looking at Andrew.

"You have had some bad days, Dinah?" said Edward.

"I would rather it had been any one else, except perhaps Andrew," said Dinah.

"But I hope you won't always feel that," said Edward. "Other people are nearer to you, in age, in everything. One is, Dinah. If some time when you are yourself, you will let him be."

Dinah raised her eyes, not to Edward's, but to Andrew's; and their helpless resolve passed between them. They could only let the light creep into what was before them, the future made unfaceable by the stress and pity of Sophia. Robin stood by them, silent, but did not leave them. He had grown older in the last days.

"Well, do not let me languish without a human word," he said at last. "Patty would not like you to do that to her baby."

"How is Patty?" said Edward. "Dear Patty!"

"She is a father to us and a husband to Sophia," said Robin. "A mother to us she has always been, or we shouldn't have had one. We have had no other during the last days."

"That is not quite true," said Andrew.

"No, but let us all speak with a lack of decent feeling," said Dinah, her voice seeming to rise up towards her own. "It is time we did something out of keeping with the dignity of bereavement. It is a bad kind of dignity."

The talk went on over unreality and doubt, but it went on. It was something, and the need of something was great. Sophia, coming out of her room, in reaction from a bout of violent grief, in which she had knelt at her husband's bed and sent her cries through the house, found the study deserted and dark.

"Have they gone to bed?" she said, hardly expecting to address a silence, and feeling the jar of the first break in the submission to her sorrow. "Is no one here?"

She turned with a heavy sigh, and went upstairs, her knees moving wearily, and her rustling weak. She stood on the threshold, pale and tragic, with her plain hair and widow's dress.

"So you are in here," she said. "Well, Judith; well, Edward. How are both of you?" Her tone showed that she felt it heroic in her to ask.

"How are you, Mrs. Stace? That is the important thing," said Edward, springing to his feet. "I hope you feel as well as you can expect?"

"Yes, that is how I feel," said Sophia. "As well as I can expect. And that is not very well."

There was a silence so long that there seemed no reason to break it.

"So you are all in here," said Sophia.

"Yes. The table was being cleared in Father's study," said Dinah.

"That would not have taken very long," said Sophia, looking straight at her daughter.

"We thought you might come down to the study," said Robin. "You wouldn't have wanted us all talking round you."

"No, I should not have been up to that," said Sophia, almost dreamily. "I heard your voices as I came in. I should not have the endurance for it."

There was another silence.

"Well, I will go down there again," said Sophia, "down to Father's room. Perhaps Miss Patmore will come to me. Good night, all of you. I think I shall not be equal to seeing any of you again this evening."

"Dinah, don't sit there with that expression," said Andrew. "It won't do Sophia any good for every one to get a horror of her. She had better be pulled up in time."

"She does look terribly ill," said Judith.

139

"Oh, there is every excuse for her," said Robin. "But she needs other people more, not less, for that."

"Throwing away friends when we most need them, is a thing we are all apt to do," said Andrew. "I hope you won't let us do it, however much of a strain you find us."

"Oh, we will be on the watch," said Edward. "We shall always be at least as much as friends."

But Sophia had done her work for the moment. The three accompanied the guests to the hall, and turned at once into the study.

Their mother was sitting in her usual chair, opposite her husband's, turning over old letters. She looked up with hard, questioning eyes.

"Well, so you have come in to see me?" she said.

"Are you all alone?" said Andrew.

"Yes, dear boy, you see I am," said Sophia. "What should I be but alone? You were all upstairs."

"I thought you said Patty was coming to you," said Robin.

"No. I did not ask her," said Sophia. "I will not go about begging people to be with me. I will be by myself. I should have this awful solitude at heart, anyhow. I will not perplex people with a grief beyond their conception. I will not interfere with their pleasure, as they are ready for it. But I should not have believed they would be prepared. That is where I was wrong."

"We can understand now, you and I, how Dinah and Andrew felt, when the break with Gilbert and Carrie had to come," said Robin.

"Oh, no, my boy, that is different," said Sophia, looking for a moment as if she did not follow, and then almost giving a smile. "Father is not like other people, for losing him to be just like giving up any one else. And they did not really lose Gilbert and Caroline. Oh, for a glimpse of Father in any way! If I could just see him, or hear his voice, or know he was on the earth! But I tell you one thing it will do, my dears, this little sorrow you have had, that seems big to you, now you are young. I will give you some little inkling, though faint and far away, of what your mother is suffering. So that we may be drawn closer; and you will find that a compensation. When your own troubles loom large to you, both this and missing Father, because I know you miss him, you will think of me, and be both pitiful and thankful."

There was a breath as of laughter silenced before it was heard.

"Poor children!" went on Sophia. "You have had some dark passages in your youth. But at your age things will soon be bright again. And you were having some better times this evening, upstairs with Edward and Judith, weren't you? I heard your voices as I came up from finding Father's room dark. So you mustn't be too dreary when you are with me; for that is giving a wrong impression, isn't it? And I trust something will come into your lives to take the place of what has gone. You mustn't let my sorrow be a damper on you; and I don't think you mean to let it. But I don't keep from you what I am suffering. I couldn't go on alone, feeling that nobody knew. I have not quite so much courage. You have not so much yourselves, that you can't understand me there. Now, run away, and leave me to read Father's letters. Each one of them is a little part of him to me. Not that I need him to be brought back. He is always with me. Do you remember who was sitting in that chair five nights ago?"

She pointed to Christian's chair.

"Yes," said her children.

"Five nights!" said Sophia. "And it seems five years, fifty years. Well, you may go, my little ones. Run away up to your own study. You are fond of that sanctum, aren't you?"

"Well, Sophia would soon have broken the spell of Father's study for us," said Robin. "It was hardly to be supposed that we could eat and drink and live in one room, all of us, for ever."

"Or be freed from the obligation of our own study," said Dinah.

141

"Do you remember who was standing in this doorway half an hour ago?" said Robin.

"What a moment it was, and how intolerable that it should be!" said Andrew. "What have we all done, that we should be tortured and deprived of a minute's ease, at one of the worst times of our lives? It isn't going to be possible. Sophia will find herself without human companionship."

"She will find herself in that case tonight, if she comes to my bedside," said Robin. "It is not in my mind to keep awake, to be worked on, because this is the day of Father's funeral. It is not likely we should forget it. God knows we have lived through it. We don't need to be reminded that Father was cut off at fifty-eight, with twenty of his good years before him. 'Do you remember who was lying in this bed last night?' Say that to Sophia, if I breathe my last before the morning. If any one ought to remember me on my pillow, it is Sophia. Good night, and luck to your counsels."

Dinah and Andrew looked at each other.

"Dinah, Robin does not want it to happen," said Andrew.

"No, and because he thinks it had better not," said Dinah. "We can depend on Robin."

"The point is, can you bear the life here with Sophia?" said Andrew. "Can I do anything in it? Can we face it together?"

"I don't think we can," said Dinah.

"Dinah, it will have to come to pass," said Andrew. "We shall have each other; that is one thing about marrying in Moreton Edge. I shall take a house in the village, and let the Manor to Sophia. There would be no good in leaving the place, as my later years are to be spent in it. And we should have Sophia; and if we are freed from slavery to her, that is a great thing."

"Yes," said Dinah. "Sophia is the only person who really takes an interest in us. Robin and Patty take an interest in so much else. It is natural in Robin, but bad of Patty, not to have only us. We should keep Patty too by staying here. But how about Patty, living in the house alone with Sophia?"

"Sophia might be easier, with more outside to engage her thoughts," said Andrew. "And if it were impossible for Patty, she would have to come to one of us. Sophia would really be better without a slave."

"I don't think people are really happier, without the advantages they misuse," said Dinah. "I wonder if Sophia has ever considered us as little as we are considering her. It would be unmotherly of her."

"Oh, yes, Dinah," said Andrew. "We have not taken more from her than people must from their parents; and we have had a great deal we had better have been without. Don't get notions of sacrifice into your head."

"I am not getting them," said Dinah. "I have just been arranging quite other ideas with you."

The door opened, and the two looked up with a start. Robin stood there in his dressing-gown.

"Do you remember who was standing in this doorway an hour ago?" he said, sauntering across to the window. "Well?"

"Well, it is this, Robin," said Andrew. "We see you want to know, and we understand each other. Something may happen, and something may not; and whatever takes place, does so, do you see?"

"Right. I see," said Robin, turning on his heel.

"Well, I am touched, Dinah," said Andrew. "Robin has remained out of his bed, and risked his interview with Sophia, to know what is to become of our futures."

"They say that sorrow makes people over-sensitive to kindness. That is what is happening to us," said Dinah. "Of course we are sensitive in everything, I trust over-sensitive; and kindness is always a thing to be esteemed. Our duty is to go down and talk to Sophia, until Robin is asleep."

CHAPTER VII

"Dear Caroline,—Will you ask Sarah and me to tea with you to-day? It is our first afternoon since our return from London. You can't be engaged so soon after losing your brother. I say 'your brother,' to go on flattering you, as I am jealous of your having Christian Stace in your family. We can't ask ourselves to the Staces, as just now any advance must come from them; and no advance has come from them to us. I can't always give these dubious parties; for people look in that light at simple, candid probing of our friends' business. It might give a wrong impression of Sarah; and I have not the gift of making them a success, though it does seem I am just the person who would have it. You have heard about the last one, because it was a failure, and we had it to discuss your affairs. Sarah would write this note if she knew it was to be written, and I send you her love.

> "Yours ever,
> "Julian Wake."

"What is this message from Caroline about her being delighted?" said Sarah, coming into the parlour.

"It is about tea this afternoon," said Julian. "She will be delighted to have us to tea. It is hospitable of her."

"Did you suggest that she should invite us?" said Sarah. "You did, Julian. No wonder you didn't tell me."

"No, no wonder," said Julian. "But you must see that we can't go to the Staces, and that therefore I had no choice but to approach the Langs."

"Why didn't you ask them here?" said Sarah.

"Well, about that, I had a feeling so delicate that perhaps no one but me could follow it. I thought that, after our not having seen them since they found that their mother had married and had a son, and forgotten to tell them about it; and that they had been meaning to marry their nephew and niece, it would be better for them to be the hosts."

"I see," said Sarah. "I hope Caroline and Gilbert won't see too."

"I believe you are showing a greater delicacy than I am," said Julian.

"Delicacy does show itself so," said Sarah. "But I don't think they will notice this."

"Then it is wasted," said Julian. "But delicacy has to be, if it must escape observation. I hope I shall not betray any this afternoon."

"I trust you will not," said Sarah.

"Well, Caroline," said Julian, when the hour came, "I am sure you are not conscious of doing us a favour. I know you think it is we who are conferring the kindness. I really do understand about the feelings of hosts. And you do not feel superior to us, because you have proof that your mother had more than one proposal, and we have only the assurances of ours, that people give no credit to, in their embittering way; or even because you have not had Edward and Judith preferred to you."

"No, we are conscious of no advantage," said Caroline.

"Sarah," said Julian, as the maid caused a clatter for a moment, "I have not been led into any delicacy, have I?"

"No, none at all," said Sarah.

"Have I evinced a lack of it?" said Julian. "Has such a thing come upon me?"

"It has fallen on Caroline," said Sarah.

"Well, that was a brave speech, Julian," said Gilbert, coming to shake hands with his usual smile. "Everything brought into the light, and nothing left to leap out upon us! We are beginning to leave off feeling branded, but all our friends seem shy of us. It is all too like an ancient tragedy for them."

"People are so educated," said Julian. "It is unaristocratic of them. They might all be tutors and governesses."

"And we don't know now who Mother's first husband was," said Gilbert. "She died before she told us. He belongs as much to the realm of imagination as your mother's lovers."

"But my mother's lovers do not belong there," said Julian. "I have just explained about it."

"His place is the sphere of speculation," said Caroline, "an ominous position for him, and for us."

"I wish he avoided the world of the actual," said Gilbert. "He hastened Mother's death, for I am sure he did; and very likely Christian's as well. He has torn Andrew and Dinah from us, and left us a most complex relation with their family."

"And given you the right to refer to Christian Stace as Christian," said Julian. "You must not look only on the dark side of things. Perhaps you even called him that. I wish I had. Simple goodness is the only thing I feel really at home with. I only admit to very chosen people how hard I have to try to be at home with the other things. But don't I seem at home with them?"

"Oh, not too much," said Sarah.

"No. I meant just to the right extent," said Julian. "It would be horrible to be too much."

"Mother liked Christian better in one day than Caroline and me in thirty years," said Gilbert. "We have never said that to any one else."

"Then you are right to say it to us," said Julian. "Say some more to us. What do you call Mrs. Stace? I ought not to ask, but I must get to know."

"We look at her definitely before we speak, and talk rather loud," said Caroline, "so as not to call her anything."

"And go to the house instead of writing notes," said Gilbert.

"Thank you so much," said Julian.

"How are things at the Manor?" said Sarah.

"Darkness, bridged by Sophia's tragedy and Dinah and Andrew's endurance," said Caroline. "Robin is often away."

"We don't go there much. The link seems to be gone with Christian," said Gilbert.

"But Edward and Judith go there much?" said Julian.

"Yes, that is the lie of things," said Gilbert. "Our relationship is regarded by Sophia vaguely since Christian died."

"Not exactly coldly, to do her justice," said his sister.

"What a blank Christian Stace's death has left!" said Sarah.

"You have the gift for saying those things, Sarah," said Julian. "I often think it is fortunate that gifts are rare. I am not speaking to wound you. I don't mean to belittle blanks. I try to be a person to leave a blank. I quite dread to die, because of my blank, the poorness of it; and I know one ought not to dread to die. I know your blank will be better."

"I shall try now," said Gilbert, "until the effect of troubles has worn off. I am affected by everything in the common way. I am rather ashamed of my mother's blank. It ought to be better, though she did not try."

"She tried to manage without one," said Caroline.

"But she ought not to have succeeded," said Gilbert.

"She did not know what it was to repent. That was so brave of her," said Caroline. "I am always repenting."

"I wish I could be," said Julian. "I believe I shall never break myself of the unmanliness of having no real ground for remorse. I really might as well be Edward."

"This about Andrew and Dinah and the Drydens? Can it happen?" said Sarah.

"It can," said Caroline; "and we can't know how much our own position causes our dislike of it."

"Only partly," said Gilbert. "Sarah and Julian see it as we do."

"I cannot bear it," said Julian.

"Did you ever want to marry Dinah, yourself?" said Gilbert.

"You should not take advantage of my asking unjustifiable questions to do the same," said Julian. "What is the sense of your being preferred to us, if you are in no way above us?"

"We have lost our advantage," said Gilbert. "We cannot do all the answering."

"There is a great deal to be done," said Julian. "Well, I wanted to marry her enough to be rather angry when you were engaged to her, and quite angry now that Edward is, but I suppose not enough to make a timely effort myself. I have not made it, and been repulsed. My anger has nothing personal about it. Shall we get to abuse of Edward? That is another thing in front of us. Ought we to go away from the women to do it?"

"No, that is the worst of Edward," said Caroline. "It is not necessary."

"It is the worst of him," said Julian. "But many things are very bad. His self-esteem is so deep, that he has never even seen it. And to have a fault and not the humiliation of it is so dreadful for other people. All the rest of us come between Latimer and Cousin Peter in self-esteem. Latimer has most, and Cousin Peter least. Edward comes above Latimer."

"That is profound," said Caroline. "I always knew it about Latimer; but about Cousin Peter it is so deep a truth that it might lie hidden."

"That is what I thought," said Julian. "I do like to be talked about in that way, and not just as such a good brother, which is really complimenting Sarah. I wish people would realise my needs."

"Well, let us get on with Edward's," said Sarah. "We are doing him now."

"It is his needs that are the matter," said Caroline, "the chief one of them being Dinah."

"He has no needs," said Julian. "If he had, I would hardly grudge her to him. Even Latimer in a negative way has them, for an occupation not degrading, and a modification of his father; and Tilly has them fiercely. Edward is without them."

"Shall you and I repair to the garden, and leave Sarah and Caroline to undertake Judith?" said Gilbert.

"We must not go apart in that spirit," said Julian, "because even if women are more inclined than men to criticise their own sex, I cannot agree to it. I have taken too much pains with that side of my nature—I mean that aspect of it."

"Well, you and I have done our best with Edward," said Gilbert.

"He has escaped us. Evasiveness is an unsuitable quality in a clergyman," said Julian. "We will retire and do better."

"Well, we are left to talk about Judith," said Sarah. "I have not much to say about her, have you?"

"Nothing with regard to Andrew," said Caroline. "She will marry him if she can. I would have done it myself. If any woman ought to understand it, it is I. I have got over my feeling of romance about him. I think I had it. I hope in a way I had. If not, I shall never have it. It has happened with me, that it has been too hard to hold to it, as things are. But if only people would marry him and Dinah, who would keep them for each other, and for us!"

"And Judith will not do?" said Sarah.

"No, she will not," said Caroline. "And now she has been more utterly destroyed by us, than Edward by our brothers. I think we have a neater hand."

"Oh, you don't know what a thing we have just made of him," said Gilbert, going past the window.

"You are giving a wrong impression," said Julian. "You know what women read into such hints. Women have to cling to their illusion about men. I even said a generous word about him."

"I did not. I am not going to," said Gilbert.

"I should hope not," said Julian, "when we have come on purpose to hear you do the opposite. There is something you owe to guests."

"I think we had better stop imposing the demands of the uninvited," said Sarah.

"I do not think so," said Julian. "I asked myself in my mind for longer than this. I want to sit with Caroline, while you walk with Gilbert. That is the sort of thing we have to bear the sight of, even with bitterness."

"Well, perhaps doing it may bring out our native sweetness," said Sarah.

"If I have any, you shall see it," said Gilbert, helping her out of the window.

"Sarah," said Julian, on their way home, "it is a pity we are not capable of real romance."

"Is it a pity?" said Sarah. "I see it is a fact."

"Yes; because we might leave a better blank," said Julian.

"And have a less bad one," said Sarah.

"Do you find the blank bad, then?" said Julian, looking at her.

"Oh, there are worse things than blanks," said his sister.

"Oh, it is really bad," said Julian. "Perhaps it is. You are brave to face it. I am glad it is not so bad that it can't be faced."

"Oh, I can face it easily," said Sarah.

"I wonder if I can," said Julian. "Perhaps not easily, but possibly with that peculiar courage I have of my own. Perhaps I have always turned my eyes from it, in a way that needs a truer courage. The easier and less active things do need that. Well, I am going to use my own courage, not the truer one. I think a courage different from ours need not be considered, Sarah."

CHAPTER VIII

SOPHIA SAT AT her breakfast table ten months after her husband's death. Christian's place at her own right hand was set as it had always been. Dinah sat with this gap between her and her mother.

But in spite of Sophia's insistence that all things should be the same, the sameness was less than the difference. Sophia's beauty spoke more of simple care for itself than of desire to enhance it. The impression she gave was simply one of widowhood. Her bearing seemed calculated to suggest the one thing. The whole of her inner life seemed focussed towards it. And the difference had gone beyond herself. Signs of economy and carelessness had crept into her home. The sons and daughter looked older and out of heart. Sophia was bent on harbouring her stores for their future, and seemed to give little thought to the sacrifice of their youth.

She overstressed the significance of her widowhood, magnified her married happiness, and forgot what she had daily taken into account in her husband's life, that his feeling was for the personality she presented as herself. It stood simply that her children could not leave her while her widowhood was young. She regarded their share in her sorrow less as a claim on her sympathy than as a support of their duty; and their married life as, even in their own thoughts, subordinate to the ending of her own.

But she was looking at them today as she more often looked of late, as if their acquiescence in her life was not what she wanted for them, or from them for herself.

"We are not a cheerful party, are we?" she said.

There was no reply.

"We are not a cheerful party, are we?"

151

"No, we are not," said Robin. "We have not much reason to be."

"Are we?" said Sophia, looking at Andrew and Dinah.

"No," said Andrew.

"Can you only speak in monosyllables, my son?"

"Nothing more was needed then," said Andrew.

"Oh, I don't know," said Sophia. "I don't think you all ought to sit, dreary and monosyllabic, and make no effort at intercourse, just because your mother is in great sadness and loneliness of heart, and never spare her an encouraging word. When my life is broken, I don't want less from people who are supposed to love me. I need more."

"You exact too much from people in that position," said Andrew. "You have gone too far."

"Oh, do I? Well, I don't get it then," said Sophia. "I don't know what I have had, I am sure, to be taken so much into account."

There was silence.

"What do I get?" said Sophia. "What do I have, Andrew? It was you who spoke of my wanting too much."

"Andrew did not say you had it. He said you claimed it," said Dinah, trying to speak lightly. "We all find that difference."

"I don't think you should let me find it. I hardly consider that you should. What do I need? A little sympathy and fellowship just for an hour or two a day, the hour or two you are with me. You don't spend much of your life in my dreary presence, and you have your own meals while you are doing it, so that the time is not wasted, even from your own point of view. What are you laughing at, Robin? It is not so much for a widowed mother to ask, to hope for from her children, whom she gives her life to, is it?"

"It is too much when it is met by everything that forces it back," said Andrew. "And you do not give your life to your children. You devote it to your sorrow, as you say yourself. We can't go on offering and offering, with no result."

"It is really not for you to talk about fellowship," said Dinah, still using an easy tone. "You have very few gifts in that line for us to inherit. I am sure you do not expect us to be more than equal to you."

"We were exhausted by it all four days after Father died," said Robin.

Sophia was silent, pacified, as always, by the other point of view.

"Well, well, I must not expect it. I must not hope that you can know what I feel. How could I have had Father for my own as I had him, if any one knew? You are young, and must live your lives for yourselves. You have been brought up to think of your own claims. You are right, Robin. You were tired of it, exhausted—that is your word, is it?—tired of me and my despair, four days after Father died. I remember that you were."

"In that case, you were rather optimistic this morning, after ten months," said Robin.

"I was speaking of you, my dear, not of Andrew and Dinah. Ten months is a short time to forget a great sorrow in."

"You might have spoken of yourself," said Robin. "There are signs of your having had something near to enough."

"That will do, Robin. That way of talking really disgusts me," said Sophia. "It is a nasty, cheap, second-rate kind of talk. I can't think where you get it from."

"From you," said Robin. "You and I are adepts at saying just the thing at the moment, that a decent person would not say. I have the excuse of your example. Dinah and Andrew are above being dragged down by it. So was Father, though he was never put to the test."

"Yes, Father was different, above everything," said Sophia, as if to herself. "Above everything, above me, above us all. I know he was. I am the first person to say it, the only person who really knew it."

"Above you and me, certainly," said Robin.

"Oh, above every one, my boy," said Sophia, in a tolerant tone. "But Andrew and Dinah are very like him. They are, my dear companion-children."

"Suddenly remodelled to your pattern," said Robin. "Well, we are having some chat now."

"I think you had better go away, Robin," said Sophia. "I can't feel I want you here any longer. The others can stay with me for a little while."

"We must all of us go this morning," said Andrew, striving for a natural manner. "We are going to explore the valley on the other side of Moreton Hill with Judith and Edward. We ought to be looking out for them almost at once."

"Oh, you are going to do that today," said Sophia, after a pause. "That is what you have been thinking of then, while you have been sitting there, so dull and still! I need not have reproached myself for being vexed with you, when you were really out of spirits. You have your own lives that I do not share. I must get to know it. Not that I want to share them; I have no heart. But I don't think you had so much reason for drooping in your chairs, so martyr-like. I don't think there is much of the martyr about any of you. I need not be afraid of it."

"I don't think you need. But you are not," said Dinah. "We very few of us have much fear of other people's having much of the martyr about them."

"You make demands on us too easily for thinking that," said Robin.

"Well, well, run away, little martyrs," said Sophia. "You are determined on that character, I see. I won't make demands on you. I mustn't bring you up as I have, and then expect a return. I do see that. But I don't know what you mean by saying I make them easily. Well, run away, my dears, and have a good day. There may be other troubles in front of you. And already you think you have had enough. And I know you have. I would keep it all from you, if I could. But I am afraid I cannot. Life cannot always be

154

made smooth for us; and I fear your young life is not very smooth. But you may make your escape from it all today."

"Sophia seems determined on our disastrous future," said Robin. "I suppose she judges from the precedent of our past."

"What else is coming on us?" said Dinah. "Are we related to Edward and Judith through the unknown grandfather?"

"I don't know. It may be something to do with Sophia," said Andrew. "Have you noticed anything about her lately, apart from trouble and nerve storms and all that? Anything about herself?"

"There has been nothing about herself lately apart from all that," said Robin.

"Yes, there has," said Dinah. "I think I have seen it without knowing it. She is not as strong as she was. She gives up things more readily. This struggle at breakfast today. She seemed to get tired of it, tired by it. She has often been like that in the last few months. She does not hold on to the end. Is there anything wrong with her? Shall we have to give out any more sympathy? We shall be done to death by it all."

"There can't be anything serious the matter with her," said Robin.

"We ought to be able to say that of Sophia," said Andrew. "It will go hard with her if she can't control her own fate. But we can't say it of any one."

"What is the use of all that power," said Robin, "if it isn't to be any good?"

"Power has never been any advantage to Sophia," said Dinah. "It has worn her out, and every one who would have served her. Are you anxious, Andrew? Has she said anything to you?"

"The last few days she has dropped a hint or two, as she did to us all just now," said Andrew. "She always does first to me, you know. But I dare say it is nothing. It can't be going to happen, that Sophia is not mistress of herself."

"I suppose she was expecting sympathy at breakfast," said Dinah. "How like Sophia to exact compassion for something she had not revealed!"

"We can't go and say good-bye to her," said Robin. "We should never get off."

"It would give us too much preparation for a day's pleasure," said Dinah. "The day can hardly come up to the reckoning at the end, the middle; for we have to be back at four. It could not stand both."

"Have you seen any difference in Sophia these last weeks?" Andrew asked Edward, as they set off. "We think she does not seem herself."

"Oh, no, none at all," said Edward. "She is wonderful. A little changed since your father's death, of course."

"Yes, she must be marvellously strong," said Judith, "to have gone through what she has, and then to do what she does! It would wear most women out. I should not like to face it."

"Nobody would like to face what she has," said Robin. "Doing what she does is to the good. It comes from having control. And women are not so easily worn out."

"Oh, you don't know," said Judith. "How can you? You are not a woman."

"I am afraid she is not marvellously strong," said Andrew. "She has always put a great strain on herself, both when it has been necessary and when it has not. She has taken more out of herself than most people."

"And so she has to be troubled about more than most people, who wisely avoid needless strain," said Judith.

"Yes, she has to be, Judith dear," said Andrew. "That is the gist of the business. Necessity has us as her slaves, and we drag you both in our wake."

"We must stop using 'both' on this family basis," said Edward. "It is time that Dinah and I, and you and Judith began to be the pairs."

"I assure you, you shall be," said Robin. "As soon as Sophia is in better spirits—and she is giving the most promising signs of chafing at the routine that low spirits impose on her—I will begin to be such a son to her, that Dinah and Andrew will become merely quiet memories."

"We shall both be here in the flesh," said Andrew. "Judith and I will take the empty house in the village, and eke out our living with Sophia's rent for the Manor."

"I am glad I am only to be mistress of the house in the village," said Judith. "I should feel very unsuited to order the Manor."

"Any one would feel unequal to that, with Sophia alive," said Robin. "The person who will be really unfit is Dinah for the parsonage."

"Oh, people need not identify themselves with the people they marry," said Edward.

"No, that is what I mean," said Robin.

"Robin, the people who will be unsuited are you and I as brothers-in-law," said Edward, laughing.

"Oh, pass over me as a brother-in-law," said Robin. "Think of Sophia as a mother-in-law, and concentrate your powers."

"There is no problem to me there," said Edward. "I have a great admiration and affection for Mrs. Stace."

"I trust I may remain your only problem," said Robin.

"Affection for Sophia leads into many dark ways," said Dinah; "and the admiration is no help, as she takes it for granted, and gives no credit for it."

"I don't wonder at that," said Edward.

"I hope you won't ever wonder, Edward," said Robin.

Sophia, left to herself, went to the study and stood by the shelves, turning the leaves of some books in places she seemed to know. Then she went upstairs to Patty's room.

"Well, Miss Patmore, so I am left alone today. What time will they be back?"

"Oh, quite by four," said Patty, looking up cheerfully. "They will be home in time to have tea with you."

"I didn't ask that, to have that said to me," said

Sophia, with tears in her voice. "I don't care if they are here or not to have tea with me. I am not searching about for people to have tea with. I am not dependent on any one for a meal. It is I who organise those things for other people. And I am always alone, always by myself at heart. So what difference can it make if people are back for their tea or not? They will probably attend to such matters for themselves. I only asked because I am interested in them."

"Well, they will be back by four," said Patty.

"Do you think they are happy with Edward and Judith?" said Sophia.

"Oh, yes, I think they are," said Patty. "They seem to enjoy getting away with them. It has made a change for them."

"Yes, I see. I understand what you mean," said Sophia, with conscious slowness and sadness. "I knew I should have to hear that. You mean I am too middle-aged and wrapped up in my grief, to be a companion for them any more. I know what is in your mind. But perhaps it will not go on much longer. Perhaps I shall not be here, to tire and trouble any of you for a great while. Then, with my love and understanding gone from them, will Edward and the girl be enough for them? That is what I want to be told."

"Oh, yes, I hope so," said Patty, not knowing what to say, and not giving much significance to Sophia's words.

"Yes, I see what it is," said Sophia, turning away. "I have talked so much about my sorrows and myself, that people do not listen to me now. They think I do not mean anything. But I have never meant nothing, if they only knew. I shall have to put things very plainly to make them understand. Well, I will not do it now."

She left the room; and Patty, looking simply relieved, began to sing over her needlework.

Sophia heard her, and gave a sigh outside her bedroom door that reached the landing above. At luncheon, which Patty shared with her, she showed she had been crying; but Patty read little into what she took for one of her habitual

fits of tears, and talked until she lapsed into silence from
lack of response.

"Yes, I am a dreary companion, Miss Patmore," said
Sophia at last. "I know I am. But you do not know how
much reason I have to be low and sad; what I have on me
just now. I hope you will never have to face alone what I
am facing."

"Oh, you must try and cheer up," said Patty. "It really
is your duty. It is time for you to make an effort. It would
be better for you, and for every one, for the children most
of all, if you could be a little more like yourself. You ought
to have more change. It would be healthier for all of you."

"Better for all of us, better for the children," said Sophia.
"That is what you think of. It is they who have your concern. I know that. For no one thinks of me now; and there
was some one who thought of me first of all. Well, he is
gone. Well, who knows how soon I may go too, to be with
him? Now, Miss Patmore, don't listen any more to the
drone of my embittered heart. You be off to what you want
to do. I am coming up to you presently, to inflict some more
on you."

She smiled, and Patty left her, still without alarm.
Sophia came up at half-past four.

"Miss Patmore, I wanted to say something to you.
Something else there is for you to share with us in our
family woes. But I am worried that the children have not
come back. I can't settle my mind to my own anxieties, to
things that only concern me, until they are at home."

"Oh, is it time for them to be back?" said Patty.

"Yes, of course; it is half-past four. Didn't they say they
would be back at four?"

"Yes, so they did. Is it more than that?" said Patty.

"Yes, of course it is. I have just told you. Besides, there
is the clock in front of your eyes. And I have just said that
it is half-past four. They are half an hour late already."

"Well, they are sure to be all right," said Patty, adjusting
her sewing-machine.

159

"Why are they sure to be? I don't see that at all. I don't see any sense in that," said Sophia. "Why are they sure to be?"

"Oh, I think they are," said Patty, her eyes down now in self-protection.

"How rare it is to find any one who takes anything seriously!" broke out Sophia. "Here have I been worrying ever since the clock struck four, and getting more and more into torture with every minute! And here are you, going on peacefully sewing, just as if they were not out! Not even troubling to look at the clock, to see if they should be back, the children you have cared for and loved since the day of their birth! Well, what a difference there is between people! How much more of life I have had in my years than many people in half as many again! 'We live in deeds, not years.' How true that is! It is no wonder if I am worn out before my time."

"Nothing much can happen to them, five together," said Patty.

"Nothing much can happen to them, five together!" said Sophia. "Well, what a silly thing to say! Something might happen to one of them, of course. Something has happened, I dare say, while you are sitting there. And that one would be sure to be one of mine. Oh, I am so gnawed by anxiety that I can hardly stand still. I wish I could sit there as you do. What do you think they would be doing now?"

"I don't know, I am sure. They ought to be home," said Patty.

"Of course they ought to be home," said Sophia. "That is the whole thing. What I ask is, what do you think they would be doing now, as they are not home?"

"I don't know. How can I know?" said Patty. "I am not with them."

"No, you are not with them," said Sophia. "You are sitting here, thinking of nothing outside this room. But I am with them, with them in my heart. Their mother is with them, trying to hold all harm from them. Your mother is with you, my children."

She walked about, working her hands, and Patty looked at her helplessly. She was crying aloud by the time a telegram bearing the name, Patmore, was brought.

"Oh, what is it? What is it?" she shrieked, raising her hands to her head.

"It is addressed to me. See. Patmore! There is nothing to worry about," said Patty, implying that this was the case for her as well, if the news could concern only her own family. "Oh, they have addressed it to me, so as not to frighten you." Patty's tone accepted this as well thought of. "They are all right. They found the train altered, and had to come by another. The telegram is sent from Moreton Station, at three o'clock. It hasn't been very quick, has it?"

"Oh, no one knows what people go through, when they have such a temperament as I have," said Sophia, sitting down. "No one knows what I imagine, what pictures I call up, what scenes I live through with my dear ones, when they are away from my care. For the one death my husband died, I died for him thirty times. Well, now, I have something else to bring down on you, Miss Patmore. My children are safe; so I can turn my attention to myself, to my poor old self. I must come second to them; I know; I do come after them in my own thoughts. Well, you know, Miss Patmore, I don't think I am well." Sophia's voice broke and she went on, weeping. "I don't think my health is what it ought to be; I am sure it is not. I have been comparing what I feel with some symptoms described in some of my husband's books; and I believe it may be something serious, something that sometimes comes when women are hurt as I was. Of course it may not; I know I am rather fanciful. But about myself I don't think I am. I confess I am about my children." Patty raised her eyes in recognition of the truth of this. "About those I love I own that I am. But I was right about my husband. I was not mistaken when I was afraid for him. And now I may be right about myself. Miss Patmore, I don't feel I can turn a brave front to anything more without my husband. I feel, if I am to find that anything serious is amiss with me, that I cannot go on. I have borne enough."

"Oh, you want a little looking after," said Patty. "You must see a doctor, and let him put you to rights. You have had a dreadful year. You have not tried to get your spirits back. The children—we none of us have. You will soon be strong again with a little care. You must have Dr. Bateman come to see you."

"No, I don't want him to have anything to do with it," said Sophia, with a fretfulness at once easier and deeper than the one Patty knew. "And I am not discussing myself with all of you. I am talking about myself as a separate person. I must speak a word about myself sometimes. I don't want a relation as a doctor; and I don't think Dr. Bateman is good enough. My husband thought very little of him; and we must not be content with any one who happens to be near us, for me. It is very important to every one that my health should be saved. A great thing for the children whom you think so much of. And I could not bear his being so casual and calm, as if he did not care. I thought I ought to go to Dr. Lamb, my husband's friend in London. That is what it is my duty to do; but I don't know how I can make my mind up to it, with no one to help me."

"Oh, you have plenty of people to help you," said Patty. "No one has more than you have. You know we shall all think of nothing but you. That is what you must do, of course. We will take you to London, Andrew and Dinah and I; and I will go in to the doctor with you, and hear just what is to be done for you. We shall soon see you yourself again."

"Well, I feel better now that I have told you, Miss Patmore, and things are being talked about openly. You won't have me well quite so easily; but I think perhaps I may begin to mend, now that I am not staggering under it all alone. I must tell the children when they come in. I know it seems a good deal to bring on them; but they would not like me to carry this by myself. I should not like them to struggle along with burdens apart from me; indeed I should not. It seems hard on them, all these things coming one after another. I see by your face that you do think it is hard; but I can't shoulder this by myself. Even to please you, I can't do that. It is too heavy a load."

She gave a little bitter smile.

"Oh, you know I would not have you do that. We should not dream of letting you," said Patty. "We shall soon have you strong; I know we shall. See how young and well you look! I wish I could look as you do. There can't be much the matter with you, I am sure."

Patty was sure; but she had not looked at Sophia, to see her, for many months. Sophia did not look young and well. There was more change in her, though it had not touched her beauty, than that of her ten months' service to grief.

Her children were startled by her face when they returned, and wondered that the change had not struck them, and knew that it had.

"Well, my dears, have you had a happy day?" said Sophia. "So the trains were altered? Dear, thoughtful ones, to telegraph to your mother!"

"We used Patty's name out of regard for your nerves," said Andrew. "We did not show a like tenderness for Patty's."

"Well, so you have enjoyed it all," said Sophia, not wasting a word on this. "Well, now, directly you are back, there is something else I must bring out to you. You were half expecting it, weren't you? So come back here when you are dressed. You will have to be quite ready to listen to me. It is not a thing we can deal with, with half our minds. I don't seem able to stop, do I? You have a poor, weighed-down person for a mother. Unless you would like to hear now. I can see you would. Such dear companions as you are to me, through all my moods and troubles. I hate to force anything more on you; but I know you would not wish me to carry this alone. It is enough for us all to carry together, I am afraid. I have been telling Patty about it. I don't think that all is right with my health. I have had symptoms lately that I think should be taken notice of. I don't know that they mean anything serious, but I have an idea that they might. Don't look so frightened, darlings. You know I may be making a mistake."

"We will soon find out if you are," said Andrew.

"Tomorrow we go up to London to Dr. Lamb," said Dinah.

"And today we telephone to him, to know when he is free," said Robin.

"My dears!" said Sophia. "That is what it is to have one's own children to consult. Patty thought I ought to have Cousin Peter; but you say just what I knew myself. Not that Patty was not kind and good. She was. She always is. But that is what I ought to do, I know. And I will do it for all our sakes, yours as well as mine, especially for yours; but I shall have to work myself up to it. I was not thinking of quite so soon as tomorrow."

But Robin had gone to the hall to the telephone, and Sophia got up and moved about, touching the things she passed, and talking as if she hardly knew what she said. Andrew and Dinah tried to separate the signs of sickness and sorrow in her face.

"How long have you been cultivating this talent for secretiveness?" said Andrew.

"Oh, only a few weeks, my boy," said Sophia. "But if I am right about the illness, it may have been coming on for a very long time, perhaps from the time when I was hurt. But we must hope for the best. I know you do all hope it. Have you had a nice day, darlings?"

She asked this question several times with the same smile. It was a relief when the call came.

"Tomorrow at half-past one," said Robin. "The only free time he had was his luncheon time, and I accepted that."

"You insisted on it," said Andrew. "I heard you."

"Well, I don't think that can be helped, my boy, in a matter of great seriousness like this," said Sophia, not seeing that Andrew was in jest.

"Well, here is a pass for us!" said Andrew, as they went to change their clothes. "I hope we shall be able to take it as Sophia does, as a thing subordinate to any passing trifle. Well, Patty, so further things have come upon us."

"Oh, I am sure it will be all right," said Patty, hardly raising her eyes from her work, as if determined on calm. "I am certain there is nothing really wrong; I don't see how there could be." She stopped, and then began to speak, as if pent-up thought were rushing forth. "Here is the whole house run for Mother! Nothing in it that is not thought out and carried out just for her! Every one and everything adapted to be as she likes! None of you regarded at all, no one in the place considered really! We have no power to do anything further to keep her happy and well. The way she gets angry about nothing shows how much she has. No one else would dream of it. She can't have any more."

"She can't, but she will need it," said Andrew. "What she is used to won't be much good now."

"The whole trouble is that she has had too much," said Robin. "Father never knew her. She managed that with her usual success. And she has never had to put any check on herself. Most of us spend our lives doing it, and save ourselves untold things."

"The three of us do," said Dinah. "We have a terrible lot of Sophia in us. The way we understand Sophia shows that."

"Well, Patty, we go up to London tomorrow, to take Sophia to Dr. Lamb," said Andrew.

"Yes, I heard the telephone," said Patty.

"We didn't suppose you didn't know, Patty," said Dinah. "But are you coming too?"

"Yes, of course I am. It would not be right for you to go alone," said Patty.

"What is it? What are you all talking about?" said Sophia, coming into the room, her eyes at once apprehensive lest the talk might be about herself, and holding resentment ready in case it were not.

"We are planning tomorrow," said Andrew; "and who is to go with you."

"Dear ones!" said Sophia. "I think you had better come with me, my dear man of a boy, so grown up all of a sudden, to take care of your mother! And Patty, to come into the room with me. So I shall be looked after all the time. And Dinah and Robin will be waiting here to welcome me back. So I can't have more than that, can I?"

Sophia was calm and controlled the next morning, and left the house with Patty and her son, having taken more pains with her appearance than she had since her husband's death.

Dinah and Robin went down to the hall at the sound of the return. She came in looking pale and tired, but herself.

"Well, my dears," she said.

"Well, tell us just the word," said Dinah.

"Well, he says I am very ill, but that I shall get quite well," said Sophia, caressing her cheek. "So that is bad news and good, isn't it? We shall have to be very thankful, and very careful. Now, let me go to my room and let myself relax. We will tell you all about it presently. For I am at the end of my tether, as I have a right to be, after working up my courage to this, and then having a wearing day as well. Move out of the way, Robin dear. Don't stand in the middle of the hall, dear boy."

"I wonder what would have happened if we had been stationed anywhere else," said Robin. "Well, what about it, Andrew?"

"Let us go up to the schoolroom," said Andrew, who looked as weary as his mother. "Things are like this. I went back to Dr. Lamb, while Sophia and Patty were at luncheon, on the excuse of wanting a walk about London. He says she will get better. 'May get better', were his words to me. But I don't know that he thinks so. She has some internal illness that is mortal; but it has come where it does not cause much pain; and that is why she has found it out so late. It is very late, it seems. It may have been coming on for two or three years, probably as the result of her accident, as she thought herself. Of course Sophia knew. Dr. Lamb says it will yield to treatment. 'May yield to treatment', he said to me. I think he means it is too late for anything else. I don't believe he has much conviction that it will yield. I don't say he is without hope. I think it is just that. May yield, and very likely won't. That is how it is."

"Have you told Patty about your going back?" said Robin.

"No," said Andrew, "but I expect she guessed. She looked at me in the train as if she did."

There was a long silence. Sophia's children, in imagining the time when they should lose their mother, had thought to feel grief that they could feel no grief. Now under the threat of the loss, they found it was grief that they felt. The same thought came at one moment to Dinah and Andrew, that their marriage had meant for them not only their escape from their mother, but their mother in the background, almost as the background of their lives. The same words came to the lips of both.

"If only Sophia had been different!"

"Ah, that is what she hasn't been," said Robin. "Now is the time for remembering it. There is no sense in straining after what we might have felt. We can never grasp what we might have had. We must simply clutch at the compensation for what we have missed. How I am getting to talk like a grown-up man! Well, there has been plenty of maturing experience lately."

"So Sophia and Father were beneath the sword together!" said Dinah. "Sophia was supporting Father, under it herself! It is a mercy her heroism was unconscious. We have not suffered quite to the last. We did not suspect a bright side to things, though we might have, as only one of

167

our parents appeared to be doomed. It was hardly whole-sale enough disaster for us. But can it be so complete as to include Sophia? She must count so especially. Father can't be called any preparation for her, and we can see she doesn't find him any."

Patty opened the door.

"You know that Mother is alone in the study?" she said.

"Patty, you know what I did this afternoon?" said Andrew.

"You went back to the doctor?" said Patty.

"And you know what he said to me?" said Andrew.

"That things were not so good as he said to Mother?"

"Yes," said Andrew. "Sophia does not guess, does she?"

"Oh, no, no," said Patty, her face at once distressed and yearning.

"I will tell you the conversation word for word," said Andrew. "We must go down now."

"Oh, yes, go down," said Patty.

"Well, my darlings, I was beginning to wonder when you were coming," said Sophia. "Are we all to have a talk together?"

They sat in a group, Andrew with his mother's hand.

"Well, so I have to confront the possibility of not being here long," said Sophia, her tone showing that she was not facing it, that she felt her future to be somehow her own. "I wonder how many people have had to meet that prospect. A good many, I suppose. I hope I shall be able to come up to them in resolution, that I shall not be the one to fail, to be faint-hearted. I must gather up my courage. But I confess that I begin to feel it ebbing."

She fixed her eyes on her children.

"I feel it falling from me," she said. "Father little knew what he was leaving me to face."

She stopped, as if her words awakened thought; and for a time was silent. At dinner her mood seemed calmer.

"Well, we have to accept what has come to us," she said, "and bending under a burden, yet do our best. We can do what we can to help ourselves. I think of your lives more than of my own. And there may be something we can do. I think there may. And I know the burden is not all mine. I see it is not, my darlings. Well, one thing I have to be thankful for, and that is my children. No one ever had such children. Whatever I may have before me, I have been set apart for that blessing. I must take that thought with me, as I try to go on, not knowing what I am going to, to what duty here or elsewhere."

She smiled at them, and fell again into silence, but remained through the evening in the easier mood. The next day she went up to Patty's room.

"Miss Patmore, you know I have something on my mind, whenever you see me. You will think you will never come to the end, and I dare say you may be sure of it. You remember the question of some papers in my father's desk, that troubled me before my husband was taken? He was going to search the desk, when this happened that has darkened all our lives. Well, I have that feeling again, that the desk should be opened, in case there is anything there that my father did not destroy. I feel as if nothing would go well until that is faced; as if we were all clutching at hope for me, with something at the back that will make all our effort of no avail. And whatever we find, and have to do because of it, we shall feel that no omission lies behind us unatoned."

"Oh, no, I should not do it," said Patty, who had listened with her eyes down, and now only half looked at Sophia. "I should not think of it. You must just forget it, and go on fixing your thoughts on getting well. That is what the doctor said you were to do. You must obey him in all that he says. We must be able to tell him you have followed his orders to the letter. You must not give your mind to any-thing else."

"Yes, but what if all my striving is of no good? What if all my concentration is wasted? I have a conviction that that is how it is; that I should get back my health perhaps, if this were once behind. You know I had the feeling before, when we were anxious about my husband. I ought to have held to my resolve, and forced myself to carry it through; spurred myself to rise to my duty, with my life shattered about me. That was the demand on me then. But I felt that, if I had lost him, just when he was going to deal with it, there was not anything in its being done. But you see, it had not been done. Perhaps it would have saved him, if it had been gone through with in time. We can't know. And I have a sense that we are losing days that may be precious for me, for you all. You see that I mean what I say, Miss Patmore? Oh, don't torment me by being blind to it. I ask you not to try me in my failing strength."

"Oh, yes, yes, I see," said Patty. "We will get it over at once. Let me have the key; and I will go and bring back whatever is there. I don't believe there is anything. The desk doesn't make any sound if you shake it. I have tried. But I will look; and there will be an end of the uncertainty."

"I don't know if you ought to do it. It is my duty to do it with my own hands," said Sophia, weighing her keys in her fingers. "But I feel as if I had done so much, borne so much, and was so frail and fading myself, that the impulse fails. And yet I shall feel no peace until it belongs to the past. I shall not be able to give myself up to trying to get well. And I know that if I do not set myself to it soon, it will be of no good to turn to it. Something gives me that message."

"Let me go at once, this minute. Let me have the key," said Patty.

"I think Andrew might do it," said Sophia, with her head bent down. "It is for him to represent his father now. It is what his father was doing, the last thing. He must take his father's place. I will go and rest, and some time, when I find the strength for uttering another word, I will tell him."

She ended almost in a whisper, and went with heavy movements out of the room. Patty sat with a look as of eagerness struggling with despair.

"Andrew," said Sophia, going at once to her son in his study, "I want you to do something for me. No, sit quiet, my boy, and listen to what I say. I am only equal to saying it once. I am fit for less and less, it seems to me, as the hours go by. All three of you, be still, and listen. There are some papers, at least I think there may be, in the desk in my bedroom. It used to be Grandfather's room; and I remember he spoke about putting some papers in his desk before he passed from us. And I forgot about it, with one thing after another crowding on me, poor child that I was! I am thankful you have not had the youth that I had. And just before Father was taken, it came into my mind; and he was going to make sure, when he suddenly left us. You remember he was sitting at the desk. And then it went out of my head again; and indeed no wonder! And now I think that whatever is there ought to be examined. It has been borne in upon me since I have known I am not well. I feel that we cannot expect things to be right for us, if we do not do what is our duty on our side. So Andrew, some time, not this minute, because I don't want to know just when it is, go to my room, and unlock the desk, and see what is there. Here is the key; I will put it on the chimneypiece. Remember it is here, Dinah. And whatever it is, we shall know about it together. It may be nothing. And it can't be anything that can do us much harm, can it!"

"I don't see that it can be anything much at all," said Andrew. "What manner of document can it be? Was Grandfather in the habit of locking papers up? Is it anything about Father's parents, do you suppose?"

"It probably is something about that, if Grandfather made a point of it," said Robin.

"I don't know that he laid much stress on it," said Sophia. "I don't think it is anything to do with that, my boy. I have an idea, though it may be only a sick fancy of the last days, that it may be something about money, some directions he wanted carried out."

"It can hardly be that sort of thing. He would have given

anything of that kind to the lawyer," said Andrew. "It would have been put in his will."

"Well, we can only see what it is," said Sophia. "It may not be anything of much significance, as you say. He might have given more explicit, more general instructions if it was. But he was so old that we cannot tell. He may have had any kind of fancy, and done any strange thing. But we owe it to him to consider his wishes, even if he was hardly himself when he had them. So you will attend to it for me, my son. I must go now and try to rest. I must not be deterred from keeping at bay the real threat over us, for all our sakes."

"What else is coming upon us?" said Robin.

"Oh, nothing, I think," said Andrew. "Our paternal grandfather, at the worst. More likely some old letters, with directions about burning them, or something."

"People never destroy for themselves," said Dinah. "They leave every kind of giving up for other people."

"Well, Patty, what are you edging into the room like that for?" said Andrew.

"Well—how warm it is in here! Was that Mother going downstairs? Are you going to open that desk some time?"

"Yes, Patty. Andrew is going to open it at once," said Dinah. "For fear you should die of curiosity at a time when we can ill spare you."

"Oh, I am not inquisitive about it," said Patty.

"No, I believe you are not," said Dinah, looking into her face. "I perceive that you know all about it."

"Indeed I do not," exclaimed Patty.

"I envy you your temperament, Patty," said Robin, as they went downstairs. "It is such a very mild eagerness that I am feeling."

"Oh, I do not want to know," said Patty. "I dare say it is only some letters or written messages. It might be as well to tear them up, without troubling about them, for fear they might be worrying to Mother."

"Oh, no, Patty, we can't do it in that way," said Andrew,

taking a chair to the desk. "What a superior bedroom Sophia has!"

"Sophia is a selfish mother, to know about comforts that she does not provide for us," said Dinah.

"I am now sitting at the desk where my father sat, with the same purpose," said Andrew. "Sophia did not seem to be struck by my pathos in this position."

"I hope you will not be taken, Andrew," said Dinah. "A second shock for Sophia would be too much upon Robin and me."

"Oh, don't make jokes," said Patty. "It makes me feel nervous, somehow."

"There is nothing in this desk," said Andrew. "Be easy, Patty. I should have been taken by now. Perhaps I am not ready to go. Yes, there is something, a letter, one letter in a broken envelope, addressed to Christian Stace, to Father. I may as well read it. I suppose that is what I am to do. 'My dear son—' "

He stopped, as his eyes went down the sheet. His brows went up, and his lips apart. He read the letter, and turned his head aside.

"What is it?" said Dinah, moving to take it from him.

Andrew made a gesture to prevent her, but gave it into her hand, as if seeing the uselessness of withholding it. Dinah held it for Robin's eyes to follow hers.

"Well!" said Robin.

"Is it anything?" said Patty. "Had it better just be torn up?"

"Patty, you know what it is," said Dinah. "The envelope was broken. You had got at it somehow."

"I hadn't. I never had," cried Patty. "When I came in, and saw Father at the desk—"

"Oh, I see," said Dinah, moving back. "You found Father at the desk. That is what it was. He was sitting at the desk; he had read the letter. It was that and not the stairs; I thought it was not the stairs. Well, it was only the same shock for him that we are having now. It is not such a great one. We must think of that. That is all it was." Dinah, as she spoke, looked suddenly like Sophia. "You put back the letter and locked the drawer. No wonder you wanted it to be torn up. Poor Patty! I wonder you did not do away with it."

"I wish I had. I wish I had," wailed Patty. "I ought to have. I would have, if I had had a moment to think. But it happened so in a minute. I had no time. I could not wait, with Father there as he was, to think what was best for all of you. What exactly is in the letter? Let me see it."

"Read it, Andrew," said Robin. "We are none of us in advance of Patty in regard to it."

Patty sprang and shut the door.

"My dear son," read Andrew, "I write to you as my son, now that I am old and soon to die. You are my son. I met your mother at a friend's house, where she was a young governess. I was not married to her. I was pledged to Sophia's mother. But I know that all is well with her, and she knows that all is well with you. You see that my daughter, Sophia, is your half-sister, and that I rightly treat you and provide for you as my son. You and she are my only children. My life has not been an hypocrisy. I did the one wrong in the mood that preceded my second marriage. To me, and I hope to you, it was a wrong. This letter is the way I take, to guard you and your sister from what must not be. I leave your sister to you, as your sister, my dear son.

"Your loving father,
"Andrew Stace."

"Well!" said Patty.

"Well, is that all you can say, after ten months' preparation?" said Dinah.

"Could this happen to any one but us?" said Robin.

"It has not happened to us. It has made us," said Dinah.

"Heaven help us!" said Robin.

174

"Heaven helps those that help themselves," said Andrew. "There must not be a word of this. It must be kept as dark as it was in the desk. Not a word amongst ourselves. We must be oblivious of it. You must forget it, Patty."

"Oh, I have forgotten it," said Patty. "Not a word will come from me. I have made myself not remember it for so long, that I am used to it."

"You must be accustomed to hiding knowledge," said Dinah. "I pray that your practice will stand you in good stead. How about Sophia? Shall we tell her? Or tear it up and say there was nothing in the desk? Or make up something? We must decide."

"And about other people?" said Robin. "The Drydens? Caroline and Gilbert? The unknown man their mother was married to the first time, not married to, was Grandfather."

"He had to be used a good deal," said Dinah. "No doubt there was a dearth of people like him."

"I should hardly have thought Mrs. Lang would keep back the truth," said Andrew.

"She wanted to save Father from knowing that he and Sophia were brother and sister," said Dinah.

"Oh, hush!" said Patty.

"Yes, that is the attitude, Patty," said Andrew. "Yes, that was it, of course."

"So Grandfather had a romance and a natural son," said Robin. "I must say I follow his keeping it dark, when you think of the personality he foisted on the world as himself."

"Hush, hush!" said Patty.

"To him it was a wrong. He seemed to think that made it better," said Dinah.

"That was his personality," said Andrew. "This slip was not significant, and great significance would have been given to it. That is why he concealed it. I see why."

"One slip was not such a bad allowance for the time between his two marriages," said Dinah. "It was only a few months. And he was already pledged to Sophia's mother!

Well, it was evidently time he was plighted to some one."

"No doubt he was helpless," said Andrew. "But the concealment was a grave mistake."

"He thought he had put it right," said Dinah. "He meant to guard against harm's coming of it during his life, and for Father to know it at his death. What light this throws on his objections to Father's marrying Sophia!"

"Complete light," said Robin. "I share the objections. I never thought to have so much in common with my maternal grandfather, my paternal grandfather, my only grandfather."

"We must be quiet. We shall have to learn not to know it," said Andrew. "We must tell Judith and Edward in fairness, and because we could not start other lives on secrets. We have learnt better. And if it makes no difference, they must forget it too."

"I should not tell them. Oh, don't say a word to them," said Patty. "Don't breathe a syllable to a soul. It will only come out. I should not tell even Mother. She might let anything escape when she is upset. You know how she says things, and expects people to take no notice of them. Is that Mother calling?"

"Yes, it is. I wonder it has not been before," said Dinah.

"We must go down," said Andrew, holding the letter. "Some one must go. Shall I go, and make up something? Sophia must not know."

"Andrew! Dinah! Miss Patmore! Are you all in my room? What are you all doing in there? I told Andrew to go in."

Sophia came into the room.

"What is it all?" she said, sitting down at once, as if wearied.

Andrew stood uncertainly. Patty shut the door. Sophia looked at her closing it, and repeated her question.

"Oh, it was nothing," said Dinah. "There was nothing there."

"Yes, there was something, my child," said Sophia.

"People don't talk in a room together for ten minutes about nothing. I came part of the way up the stairs, and heard your voices. Tell me what it is."

"Oh, it was nothing. Nothing at all," said Andrew. "Just a piece of paper, with a message on it from Grandfather to Father, telling him to take care of you, and that sort of thing, but not exactly for your own eyes, you know. We were talking about how odd it was, that it should be only that. I don't even think I have it; I don't know whether it is here."

He fumbled in his pockets.

"Yes, you have it, my dear," said Sophia. "I see it there. You are pushing it into your pocket. Don't fidget with it; don't crumple it. Yes, that is grandfather's paper, and his writing, his weak old writing, poor old man! Let me have it. Give it to me, Andrew, when I tell you. Do you wish to make me more ill than I am? I know you all want to spare me something; but I should have no peace after this. I am prepared for it. There is no good in the thing's being done, if it is kept from me. It is the whole point of our doing it, its part in my life-story. It would still be on my mind. I should still feel I had no chance. Is this all, this letter? Was there nothing else?"

She looked into Andrew's face, but his tone, as he said, "Nothing else," sent her eyes down to the page. The change on her face was less than her children had feared.

"So this is it," she said. "This is the explanation of it all. That is why Grandfather did not want Father and me to marry. Do you know what I thought? Well, it is no matter now. I wonder nobody ever suspected this. I dare say people did think of it; but Father's marrying me would put it out of the question. So that is how it was. It seems so strange, with Grandfather so strait-laced; but one never knows. That is why Mrs. Lang did not tell Father who his father was. To prevent him from knowing this. Well, it was wise of her. Whatever she was, she was a wise woman then. I could see she was a wise woman, worthy to be

Father's mother, by the time she met him. So I am Father's sister. Well, I am not troubled about that. It only seems to draw us closer. But you must not think of it, my dears. You must not know it. It would be a great disadvantage to you, unspeakable, worse than you can realise. Poor children, you have had enough to overcome. But this need make no difference. It has had no ill results; indeed it has not. You couldn't be better in any way than you are. And things are straight and clear now, and I am leaving nothing undone. Miss Patmore, you must never speak of it. You never should have known it; but you are one of us."

"Oh, no. I have hardly understood what is in the letter," said Patty.

"Do you know what I thought?" said Sophia. "I thought it might be a will, leaving everything away from us, if Father and I should be married. I knew Grandfather had something on his mind the day before he died. He talked about a will." Sophia felt her children's eyes on her face. "Or I think he did. And then he was supposed to have burnt it. And it all went out of my head with the shock of his death. He must have changed his purpose. Old people do that easily. Well, I can go forward now with a good heart. But you must be utterly unconscious of it. I am glad that Father never knew it. I am thankful he was spared that. Perhaps it was meant that, as he was not to be here long, he should pass away before he knew. Not that he would have minded anything that drew us nearer. I feel that."

She stopped as she caught a glimpse of Patty's face.

"Miss Patmore, did he find the letter? Did he unlock the desk and read it? Tell me. You wanted to go and open the desk by yourself. You had some reason. You had seen the letter. You knew he had read it. You guessed. Tell me how you found him."

"Oh, no, no. I am sure he had not read it," said Patty. "I could see he had not——"

"Tell me how you found him," said Sophia.

"I found him just as you saw him," said Patty. "I know he had not seen it. He was just sitting at the desk. The desk was still locked. The key—"

"I see," said Sophia, in a quiet, even tone. "There is something else for me to face. I should not have thought I had come to the end. That is not for me. He opened the desk, and read it, and was alone with that shock. And his heart failed. And you kept it from me. I have been saved from knowing it for ten months. You saw it was best for us not to know. You locked it up again. Was the letter open, Andrew?"

"Yes, the cover was broken," said Andrew. "There is no keeping anything from you."

But Sophia did not smile.

"And now you do not want me to know it," she went on. "Yes, I see. It was good of you, Miss Patmore. You meant to be good. You have always been kind and good to us. And I think it would have killed me at the time, to think of his reading it there alone. You judged rightly in that matter. I could not have borne any more. It did all but shatter me, what I went through. Perhaps it has brought me to my end. Well, I can bear it better now, knowing that he met this there by himself. I may not be so far from going to him now."

"It did not need so much of a shock to stop his heart in the state it was in," said Dinah. "The doctors thought even the stairs might have done it. The revelation to him was only what it has been to all of us. We are not suffering so much."

"Darling, that is a comforting thought," said Sophia. "And whatever comes of it, I shall always be glad that he and I lived our years together. I can't be sorry for that. And if it had been discovered, we couldn't have had them. And I shouldn't have had all of you, not as you are, not like Father. How like him you look, Dinah! And no other children could have been what you have to me. So I can't regret it. It may be wrong, but I can't. And now go away,

179

and leave me to think of it alone. And just forget it. Do you understand me? Really be unconscious of it. Never speak of it, even to each other. Only remember it enough to be on your guard, if there should be need. I hope no need will come. People must always think we know nothing about Father's father, as they think now. They must always have that impression. You understand me, dear ones. You are old enough to grasp that this might be an infinitely serious thing for you. Now go, and think and talk of other things. Miss Patmore, you will stay with me for a little while? What mazes of life we have been through together, you and I! We little thought, when we first met, of all there was before us."

"It isn't a thing they would naturally include in their forecast," said Dinah, "even Patty and Sophia."

"Shall we ever be able to face it?" said Robin.

"No, we shall not. That will be our solution," said Andrew.

"It is a good thing we did not add a marriage to an aunt and uncle to it," said Dinah.

"Do you take in what Sophia has behind her?" said Robin. "Keeping a will locked up for twenty-eight years, as far as her intentions went! Fancy meeting us every morning with that breakfast table thought!"

"Sophia has other thoughts at breakfast time," said Dinah, "smaller, worse thoughts. I hope we shall be able to emulate her, and avoid the worst thought of all, that we are apart from our race in the thing at the root of our being. We have always seemed to be something of the kind. Perhaps the truth behind us was working itself out. Well, it has done it now. Perhaps it all had to be planned to make us what we are. Sophia keeps on complimenting us on that score; and Sophia is not prone to take rosy views of human quality, certainly not maternal ones."

"It doesn't seem to have done us much harm," said Robin.

"Oh, so many things have gone to the spoiling of us,"

said Andrew. "Our unnatural life, our want of friends, our thraldom to Sophia, in her success, her sorrow, and now her sickness. We can't tell what has or has not worked our undoing."

"We can," said Dinah. "All those things have done ill by us. We can tell it quite well. You have just told it very well. But the main thing does not seem to have done us harm."

"It has not done you any," said Robin.

"Sophia has taken her own way even more than we knew," said Andrew. "She incurred the disinheritance, and would not be disinherited."

"Fate has tired of it," said Dinah. "We all get tired of Sophia's way. She cannot be managed except by making most things matters of life and death."

"Well, she hardly can," said Robin. "Did you mark her summing up of everything in a second? And isn't her lying masterly? Patty's is the feeblest thing beside it, and Patty's is a deal above the average."

"We ought to be good at double-dealing," said Dinah, "brought up by those two women. All our life will be a call for it. With a twofold share of Grandfather in us as well, we should come through."

"It is firm of Sophia to plume herself on the union and its results," said Robin.

"Oh, hush, as Patty would say," said Dinah. "We none of us think the offspring so bad in each case. We shall get to the pluming. We shall see ourselves the victims of darkness and tragedy, and feel ennobled by them. The worst of it is, that I believe we are being ennobled."

"Why was it so important that the old man's life should be thought to be without a blemish?" said Robin.

"Of course it was a great thing to him," said Andrew, "just as it is to you that yours should be held to be be-smeared with every blemish. To do him justice, every one assumed it was without. He was more successful than you. We see that, by no one's suspecting that Father was his son."

"Father was not like him, was he?" said Robin, "or like Sophia?"

"He was too like Mrs. Lang to be really like either of them," said Dinah. "But it was said that living together had given them all resemblances. It all fits into place now."

"After all, it was only one slip," said Robin, "unless he only confessed to the one he was committed to."

"Boasting of your London life at this moment!" said Dinah. "I wonder whom Sophia thought she was depriving. Cousin Peter perhaps. If so, can we question the course she took? We have always deprived him of everything possible. I suppose the matter had not her consideration."

"Talking, darlings?" said Sophia, opening the door, her tone at once deprecating the subject of discussion, and recognising that it was inevitable. "I have come up because I want a little time with you. I feel I must have it. I know I have told you not to speak about all this, to forget it. And we will never utter a word about it after today. It will be simply a sort of dream. It is just a strange tale already. But today I knew I must come to you. I am in a state that I can't explain. There is a great darkness over me. I can't get it out of my thoughts, that Father went up there alone, and was there alone with that shock, and died there by himself, and that he was there by my word and will. I feel as if it was I who caused his death, because of what I had left undone; as if I had been made to give him that mission, for his heart to fail; as if his health had been brought into that state because of me. Oh, my husband!"

Sophia bent her head on her arm, and her children looked at each other. There was something about her that was more than the moment's change. Die and death were not words that used to come from her lips. She had gone to her end, to where danger was no more for her. Robin got up and pulled his chair to her side.

"Here, sit down," he said, with a roughness that she did not misunderstand.

"Are Edward and Judith coming tonight?" she said,

leaning on the chair, and giving him a tender look. "Then I will go in a moment. I don't want them to see me like this. Dinah dear, brighten up, and go and put on some other dress. You want a little helping with your looks tonight. And be yourselves with Edward and Judith. How I am always having to tell you that! Poor children! Such sweet selves! You know you have just to forget it all. We shall all forget it after tonight. Have you forgotten it?"

She laughed, and went with a sudden energy out of the room. The door was hardly shut when Patty opened it.

"Judith and Edward are on the staircase," she said. "You won't say anything to them? Not a word!"

"Oh, no, we shall not breathe of it," said Andrew. "It is as if it had never been. It was a play we played. All right, Patty."

Patty shut the door

"It is best to say that," said Andrew. "But we must tell them, of course. We will get it out at once, and then I hope never speak of it again. But it is wiser to keep our revealing it from Sophia and Patty. It will prevent Patty from being unguarded herself, though I believe she would die in defence of any family secret of ours. I am not sure that Sophia is any too safe."

"I am sure she is not safe at all," said Robin. "She is hardly fit to be. What a plight we are in!"

"Well, you all look rather tired," said Judith.

"Tired?" said Robin. "It will be some time before we get to that."

"Why, what is it?" said Edward. "We passed Mrs. Stace on the stairs. She looked so pale that we only just spoke to her. Is anything amiss?"

"You must have some preparation, Edward," said Andrew. "Men are said to be more conventional than women, and your shock may be greater than Judith's."

"Why, what is the trouble?" said Edward. "A mere breach of convention will not worry me."

183

"It is really just so much," said Robin; "but it will do more than that for you, Edward."

"Are you uneasy about Mrs. Stace?" said Judith.

"We are very anxious about her," said Dinah; "but that has come to seem an honourable anxiety."

"Whatever do you mean?" said Judith.

"We can't tell you while you talk of it in that light voice," said Dinah. "We must do some more leading up."

"Well, go on preparing the way," said Edward. "Has it come on you lately?"

"Yes," said Robin. "This afternoon."

"It has always been on us," said Dinah, "but we did not know."

"Oh, it is something that has been found out," said Edward. "Oh, have you discovered who your father's father was?"

"It shows how people's minds are occupied with our affairs," said Dinah, looking at her brothers.

"Well, your affairs are mine, Dinah," said Edward.

"Go on, Edward, and find out," said Robin. "Then we shall not have to tell you."

"We could not do that," said Dinah. "We see that now."

"Are we so difficult to tell?" said Edward.

"Not above the average," said Robin.

"How do you know?" said Judith.

"It came out in a letter," said Robin.

"Oh, a letter has been found, explaining who your father's father was!" said Judith.

"The intuition of women! How utterly true all common theories are!" said Andrew.

"That is sad, to be an instance of a common theory," said Judith.

"Judith, how terribly without preparation you are still!" said Dinah.

"Well, it is simply that, isn't it?" said Judith. "You simply have to tell us who your other grandfather was."

"Simply that," said Dinah. "It is too simple. The lack of variety is the trouble."

They all began to laugh.

"The intuition of women, that is such a common thing, fails me now," said Judith. "Perhaps that is more original."

"Oh, Judith, do summon it to our aid," said Dinah.

"Well, who is the other grandfather?" said Edward. "Let us come to it like that."

"There isn't any other," said Dinah. "There is only the one."

"It makes us hysterical," said Robin. "It is that kind of thing. Now, for your intuition, Judith. Dinah has really told you."

"How do you mean?" said Edward.

"Yes, that is it, Edward," said Andrew. "There is only the one." His voice shook as if for several reasons. "My grandfather, Andrew Stace, was my father's father."

"Oh, well, people used to think that at one time," said Edward. "I have heard it said that they did. It was a natural thing to be suspected, I suppose. But it couldn't have been so, because your father married your mother."

"It was so," said Andrew.

"What?" said Edward.

"Yes, that is the truth," said Andrew. "A letter has been found from my mother's father to my father, explaining that he was his son."

"But he would not have allowed the marriage between your father and your mother," said Edward.

"It never had his sanction," said Andrew. "He prevented it in his lifetime, and left this letter, explaining the truth, to be opened at his death. The letter was not found. It has been found today."

"Are you sure the letter was written by him?" said Edward. "It is a thing that might come into any one's head."

"Quite sure," said Andrew. "It is odd that I should be

insisting on the truth of it. But we must get this over once for all."

There was a pause.

"This is a thing to be absolutely silent about," said Edward; "to be so silent about, that it does not come to our lips when we are alone, does not enter into our thoughts. It must not be breathed to a human being. It must hardly be mentioned among ourselves."

"It must not, Edward," said Andrew. "It has not been. No one knows but Sophia and Patty. No one will know. We have told you from a sense of what is right to you; and it is fair to you that you should be clear that it is the truth. We could not start life with you—if we start it at all with you now—on this hidden knowledge."

"We do appreciate your telling us," said Edward. "It must have been a great effort. Of course it makes no difference. We thank you very much for your courage."

"Was Mrs. Lang your father's mother after all?" said Judith. "Was she married to your grandfather?"

"She was his mother," said Andrew. "I will show you the letter some time. They were not married. My grandfather was engaged to Sophia's mother, when he heard that the child who was to be our father, was to be born. Mrs. Lang gave Father the facts without the names; but we thought the story of the marriage was better to tell. You will understand that. We were not the only family involved. It is easy to see why she did not reveal to him the whole. Grandfather adopted his own son."

"It is bad for Caroline and Gilbert," said Judith.

"How, bad for them?" said Robin. "Oh, you mean that their mother was not married when my father was born. They know that. They only don't know who his father was."

"They need never know," said Edward. "If so many people are to know, it will cease to be a secret; and that is unthinkable. It is nothing to do with them, or with their parentage. It does not touch them."

186

"There is no reason for telling them," said Andrew.

"Oh, they must not be told," said Edward.

Robin looked at his face.

"How did you come upon the letter?" said Judith.

"Sophia remembered Grandfather's putting some papers in his desk before he died," said Robin. "She told Father, and he went to look for them, and it was probably the shock of this letter that caused his heart to fail. We did not know at the time. The desk got locked again, and Sophia remembered again yesterday."

"What a tragedy!" said Judith.

"Yes," said Robin.

"You are all full of courage," said Edward. "Now let us talk of something else."

They spoke for a while of the same thing, and parted to avoid returning to it. As the three came up from seeing the Drydens to the door, Patty was on the landing.

"Remember we have said no word about it," said Andrew.

But Patty did not ask. She looked at them in silence and dropped her eyes as they passed her.

"Well, Patty knows we have betrayed our trust," said Dinah. "I know her look when she has found out something. And not speaking always means guilt with her."

"Why should she feel guilt?" said Robin. "That seems our business."

"It is generally Patty's," said Dinah. "I suppose for listening at the door this time. But I don't see why she should feel it. I am sure she has a right to know everything in the house. She may even feel it the thing to do, in this home of duplicity. I am glad she has some compensation for living here. It is a good place in a way for Patty to live in."

"There are certainly things to know," said Andrew.

"And they are getting known," said Robin.

"Oh, they have had to go just so far," said Andrew. "No one really knows."

"You and Dinah and I know," said Robin. "Edward and Judith know. Sophia and Patty know. Pretty good for no one. But no one as yet. Any one else will be some one."

The next morning at breakfast Sophia looked ill and old. She hardly tried to eat, and her hands trembled over her tasks at the head of the table. Dinah offered to deal with them for her.

"No, no, darling," said Sophia, beginning a second time. "I can look after you all just a little while longer. I will care for you while I can."

She smiled, but in a minute gave it up, and sought her children's faces.

"I don't know how to describe my state to you," she said, relapsing into the stooping posture that was getting familiar. "I know you must be worn out with my griefs and troubles; but I must depend on your love. It is the only basis of my tottering life, the one thing that holds me from falling into the abyss. A great oppression still seems to be over me, a great cloud. It is as if I could not get strength to rise out of it, struggle as I will. And I have not striven so very hard. It may be that my struggling time is past. It is not only that I feel as if my days on earth were numbered, though I think they must be numbered now." She smiled, and her children saw that she did not believe what she said, though they were beginning to believe it. "It is that I feel that this great blackness has come between Father and myself; as if this that we were to each other, has taken away all our romance from us. As if, when I go to join him, there will stand a barrier between us. Though, if I had let the truth be discovered, we could not have had each other, not as we did. I could not have been your mother, you dear children of our love. I don't know where to turn my eyes for light. My way is dark, as I go alone into the valley of the shadow."

"Your oratory is most telling," said Andrew.

Sophia laughed, and her eyes had a flash for a moment. "In some countries it has been normal for children of

188

the same father to marry," said Dinah. "There is no need to make too much of its happening once."

"Dear one, what helpful things you do think of!" said Sophia. "Doesn't she, Andrew? Well, I must give myself up to trying to get better for all your sakes. I must resolve to think of nothing but that."

She glanced at Robin.

"Don't you want me to get well, then, Robin?" she said.

Robin's fleeting thought had crossed his face. It was one of many, at variance with themselves.

"What a question to ask!" he said. "I shall not answer it."

He was silent to the end of the meal.

"Really, Sophia cannot wonder if we rejoice sometimes at the prospect of freedom," he said, when they were upstairs.

"She doesn't wonder, evidently," said Dinah. "She took to the idea readily when it was presented to her."

"You might draw a veil over your moments of inner gladness," said Andrew.

"I own the thought did cross my mind," said Robin. "As I say, how can it not at times?"

"See it doesn't disfigure your face again," said Dinah.

"Sophia believed my implied lie," said Robin; "and it was only partly a lie."

"Sophia is always soothed by lies," said Andrew, "even by whole ones, as I suspect she took yours to be."

Patty came in, and stood before them, shutting the door behind her.

"What have you been talking about at breakfast? The maid who was doing the hall came down to the kitchen with a regular muddle of a tale. It will be out all over the place, if you are not careful. It is all but out now. I did my best to put them all off, but I don't know how far I have done it."

"Oh, well, Patty, if people will listen at doors, we are helpless," said Dinah. "We can't allow for that, though it does seem the rule of the house. And we have to talk to Sophia about it. She can't keep it off her mind. How is she to make an effort now, for the first time in her life? If people will leave no stone unturned, to find out what they ought not to know, they must go on turning stones. There are some more to turn. Sophia must be served until the end."

CHAPTER IX

SOPHIA WAS SERVED until the end. Soon after this the service became constant, and it was seen that the end was near. The time was one of relief and surprise to those who served. Sophia, who had gone in storm through her life, drew in calm to its early close. Sophia, who had never brooked a challenge to her will, seemed to bow to the extinction of herself. Her nature protected itself, and in the moods when she greatly wished to live, she felt she would not die. It was not Sophia's personality that was diseased. Moreover, did she always so fiercely desire to live? Had life been so sweet to Sophia? More was learnt of her in her numbered days. In her thousand asseverations, that life could offer no more to her, had there been the touch of truth? Was there truth at the bottom of Sophia? No doubt had been accepted of her strong grip on life. Her children, who had thought to lose her many years later, had never foreseen that the tide of her life would go out with so little violence.

Peter supervised her illness under the London doctor's guidance. His willing, consistent kindness was a great support. No strain came with Cousin Peter. His nature seemed worked up to yield its best to this need. He read and talked to Sophia with a greater ease than when she was in health. The only trouble that came with him was his guilty awareness of the greater ease.

Sophia was true to herself to the last; and in this her first and last helplessness laid her hand on the future she would not see.

She had come to seem to change with the days, and her children seldom left her. True to herself, she accepted as a matter of course their constant companionship. She seemed to feel at once a presence withdrawn. The changes were sudden and complete in a moment, and they were all on the watch for them, and alive to the one that came.

She raised herself a little higher in her chair, and began to murmur to herself.

"Just dying!" she said, in a voice of realisation kept to resignation by her weakness. "Just dying. It is just that."

"Oh, no, no. Come, what are you talking of? It is not like you to speak in that way," said Peter.

"No, you have been watching me," said Sophia, turning her eyes to his. "That is true, Peter. It is like me to sit and get weaker, while other people round me know. That is what I have been doing. I see what it is."

"Oh, come, you mustn't say things of that kind," said Peter. "Not a good patient like you."

"No," murmured Sophia. "No, he would not like me to, Christian would not. He would wish me to do my utmost to get well; and then, if I could not, to go to meet him with a good courage. I shall go to him soon now. I have not often felt it as I do today. And it will not make any difference that it has been found out. He will not mind that we were brother and sister. He will help me to reach him just the same. It was not our fault that we had the same father. He was my husband. He was."

"Yes, yes. He was indeed. I don't know any one who was more husband than he was," said Peter. "Your being brought up together made you all the more to each other. You understood one another so well."

"Yes; but it would have been better not to keep it a secret," said Sophia, raising her eyes. "He should have told us, my father should. But he meant it for the best; and if he had let it be known, we could not have married. So I don't really wish he had; I can't wish that. It would have been best if there hadn't been that letter." She gave a little smile. "That is what I really wish. Then we should never have known."

"She is getting fancies," said Peter, looking round. "She is very weak."

"Yes, yes, she is," said Andrew. "You are letting yourself imagine things," he said, in a calm, clear voice, bending down to his mother. "You are not thinking what you are saying."

Sophia looked at him for a moment.

"No, I am not thinking," she said, with a faintly startled look. "I am not remembering; and I said I would. I am very ill. He understands I am very ill." She made a gesture towards Peter. "It was he who said I was." She turned to her cousin, herself. "That was not true, what I said about Christian and me being brother and sister. You guessed I was getting fancies. Andrew and Dinah will tell you I am getting them. Christian and I were not a real brother and sister. Nobody is to know about it. They will tell you."

She nodded and closed her eyes; and Peter stood looking down on her.

"It is a strange thing, but that was a rumour once, long ago," he said, "that your father was Andrew Stace's son. A natural report enough. But of course it died down when he and your mother married. She must have got hold of it."

"Yes, she must," said Andrew. "We have heard that it was a rumour."

Peter still stood looking down at Sophia.

"Has a letter or anything been come upon lately?" he said.

"Yes, a sort of letter of farewell from Grandfather to Father," said Andrew, "telling him to take care of Mother, and that sort of thing. That is what she is thinking of. Nothing much in it, but an intimate letter, not one to quote from."

"Oh, no, no. Not one to quote from," said Peter, still looking down. "Well, Andrew, I must be going for today. You may count on me tomorrow as usual. I will come in in just my ordinary way."

Sophia roused herself.

"Tell him," she said, with a touch of her old command, "that it is not true, what I said. Tell him I said it because I was ill, that I did not mean to say it. Because nobody is to know. I will not say it again."

She smiled at them, and closed her eyes.

Peter turned away from her.

"Well, good-bye, Andrew, good-bye, Dinah. I hope there is nothing more to fall on you. Those words are from the bottom of my heart. No, don't touble to come out with me. Don't trouble to do that today."

"Ought we to send a message after him, to tell him to keep utterly and to the end quiet?" said Andrew. "Or wouldn't it be the least good?"

"It will be better simply to contradict whatever he may say," said Dinah. "To say that Sophia was wandering, got puzzled about the old rumour, anything. People can't dispute it to our faces. To tell him to be quiet would be to give the whole village the truth at once. He may as well do that for us. He isn't going to lose any time, we can see. It all comes to the same thing in the end."

"It is as bad as that, is it?" said Andrew.

"Who would have thought that Cousin Peter would be so quick on the truth?" said Robin.

"It didn't need so much aptness," said Andrew. "He had heard the report. And it is simple minds that grasp the one thread, that seem quick. There is so much they don't reckon with. They work along one line."

"And Sophia told him plainly," said Dinah. "There is no need to account for it in such a difficult way."

"Sophia?" said Sophia, opening her eyes, and fixing them with smiling reproach on Dinah. "Sophia? Oh, you naughty girl! That is what you call me, is it, when I am not listening? Just because I was asleep!"

She closed her eyes.

"A day of revelations!" said Robin. "Cousin Peter is not the only one who will sleep the wiser."

"Not by a long way," said Dinah.

Patty entered in outdoor clothes, cast her eyes round the room, and began to talk in a low, agitated voice.

"Well, I don't know what is coming on us next. I met Cousin Peter in the drive, and he seemed to know about everything. He asked me all sorts of things, and I hadn't an idea what to answer. He as good as implied that Mother had let it all out. I begged and prayed him not to say anything, not to let it go further; but one is never sure with him."

"Well, you told him it was true, then, Patty," said Robin. "Sophia informed him once. You confirmed her statements. It seems probable that he has taken it in by now."

"Well, I couldn't guess he was going to talk about it," said Patty, almost in tears. "I was taken by surprise. He ought not to stop me, and ask me questions he would not dare to ask you."

"He ought not indeed, Patty," said Dinah. "You have never taken a juster stand."

"Never mind, Patty," said Andrew.

"No, don't be troubled," said Dinah. "Sophia has told Cousin Peter. We have told Edward and Judith, as you know. We have done our best to spread it about. We can't complain if we have succeeded."

Sophia looked up at them.

"I don't like to keep being called Sophia," she said. "You must not go on doing it because I am ill, and don't notice. You naughty children! Miss Patmore, I will go to my room now."

She rose from her chair with Andrew's help, and went upstairs supported by her sons.

"What did you keep on laughing at?" she said. "I don't see much to be amused at, in the way we are situated now."

"Oh, a lot of silly little things," said Robin. "We thought you were listening."

"I didn't give anything away to Cousin Peter, did I?" said Sophia, sinking into a chair.

"Oh, no, no, nothing," said Dinah. "Nothing that mattered at all, if you just remember not to say anything again."

"Well, I wonder what Edward would say to the course things are taking," said Robin. "I wonder what he will say; for I suppose you two will think it your duty to tell him?"

"I don't think we have any more duty," said Dinah. "I think it will spread itself now."

"Dinah, you will jest on your deathbed," said Andrew.

"No, I don't think so," said Dinah. "I am only jesting at Sophia's. Making sport at one's mother is different."

"Really, Cousin Peter's catechising Patty was criminal," said Robin. "I don't know what he deserves."

"We only know what he has got, complete satisfaction," said Dinah.

It was the custom for Edward and Judith to make an evening visit, now that Sophia's illness bound her children to the house. Edward's expression was read by Robin at once.

"Well, speak up, as a parson and a man, Edward," he said.

"There certainly is something that I must say plainly," said Edward. "I must do it once for all. I have no choice. You will be shocked when you hear it. Bateman came in today, to say a word about a parishioner who is a patient of his; and it transpired that he had heard Mrs. Stace talking about this that has been discovered. He said she was ill and wandering, but that it was quite clear what had been found out. He was very nice about it; but he was terribly shocked, of course. I simply said it must be a mistake, a delusion of Mrs. Stace's, that the old rumour had led to; but that it might do harm to talk of it; and passed it off. I felt I was justified in saying so much. We have to take life as it is. A clergyman is the first person to know that. But the thing to be firm about is, that absolute silence must be kept, if we are to have our future secure. I have grave fears already.

I hope I have put Bateman off, anyhow silenced him, as he is a decent fellow. But I would really suggest that Mrs. Stace be kept apart from outsiders, until she—until she is better or not. We must speak openly about a thing like this. I have felt that I must. It is my duty."

"Well, I congratulate you," said Robin. "You haven't missed any of it out. Did you mention to Cousin Peter that he was an outsider, as you have thought to inform us that he is a decent fellow? We both needed the information equally."

"So the parishioner and patient he really came to speak about, was Sophia?" said Dinah.

"You may be annoyed, Robin," said Edward, not looking at Dinah. "I see it is natural that you should be easily worked up about it. But I can't think any less of what I owe to Dinah and Judith, and all of us, and to my own position of trust. It is surely to your own interest that your own future should be saved; that your mother should be protected from herself while she is helpless."

"It may be to my interest, but it is hardly to hers," said Robin. "She is helpless, as you say, and we cannot take advantage of it."

"Her doctors would hardly be prepared for her being kept apart from them, in extreme illness. It is not the time they would expect it, though it is plainly what Cousin Peter ought to expect," said Dinah.

"Couldn't you make it clear to her that she must not on any account talk of it?" said Judith.

"We should not think of worrying her," said Robin.

"It is for the sake of her children, and so for hers," said Edward. "I think you regard her dependence in a wrong way; as she would not wish, if she could choose."

"No, we have tried, Edward," said Andrew, gravely; "and we have not made it clear. She is very ill."

"Well, a good deal of sacrifice has to be made in several lives, because of the end of one," said Judith.

"I don't think anything could be done, my dear," said

Andrew. "If she is not to see Cousin Peter, she must see some one else. I think there is nothing in that."

"Well, we are all in a very tragic position," said Edward.

"We are, Edward," said Andrew. "That is, Dinah and Robin and I are. You and Judith need not be. I suggest that we all should judge later, if we feel ourselves the right partners for each other in a life shadowed by this. Because the climax seems to be coming."

There was a silence.

"That is for Dinah to decide, for me," said Edward. "I do not wish it for myself."

"I wish it for you, Dinah," said Andrew. "And Edward chooses it for Judith. And so we are coupled in the way we had better be, the old way; perhaps the way we have really always been."

"Oh, well, what difference can it make in the long run?" said Judith. "Let us do what you say for the moment, and then we need not go on tormenting you while you are in trouble. You will be thankful to have an end of it for the time."

"There will be an end of it for always, unless any one of us makes another beginning," said Andrew. "That is how it is best to leave it."

"What do you say, Dinah?" said Edward.

"I do not say anything," said Dinah. "You are better at saying than I am. I won't say that I will be your sister, because in our family that seems to lead to marriage. Why didn't you deal with Cousin Peter for making the truth public, as you did through us with Sophia? A strong man doing it on purpose, to other people's harm, and a very sick woman helplessly, to her own—"

"Dinah, Dinah, you are as good at saying as ever Edward is," said Andrew.

"Oh, I don't know. Edward's method is the safer," said Robin.

"Robin, your attitude is utterly unreasonable," said Edward.

"I see it," said Robin. "A reasonable outlook would involve regarding you as a well-doing and well-meaning man. I admit that my attitude is the opposite."

"Another one of us good at saying!" said Judith.

Patty came in with a message that Sophia was settling for the night, and desired to see her children; and leave was taken under cover of her presence.

"Shall we tell Sophia?" said Andrew.

"Oh, no, I should not," said Robin. "She may be disturbed about it."

"I should rather like her to know," said Andrew. "We shall find her a better companion in memory that way. What do you say, Dinah?"

"Let us sacrifice Sophia," said Dinah.

"That from you two!" said Robin. "I wonder if Sophia knows what she has had."

"No. Her distrust of human nature has prevented her knowing," said Dinah. "Sophia demands much, and expects little."

"Well, my dears," said Sophia, lying back on her pillows. "Have you come from Edward and Judith?"

"Yes, but we are not going back to them," said Andrew, coming up to her. "We have decided that they are not good enough for us."

"What? Don't you like them any more?" said Sophia, with an air of mild surprise. "Have you given them up? Well, you know, I almost thought you would. I dare say it is better so. I have always thought they were rather shallow for you. That is partly why I did not hurry you into marrying. I was not thinking only of myself. I should have liked to know whom you are going to marry; but I am glad I know as much as I can. And in a way you will have better opportunities when I am gone."

She closed her eyes, and Andrew and Dinah looked at each other. Sophia in her weakness still strove to exalt herself. Sophia, who had never had strength for her daily life, had courage to die.

"Well, you were right to give Sophia the chance of the last word," said Robin. "She has taken it. I would have given a deal for Edward to hear her. But after all he heard Dinah."

"It is of no good pretending that we are upset about it," said Andrew, but he turned away. He was upset about something else.

"Well, we are not pretending," said Robin.

"Of course I shall always have my own feeling for Judith," said Andrew.

"So shall I always have mine for Edward," said Robin, "and one better of its kind than yours ever was for Judith. I know you tried. I needed no effort."

"We have really used Judith and Edward as an escape from Sophia," said Andrew. "I wonder what Sophia would say if she knew it."

"She does know it," said Dinah. "She referred to it. We know what she would say. She said it."

Patty opened the door.

"What is all this about Edward and Judith and your giving them up? No, I was not listening. Mother told me."

"Edward has no idea just how obliging Sophia is with her information," said Dinah.

"You imply that you think we criticise your listening, Patty," said Robin. "You do us wrong."

"But if it is about any of this, how naughty and unkind of them!" said Patty. "They ought not to mind so much about it. That sort of caring is a pretty thing. I wouldn't give much for that."

"Well, we didn't give anything for it," said Dinah; "and we expected in return loyalty and faithfulness through an impossible trial. We are Sophia's children."

Patty paused, as if these words gave her to think.

"I wish Mother would say a word to me before—before anything happens," she said, her eyes wavering away from their faces. "Twenty-eight years I have been with her; twenty-eight years I have put everything on one side for

200

her sake, everything. And she never speaks a word to me, to show that she thinks of it, never anything—"

"Oh, Patty, Patty!" said Andrew, getting up. "Sophia never says a word to any one. She doesn't to us. She regards her affection as a tribute in itself, and she has given it to you for twenty-eight years. Think what that means."

"Besides, you have hardly put everything on one side for her," said Robin. "You have dealt in that way with all things for the three of us. Thank God for that."

"We will say anything to you in our last illnesses," said Dinah. "Don't dream of not surviving us, because we can't have last illnesses without you."

Sophia's bell rang, and Patty hastened from them.

"Well, can we bring this off for Patty?" said Andrew.

"I don't think we can," said Dinah, nearly crying. "Sophia would let it out that we had prompted her, and that would be worse than nothing. We have had enough of Sophia's confidences."

"Besides, Sophia would never brook being told that devotion to her needed recognition," said Robin.

"Wouldn't she, now that she is ill?" said Andrew.

"People ought not to brook when they are ill, what they do not brook when they are well," said Dinah. "Sophia must die in peace."

Sophia died in peace. A few weeks later the summons came to her deathbed, the long awaited summons that was a shock when it came. The alarm had been given, and the London doctor had spent a night in the house; but it had happened before; and it was with feelings more of apprehension than of conviction of the truth, that the brothers and sister approached their mother's bed.

She was lying on her back, with Patty and the nurse beside her, the doctor and Peter in the room. The three joined Patty at the bedside, Robin keeping behind. For a time there was silence, and Robin and Peter moved to the hearth. Andrew and Dinah stood with their eyes on Sophia, now and then raising them to meet each other's. At last Patty spoke.

"I think—I am sure there is a change," she said.

Dr. Lamb took Sophia's wrist.

"Yes," he said, and remained by her.

Andrew and Dinah came to the pillow, and Sophia opened her eyes.

"Who are all these people about?" she said, her voice her own, her sight already dim.

"Dr. Lamb and Cousin Peter have come to see you, because you were not so well," said Dinah, the reassurance in her voice, though not its words, reaching her mother.

Sophia moved on her pillows.

"I don't want them. Dinah! Miss Patmore!" she said, and said no more.

"My name was the last word she said," said Patty. "I shall always be able to remember that."

"Yes, yes, so it was. So it ought to have been," said Peter, patting her shoulder. "It happened just as it should, as we all should have chosen. Come now into the next room, and leave them alone for a few minutes. That is best for them. We have some little things we want from you."

Sophia's children stood by her. Andrew broke down for a moment. Dinah was calm. The death, when she had known it was coming, made the least difference to her, as the knowledge had made the most. Robin stood apart, his eyes averted from the bed. Through the door, as silence came, sounded Peter's voice, ensuing on Patty's departing on some quest.

"Yes, she is the most faithful creature, the most good and loyal in the world. I say that she is. Twenty-eight years she has given herself to them, body and soul. I know, because I have watched it; I have seen it from the beginning. I only hope she will stick to them now; but I can say she will, will Miss Patmore. For it is now they will need her; it is now they will want every friend they have. Well, I for one, don't intend to desert them. It is my resolve to cleave to them through thick and thin; and I don't care who hears me say so."

But it seemed that Peter did care, for he was heard to try the door in case it should be ajar.

Patty came in with a cheerful face, and told her charges, in a tone that showed that their loss gave them back to her in this character, to go to their own room. As they went, they realised the house without Sophia, their lives without their mother. The wave of emptiness and release that came over them, held them silent. It seemed that a weight had fallen, as a weight had lifted. The survey of Sophia's life flashed on them, the years of ruthlessness and tragedy, power and grief. Happiness, of which she was held to have had so much, had never been real to Sophia. They saw it now.

"Well, I hope Patty won't go on with her open celebration," said Robin.

"There are enough gaps in our lives. It would be a pity to have to destroy her," said Andrew.

"It is not Patty's fault. We can't blame Patty," said Dinah. "She will always be able to be herself now. She is suddenly herself after twenty-eight years. We shall be thankful to see her herself, so we can't be surprised if she is a little cheered about it. It is time her spirits took a turn. After all, Sophia has always been what she was meant to be."

"It is a way people have," said Robin. "Cousin Peter was being thorough about it on the other side of that door. We shall presently have brought home to us what he has done."

"Apart from the offensiveness to us, of saying that Patty had given herself to us, body and soul," said Dinah, "he must know by now that Patty hasn't a soul, if he has watched her from the beginning, as he protested."

"He wouldn't have dared to spread it all about, if Sophia had been well," said Robin.

"We shall all have a courage we never had in that state of things," said Andrew.

"I am glad Sophia didn't bring in her religion on her deathbed," said Dinah, "but mentioned Patty instead. It was fitting, after all that had been done to her, and put on Patty."

"The thing will be out in London now," said Robin.

"Yes; now that Cousin Peter has been so entertaining to Dr. Lamb," said Dinah. "He certainly acted the host for us, and saw to it that his colleague shouldn't have a dull moment at Sophia's deathbed. We will not run over the occasions on which he has served us in that capacity. This is not a day for soliciting emotions. If we go to London, we shall have to share your London life."

"Do you really think of settling in London?" said Robin.

"We are forced to fall back on it," said Andrew. "We can't conceive of staying here."

"Then know that my life there is pure and dull," said Robin.

"You have always let us know it," said Dinah, "but we have honoured all your ambitions. And spotless dullness is what Andrew and I are so gifted at. To do you justice, you are less fitted for it."

"Can we charge Cousin Peter with his treachery?" said Robin.

"It is only being himself," said Dinah. "You heard him say he would cleave to us, declare it behind our backs. We have not too much of that. His expressions of loyalty would not have been needed, if he had held his peace. But that wasn't in him. He can't help letting everything out, any more than Patty can help finding it out; or Sophia could help hiding her real self from Father; or Andrew and I can help being spotless and dull; or you can help trying to be the opposite. It is no good to charge people with their natures."

"Then stop doing it," said Robin.

"Why, there is Edward coming across the lawn!" said Andrew, looking out later, under the drawn blind. "What does he want?"

"I knew he would be on us," said Robin. "It wasn't much good getting rid of him. Sophia has to have a funeral, of course."

"Oh, of course. It seems somehow derogatory to her," said Dinah. "We will not have Cousin Peter as host. Andrew and I must begin to be a man and woman. Sophia has left us orphans, and we must face it."

"It is a dishonour to her to be buried by Edward," said Robin. "Could Edward have locked up a will for twenty-eight years? And then unlocked it? That is the climax! Sophia and he were of a different stuff."

"Andrew, I thought you would want to arrange some things with me," said Edward. "And I hope that, apart from that, you won't object to seeing me as a friend?"

"We are very glad to see you as a friend," said Andrew, "and grateful to you for coming. Here are the three of us, all wanting friends!"

"Is everything all over the village, Edward?" said Dinah.

"Yes, I fear it is, Dinah," said Edward.

"Do Gilbert and Caroline know?" said Robin.

"No, I think not as yet," said Edward. "It would be difficult to talk to them about it, as their mother is involved."

"Yes. People would need something to prevent them," said Robin.

"Don't let me annoy you, Robin," said Edward. "I would not for the world to-day. I will settle what I have to with Andrew, and say good-bye."

"We have another telling in front of us," said Dinah. "We can hardly leave Caroline and Gilbert to hear the truth from people who find their mother's being involved an obstacle to discussing it. Such falseness of front could not augur well."

"It is a good thing you are no longer engaged to Edward," said Robin.

"Well, she is not," said Andrew. "And Edward is a good fellow, and a kind friend."

"Well," said Dinah, when Gilbert and Caroline came; "you know that Sophia is dead, and has to have a funeral?"

"Yes," said Gilbert.

"We did not know the last," said Dinah. "Edward had to come and tell us. And you know that our engagement to Edward and Judith was broken off for a reason, though we told you it was not?"

"Yes," said Caroline. "I guessed it."

"Then go on guessing," said Dinah.

"I have guessed," said Caroline. "Shall I say? Your grandfather, Andrew Stace, was Christian's father as well as Sophia's."

"How did you know, Carrie?" said Andrew. "I hear from your voice that you have known for a long time."

"It came to me when Mother was ill," said Caroline. "She was so set on dying—it really amounted to that—without telling Christian who his father was; and she cared for most things so little. And your grandfather's being fonder of Christian than of Sophia, and leaving him the estate, and being so against their marrying! And the rumours that there once were! I felt sure of it. How has it come out?"

"How clear it is now!" said Dinah, when Andrew had told the tale. "So you guessed it, Carrie, when even Patty did not. I hope Patty is not deteriorating."

"Did you say it had all got about?" said Gilbert.

"Cousin Peter has spread it about," said Dinah. "Sophia let it out to him when she was ill."

"And he put his information to that use," said Robin.

"Oh, I see. Pride in knowing, silly trust in other people, pleasure in being a faithful friend, himself?" said Caroline.

"Yes, you see, Carrie," said Dinah. "Perhaps some day we shall come upon something that you don't see. I hope not. It would have to be a dark thing."

"And it was too much for Edward and Judith?" said Gilbert.

"Well, it hardly was," said Robin. "It brought about

what was nearly happening without it. It is an ill wind—
This is certainly a very ill one. And now we all love
Edward as a friend."

"Well," said Caroline, "it is better to love him in a way
you can, than not to love him in a way you can't."

"I suppose we keep silence for ever about Sophia's thinking she was hiding a will?" said Robin, when they were
alone.

"Yes, of course," said Andrew. "But you are not keeping
it for a moment, to say nothing of for ever."

"I am Sophia's son," said Robin.

"Yes, and some sort of a cousin of Cousin Peter's,"
said Dinah. "Keep a watch on yourself."

"I will keep the watch," said Robin.

CHAPTER X

THERE HAD SELDOM been such feeling in Moreton Edge as was stirred by the death of Sophia Stace. Sophia's spirit, with its strength and the strength of its weakness, had taken hold on the place of her birth, and tore up the soil when it went.

The prominence and pathos of her figure, the power that had been in her hands, the mysteries that shadowed the background of her life, the tragedy hanging over her house: it drew the thoughts of those who knew her, and filled the church at Moreton Edge. Not to Andrew or Christian Stace had come such a throng for his burial. It was not to come to her sons.

The two sons who had followed their mother to the grave showed nothing in their faces, as they turned their backs on it, and suddenly drew on themselves a hundred watching eyes. Patty's face, as she left the churchyard with them, showed her love and pity for them, her pride in their equal company, her conviction of the unfitness of her withholding from them her protection—and indeed, with her head at the level of Andrew's shoulders, she walked, a protecting figure—and defiance on their behalf before the thoughts of the crowd. Peter, who had stood with his gaze on their backs as long as any, now transferred it to the door of the church, from which Edward would presently emerge.

"Now, run along, Tilly and Latimer. Don't stay there, staring at me, my dear boy. Come, take to the road, Tilly. I shall be following you in a moment. Do take your eyes off me, both of you. I may be at the house almost as soon as you are."

"You had better come home with us, Father," said Latimer.

"No, no; you take your sister. Do you think this the time and place for an argument? Have you no sense of what is seemly and civilised? How do you know where I am needed most? Edward wants a word with me, as a matter of fact."

"Father wants many words with Edward," said Latimer, setting off with his head high.

"Sarah," said Julian, coming to a pause, "Cousin Peter has preferred exposure of his cravings to respectable concealment of them! What an open and manly thing! I wish I were not a slave to people's opinion of me. Can you bear to think of him, discussing things with Edward, while we are sitting in the parlour?"

"Better than waiting in front of the crowd for Edward to come out," said Sarah.

"We should not have to wait for him," said Julian. "He is emerging now. It is Cousin Peter who has had that courage. And we do not have to face the crowd. Most people have gone on. Come along, or we shall have to chase them; and that would not be suitable today, hardly respectful to Mrs. Stace's memory. Well, Bateman! Well, Edward! Are you going to the rectory? We are coming with you, to talk about it all, because we have not the resolution even to disguise our feelings, to say nothing of suppressing them."

"Yes, yes, you come on and have a talk," said Peter, pausing indulgently. "You join us in a friendly word and word about. We will all have a chat together. I have sent the young ones on. So we shall be able to straighten out things without them."

"Well, but that was not thinking of others before yourself," said Julian.

"Well, I hate all this chattering, and hobnobbing, and that is a fact," said Peter, moving his head with distaste. "If there is a thing I detest, it is all this putting of heads together, and behaving as if things were so very secret, and then sweeping them from side to side all the time.

For that is what it all amounts to. So I sent the youngsters home, to prevent them from beginning it, you know."

"Well, but who is to show that initiative then?" said Julian.

"Oh! Ha, ha! Well, I don't know, I am sure. But this whole business! It is an out-and-out ghastly thing. There is no doubt of that. It is a crushing state of affairs. I am down at heart about it. It is no good pretending I am not. Why, when it all dawned on me, the whole truth, I could have—well, anything. And those poor young people up at that house, with good Miss Patmore! I could cry to think of them. Dear Miss Patmore! She has come to a pretty pass with them now. Not that she will forsake them. We sum her up better than that. She hasn't been here for twenty-eight years, without making her mark, hasn't Miss Patmore. And what I feel about them, is that I would give anything to help them to realise that I feel the same to them." Peter brought the fist of one hand down on the palm of the other. "That it hasn't made the shadow of a breach; that I am just as much their uncle, their cousin, as if none of it had happened. That is what I should like to make them believe."

"They must know it about any one who cares for them," said Sarah.

"Yes, that is what I hope, Sarah," said Edward.

"Yes, but I should like to say it to their faces," said Peter, encouraged in this line by precedent. "It would cheer me to shout it aloud to all the world."

"Oh, I should not say it either of those ways," said Julian, as he opened the rectory gate.

"Why, what have you all come for?" said Judith, coming into her drawing-room to greet them.

"Oh, just to have a neighbourly chat, after all this shattering confusion," said Peter, throwing up his feet as he walked in. "Because it has been a saddening business. If it had been only the end of Sophia—the death of my cousin Sophia, just that, it wouldn't have been so bad—it would have been trouble enough; it would indeed. But it wouldn't have been on this scale. I can't bring myself to speak of it. It isn't a thing one can put into words; all this being related in that degree; a brother and sister marrying; and their children finding it out in the way they did! Having that come on them! Poor young things! My heart aches for them."

"Do Tilly and Latimer know?" said Judith.

"Not yet, I am thankful to say. So far I have contrived to keep it from them. But they will know soon enough. People will attend to their duty there."

"I hope people will see to their knowing as well," said Edward, "that our breaking our engagement had nothing to do with the discovery; that it simply came about in the natural way by itself."

"And was a tremendous relief all round," said Judith. "To all four of us. I expect each one of us thinks he or she has the greatest relief."

"I do admire you and Judith for having such definite personalities, that things have to be broken," said Julian. "Sarah and I would always be married, if we were going to be."

"Well, I am glad to hear what you say, Edward," said Peter, twisting his moustache. "It gives me a personal relief. Because it would have upset me if the trouble had been the cause of the change. I admit it would. But as it is, it doesn't matter. I mean, all of you will soon find somebody else better, other people more suited to you—"

"I know you all think Andrew and Dinah will," said Judith.

"I am sure Dinah will," said Edward. "I trust indeed that she will."

"Well, I must be going," said Peter. "Well, we haven't had much of a talk. But then it isn't a thing that can be discussed. One can't chatter about it, and try to make it a subject of conversation. I dread the time when I tell Tilly and Latimer. I tell you I am afraid of it. Not a word

211

have I said to them. They may have noticed that I was a little down and out. Oh, well, ha! I never was one to show much of my feelings. But happily they have a good deal to fill their minds just now."

"Have they? But how out of keeping of them!" said Julian.

"Yes, yes, so it does seem in a manner," said Peter. "But they don't mean to show that attitude. When they hear of this, they will be too knocked in a heap to give a thought to anything that concerns themselves; to Tilly's marrying or Latimer's opening in business, or anything. I assure you they will."

"Oh, what about it all?" said Julian. "Are they going to do all that more definitely than they have always been going to do it?"

"Yes. Oh, yes. Oh, all that! Yes, they are. Though I grant you we have always seen this sort of end to things. I give you so much. But I haven't had time to tell any one, not the time nor the spirit. I have been so occupied with other people's affairs, that I haven't had a thought to spare for my own. I can honestly say I have not."

Peter's claim was a just one.

"How large of you!" said Julian. "But tell me quickly whom Tilly is going to marry, and about Latimer's business. I could not make Sarah look foolish by taking no notice of a sign from her. And are they obliged to marry and go into business at the same time? Does everything have to be double in this village? Have they sworn to do everything together? Sarah and I have, and I am sure Dinah and Andrew have."

"No, no, not exactly. But it fits in like that. You see, the little man in the house near the church, the corner house, with the office on the ground floor, you know; the little house-agent; he isn't such a bad little fellow; and they haven't had many advantages, poor children! They are doing all I can expect for them, I think. But I don't feel inclined to throw my hat up about it. I confess that I don't."

"Well, but is he marrying Tilly, or putting Latimer into business?" said Julian. "Taking Latimer into business for Tilly's sake?"

"Well, as a matter of fact, it is something along that line," said Peter. "He is giving Latimer a kind of partnership, apprenticeship sort of thing; more the one than the other, I am afraid. And it is because of Tilly in a way, of course. Tilly didn't feel she could look so much higher, you know. But he wants Latimer for himself. Oh, yes, he does."

"Well, we never know to whom it may fall to do great things," said Julian. "So this is the solution of the two problems of the village."

"Yes, yes. So it is. So they have been. We have had great indulgence from you all. I must acknowledge it. Ha, ha! Poor little Tilly! Poor little Latimer! They haven't done anything much. But they haven't had much of a helping hand. I couldn't do more than I could for them."

"Are Tilly and Latimer very happy?" asked Judith.

"Oh, well, they are content. They don't think they could have done any better. They didn't expect to run up the ladder a great way. I don't say but that Tilly would have put her choice on any one of you, some one else, you know. But it didn't come round her corner; and she didn't see that it would. So she has taken what she could get, and settled down to it, brave little woman! I admire her. And as for Latimer, well, so has he, poor boy! Well, it has been a melancholy day for all of us."

Peter's voice rose at the last words.

"Well, I must go and call on Dinah," said Julian to his sister, as they went home. "She has tried Gilbert and tried Edward. Surely I come next. I think I must, now that Latimer is apprenticed to a house-agent. I don't mean to suggest anything. You know I never do imply those things."

"Well, here is the house," said Sarah. "I will go on alone."

"Dinah," said Julian, "first, I have a crushing thing to say to you. Your family is not engrossing the thoughts of the neighbourhood. Tilly is going to be married, and Latimer is going into business."

"Are they really?" said Dinah.

"That is what every one asks," said Julian. "You are in no way different from other people, though you may be priding yourself on a lot apart. And I do recognise it and respect you for it. Secondly, I want to ask you what cheque for Tilly's wedding present would be thought generous. It will be equally between Sarah and me, but people may think I give the most. And thirdly, do you think we ought to congratulate Latimer on going into business, or behave as if he were already in business or above it? And fourthly, I must ask you to marry me, Dinah. If you can't leave Andrew, I might give Sarah to him; and if you do not love me, you know that respect is the best foundation; and you must have that for me, after my bringing myself to be a successor to Edward."

"About Latimer," said Dinah, after a moment of looking at him, "I should just refer to the business, and then treat him as almost more than an equal; no, as exactly and carelessly an equal. About Tilly's cheque, I must first know your income. Andrew and I have always been curious about it."

"Yes; and that means you will accept me," said Julian. "Because telling one's income goes with that settlement."

"Julian," said Dinah, "I know you have wanted to marry me almost as much as you have not wanted to; and it is kind of you to try to choose it now, with things as they are, and you are yourself as you are. And I like you to be as you are; and I need kindness now. But it would spoil you to be joined with this. It is not your kind of thing. I could only share it with Andrew, who has to share it with me, who has shared so many things with me, worse than this is to us."

"Dinah, are you refusing me?" said Julian. "If so, I shall not make known to you what my means are."

"You are always at your best, jesting," said Dinah; "and you have been today."

"Andrew," said Julian, as the brothers came in, "Dinah has rejected me, but not without trying to probe my circumstances. But I was too much for her. If it got known that they are just a little less good than people think, I should really seem like an ordinary person. But I have told you nothing. And I shall go home and discuss you with Sarah."

"You have been doing that," said Andrew.

"No, we have not," said Julian. "We have only been talking about your family, and about its being rather condensed a little way back; and how much money there will be after the death duties, and in what proportion it goes to the three of you; and whether you are more upset or relieved by your mother's death; and whether it would be best for you to move right away from it all. But that is not discussing you."

"No. You should have really dealt with us," said Dinah. "You owed us just so much."

"Well, we have told you nothing," said Andrew.

"I know you have not," said Julian. "But I should scorn to use a pleading tone."

"Well, we are thinking of a simple, open escape," said Andrew. "Of giving up the struggle here, with death duties and everything, and shaking the dust of Moreton Edge off our feet; that is, of running away from it, and seeking cover in London, where it is easiest to keep it."

"Well, shaking off the dust from anywhere is generally something like that," said Julian.

"Hardly something like this," said Dinah.

"Oh, Julian admits it," said Andrew.

"Andrew and Dinah are coming to London to find me out, Julian," said Robin.

"Oh, are any more things going to be found out?" said Julian.

"We fear not," said Andrew. "We find that Robin's London life has nothing to conceal."

"Oh, and I have envied it so," said Julian. "I have wondered how it was I could do nothing with mine. I believe even Sarah's has been better; worse, I mean. I know she gossips with her friends, and even advises them sometimes, things I so seldom do. I must go home now, to arrange about the party."

"What party?" said Andrew.

"The farewell party we are having before we leave for good," said Julian.

"Are you and Sarah giving it?" said Andrew.

"Andrew," said Julian, "you would not think of giving a party, with your mother just taken, would you? Of course Sarah and I are giving it."

"I did not know there was to be a party," said Robin.

"No, your thoughts would have been on other things," said Julian; "though I know London is heartless."

"How long have you decided to give it?" said Dinah. "Since we said we were going to London?"

"No, Dinah. You are egotistic," said Julian. "I knew troubles were not ennobling. Since I planned that Sarah and I would go too, some moments later. We should not give a party just to make up for your going."

"Will Sarah want the party?" said Robin.

"Yes, of course she will. Any one would want a party," said Julian.

"Will she want to settle in London?" said Dinah.

"Yes, of course," said Julian; "with the three of you gone from here, and Tilly married, and Latimer gone into business, and all the atmosphere of the place so different. She could not stay."

"Tilly married and Latimer gone into business?" said Robin.

"Yes. I will leave you, for that to take your thoughts off yourselves," said Julian. "It has already wrested the attention of Moreton Edge from you. I told that to Dinah; and when she rejected me, I was glad I had told her something of that nature. I must go home to see about the party's

216

being a simple one, to be in keeping with the parlour, and with your bereavement; though I don't mean that was a second thought. But I do want to be loyal to the parlour to the last."

"You had better leave us out," said Robin, "to be loyal to the size of the parlour, and to the desire of your guests to talk about us."

"We will not be passed over," said Andrew. "We need not foster that desire. It will flourish without our help. We will be the people least left out. We will give the party, if Julian will let us. It is only to old friends and relatives."

"Oh, I am quite big enough for that," said Julian, as he went. "That will be best for us all, and so healthy-minded of you."

"It will make all the difference to us, to have Sarah and Julian in London," said Andrew.

"It will bring our story with us," said Robin. "Did Julian make a jest of proposing to you, Dinah?"

"Yes. He gives us heart by his own tried methods," said Dinah. "No one would bring our story less than he and Sarah."

"You will learn a good deal in London," said Robin.

"Well, I am glad that London has something to offer us," said Dinah; "and relieved to see you yourself again, and cultivating pride in your life there. Learning is something, even if not a congenial thing. And it sounds as if you had come across some wickedness after all."

Julian went up the drive of the Black Lodge.

"Caroline, I have come in without knocking, to show the last intimacy; and to be equal to Gilbert, who has begun stepping into the parlour in that manner. You and I will be very lonely, if Sarah goes on permitting this in him. And you cannot marry Andrew, because you are his aunt. I am saying that to bring things home to you, and to show you my worst meanness, which is fair. And I cannot marry Dinah, because she has refused me. I am telling you that, for you to know all my history. That is the whole of it. I will not keep even the worst from you. I know I am no better than a woman, and how dreadful it will be to you. And I will not even tell you, that I proposed to Dinah because everything was due to her at this time, and so I did it, though I knew it would be of no good; because a true man would always avoid such an admission. And I think we had better be engaged before the Staces' farewell party, because the engagement of more brothers and sisters would be best glossed over on an occasion when people have no attention to spare from being just to themselves. We shall have to live in London, because Andrew and Dinah must have some friends; and if we stayed here, it would be our duty to take the Manor from Andrew, and we could not afford that."

"Oh, no, we could not," said Caroline.

"No," said Julian. "That is the best form of acceptance I have ever heard—heard of, I mean. Just to begin to discuss ways and means in a practical spirit. You won't expect me to have a coldness with Sarah, will you? I know you would not allow it. I won't expect you to have one with Gilbert, but I will not refuse my leave."

"Is Cousin Peter to be at the party, or is it to be just a gathering of young people?" said Caroline.

Cousin Peter was at the party, though it was to be as Caroline described. He came in, walking after Tilly and Latimer, with his chest a little expanded.

"Well, do you know, Tilly and Latimer didn't want me to come? How do you do, Dinah, my dear? It is good of you to have a welcome for three of us, to open your doors to any one at all. Well, do you understand that Tilly and Latimer tried to persuade me to stay at home? Tried to put that part on their father? That is a fact. It was a party of young people, they said. 'Well, I will tell you, you little buttons of a boy and girl,' I said, 'that I feel as young as any of you; that I am as up to things as either of you, with your old-fashioned ways.' I said something of that description to them. And then they dropped it, about its being something I was not fit for. Well, there is a nice son and daughter for you! What do you think of them?"

"I think it is generous of you, not to be too bitter to speak of it," said Robin.

"Well, I did feel rather in that mood. I felt things were a bit too much at the moment, I don't disguise from you. To be told that I couldn't join a youthful gathering, as if I were a damper and a wet blanket and I don't know what!"

"Well, but you weren't asked, Father," said Tilly, in a tone of final and hopeless reiteration.

"Not asked? Well, that didn't matter. They expected me to come. Of course Dinah wrote to you, you self-important midget, you! I shall be glad when you go off with your little man, and leave me to get my own notes. Well, here is a beautiful group of boys and girls, of brothers and sisters—and everything! Well, what I trust is, that you will some of you come together again, in some way we can't see. I can't help looking forward to it."

"I think we have had enough of such experience," said Robin. "The methods of parting chosen by Fate are so drastic."

"Well, yes, I can't contradict you there," said Peter. "But—"

"Are we not being heroic?" said Andrew. "To be simply moving amongst our old friends in the old way?"

"Yes, yes, I think you are being heroic," said Peter. "I declare you are. To be able to hold your heads up, and look people in the face—I mean that I agree that you are heroes. I, for one, am prepared to say so. What are you fidgeting and sniggering for, Tilly and Latimer? You know I didn't mean to make a joke. Whatever I had in my mind, I didn't intend that."

"Then that is your excuse," muttered Latimer.

"Well, to think of your all going to London, and leaving me and Latimer and Tilly!" said Peter, in the tone of one simply choosing safe ground. "Well, I can't bring myself

219

to look at it. But I am glad for you, that you are going to get free from all the trouble. I don't mean there is anything to run away from. I just mean that I am happy to feel you are going on, and starting afresh, and escaping from it all; though it is only love and regret and friendship that you will leave behind. I could almost wish Tilly was going too, and not going to live and marry and grow old and die all in the same place."

"You are heartless, Father," said Tilly.

"Heartless? Oh, without a heart, am I? That comes well from you, when you wanted to come away and leave me alone at home. Heartless! I should like to know to whom that word belongs."

"Oh, Father, when I am leaving you so soon!" said Tilly.

"Leaving me so soon! So you are, my little girl! And I shall fret for you and miss you every hour of the day. I shan't be the same man without you. And as for wishing that you were going to London, why, I should break my heart if you went."

"You will have to look after your father now," said Judith to Latimer.

"Yes, I shall," said Latimer, his tone implying that the office would not be a nominal one.

"Yes, he will, the dear boy! He will," said Peter, stroking his chin.

"When is Tilly going to be married?" said Julian. "Because we can't leave Moreton Edge before Tilly's marriage."

"Why not?" said Tilly's father. "Oh—I mean you could come back for it."

"We might not return," said Julian. "London might have got a hold on us, and killed our remembrance of our old life. And who can know about just impediments, if not Tilly's old companions—not know about them, I mean?"

"Oh, there are no obstacles in Tilly's family, nothing in

either hers or the man's," said Peter. "We are free of that. There is nothing of any of it there."

There was a pause.

"I am glad I am leaving the neighbourhood," said Julian to Andrew; "because Sarah finds sudden plans a strain."

"You had better say you would like cheques for wedding presents, Tilly," said Judith. "Then we shall all vie with each other in generosity."

"I would rather have things," said Tilly.

"That is rash, with so many households moving," said Gilbert.

"I'll stake my oath that she would," said Peter, in a loud voice of covering up his latest work. "She would rather have any old thing, that reminded her of any of you, than anything else in the range of possibility. I can say that without a shadow of doubt. Why, I'll be bound she would have chosen any one of you before her little man, if she could have. Wouldn't you, Tilly?"

"Well, I don't know now," said Tilly, as if loyalty must at this stage forbid this attitude.

Latimer looked as if it would be no good to sigh.

"Will you like your new work, Latimer?" said Sarah.

"No," said Latimer.

"Why not?" said Edward.

"There is nothing to like about it," said Latimer.

"Isn't there? But you will be working with your brother-in-law," said Judith.

"That is Tilly's fault, not mine," said Latimer.

"Oh, Latimer is down about it now," said Peter. "But he will get on. He and Tilly's man will turn out the best men at their job in the county. I lay it down that they will, even though they may seem a pair of funny little fellows now."

Every one avoided catching Latimer's expression, though with no need, as he did not wear one.

"Well, talking of brothers-in-law, I have a confession to make," said Edward. "I am about to possess one myself.

221

As Latimer would say, it is Judith's fault, not mine. She has been away on a visit, and this is the result."

"Well, I don't know why it is a confession," said Judith.

"Judith, dear, we do all congratulate you," said Sarah.

"I don't congratulate you yet, Judith. I have not thought yet of my congratulation," said Julian.

"You know it's an extraordinary thing, this gulf between people's opportunities," said Peter, in a tone of philosophic comment on life. "It comes of the difference in everything to do with them. That is what separates people, it seems to me, that some have chances and some have not."

"Well, is that a congratulation?" said Judith.

"It was meant to be, Miss Dryden. It was meant to be," said Peter, in a strong voice. "It was said in that spirit, indeed."

"All the same, it is of no help to me," said Julian.

"My congratulation is to Edward's brother-in-law," said Andrew. "I hope to Judith, but anyhow to him."

"I am jealous of that, Andrew," said Julian. "I am going to give it up."

"Why not say simply that you congratulate me?" said Judith.

"No, that was not my idea," said Julian. "I don't want to do it without some little touch of my own."

"I congratulate you, Judith. That is my little touch," said Latimer.

"You saucy little fellow! Judith, indeed!" said Peter.

"Tilly, you haven't congratulated Judith," said Sarah.

"Neither have Gilbert, or Robin, or Father really," said Tilly. "Julian has of course, really. She doesn't mind about me. I know it will be lovely to see her wedding after mine."

"Oh, you shall have the most beautiful wedding, Tilly," said her father. "Every one will be here for it; and it shall be the best wedding that the county—that the village has ever seen. Whatever comes after it, you shall have that."

"It will be hard on mine to follow it," said Judith. "But we shan't worry much about our wedding."

"It is clear that you will have the things that come after it," said Latimer. "I felicitate you again." He glanced at his father.

"Oh, how dreadful it will be without you all!" said Tilly, using no arts, in referring to her future.

"Yes, won't it?" said Julian. "I can't think how you will bear it."

"I shall not bear it long," said Latimer.

"You speak darkly, Latimer," said Andrew.

"I do well to utter dark things," said Latimer.

"Oh, I don't believe he will bear it long," said Peter, after a dubious look at his son. "I prophesy that he will get on in his profession, and leave Moreton Edge, and follow you all to London. That is what I foretell."

"Profession!" said Latimer.

"Well, anyhow an extra on what Andrew will have," said Dinah. "He and I will live for ourselves in empty idleness. That sounds so bad, and is so good."

"And very much the opposite life from any you have known!" said Peter. "I don't imply anything. I know you were not supposed to be living one so very different. But I shall be thankful to have you all choosing for yourselves, for a change. I can't try to disguise that I shall."

"Oh, he has tried," said Dinah to Julian.

"We shall not all be able to lead the good life," said Gilbert. "Some of us have come to an end of it. Here are you all so absorbed in Tilly's wedding; and we are wanting you to spare a little interest for Caroline's wedding to Julian, and Sarah's to me! We want them to be a success as well as Tilly's."

There was silence.

"Well, no one else does," said Caroline.

"We must not think them as important as Tilly's," said Julian. "Tilly's marriage has been much to Moreton Edge for a long time."

"Ha, ha! Much to Moreton Edge!" said Peter. "Little Tilly! She has left her impression. So she has. But about this, it is good to hear, Gilbert. It is excellent news indeed. I don't think I could have asked for better, if it could have been something to do with my own family."

"You would not ask for it, then," said Latimer.

"No, no; we must take our own affairs as they come," said Peter, smoothing his hands down the sides of his head.

Latimer looked as if his grin were a comfort to him.

"I wonder why being engaged to be married makes people feel guilty. Oh, great felicitations to you all," said Judith, her choice of word sending Latimer's eyes to the ground.

"Well, there are reasons in this case," said Peter. "I mean—what I mean is, I am rejoiced that you have pulled up again, some of you, and are forging on ahead."

"You talk too much, Father," said Latimer.

"Oh, so I am a chatterer, am I? Well, you are not, are you? It doesn't run in the family. It might be as well to hear that little pipe of yours sometimes."

"Well, you have just heard it," said Latimer.

"Oh, have I?" said Peter, not troubling to proceed on this line. "Well, you know, it's an astonishing thing, all these marriages at once. Three or four, isn't it? Four, with Tilly's."

"Yes, four with Tilly's," said Dinah. "Of the two last, all we can say is, that things are as they always should have been."

"Ah, that is generous, Dinah, very generous," said Peter, coming to a stop under the eye of his son.

"I think it is nice to think of Andrew and Dinah and Robin being always together," said Tilly.

"So it is, Tilly, so it is," said Peter. "There is a lot left for them."

"I used to think that was quite the best plan for brothers and sisters," said Judith. "But I am sinking to the level of changing my mind."

"What was Judith's level before she began to sink?" Latimer said to Julian.

But Julian happened not to hear, and Latimer desisted from lack of heart.

"People have managed both states in our family," said Robin.

"Robin, don't be so full of dreadful pride," said Julian.

"It is bound to take us in that way," said Andrew.

"Yes, it is, poor children! Yes, it is," said Peter.

"Father you had better come home," said Latimer.

"Oh, you thought I had better not start at all, didn't you? I know you decided home was the place for me. I had better take you there, you snarling snippet! People must have had enough of your phiz and squeak. Well, good-bye, Dinah. And wherever you are, my heart is with you. You will never be in doubt of that. Wheresoever you go, I shall feel the same to you. Whatever comes of anything—"

"Well, but isn't it rather soon for this loyal farewell?" said Robin. "We are not going at the minute."

"Not until after Tilly's wedding, and the date of that is not settled yet," said Dinah.

"No, well, but I seem to fancy that you are going at once," said Peter, throwing back his head. "I have a feeling that things will not be the same after to-night. And I don't prepare my speeches, because they come straight from my heart. And one can't say a thing like that too soon, for it might never come out at all. We shall all be agog with Tilly's wedding, and be thinking of nothing else. So this is what I feel, if I never get moved to say it again."

"Well, we shall have no more orations from Cousin Peter. He has promised," said Dinah. "Now we ought to say that we don't prepare our own, because they come straight from our heart. But we are not as clever as Cousin Peter; so you must wait."

"I filled Latimer's glass with wine because Cousin Peter does not drink it," said Gilbert, speaking hurriedly. "He might have thought we connected him with his father."

"We must have him often to stay in London," said Caroline.

"Do our family disadvantages admit of Latimer as an extra?" said Robin. "If Julian can carry him off as a guest in London, I shall think him worthy of you, Caroline."

"I am worthy," said Julian. "But I have not been worthy of any one to-night."

"Oh, we all came to-night to be unworthy," said Caroline.

"Dinah, let me have a word with you," said Julian. "You see, I have always been regarded as such a charming young man. And suppose my charm is not of a kind that survives youth! I supposed it. And marriage seems to excuse a lack of charm; though of course I agree that nothing ought to excuse it. And Sarah feels she would be nothing without me. I can't help her feeling it. And women seem to marry not to feel nothing. So you understand about us both."

"Yes, I understand," said Dinah.

"Well, Sarah," Julian said, when they had parted from the Langs at their home, "I hope our essential ordinariness will be better hidden in London. It is not any longer adequately disguised here. I mean our commonplace wish to settle, and our being engaged to just the people we happen to be thrown with. It is no excuse, that it is difficult to be engaged to any one else. I don't see how Andrew and Dinah can think of us as ourselves again, after they have seen us marry without being swept away by feeling, though they couldn't if they had seen us. I wish I had talked in my own strain like this at the party. It wasn't any good my having a strain. And my hardly caring whether I marry Dinah or Caroline, is so like what one discovers about one's friends. It is better to be in London while it leaks out. And it was Caroline I wanted most to marry, because of the greater cloud on Dinah's family. That is the sort of mind I am going to hide in London."

"Well, there are many there," said Sarah. "You will not reveal what you have just said to Caroline?"

"Oh, I shall not bring things out in later years, that I am silent about now," said Julian. "I am not quite so ordinary. The way I feel to Andrew and Dinah shows that I am not all commonplace. I hardly even envy them their credit for behaving well in tragedy; though tragedy is by far the best background, and every one behaves well in it; it is so worth while."

Sarah did not answer, and Julian hurried on.

"Sarah, when we feel that a double marriage makes an impossible relation; and you can't help noticing how much less well shaped my head is than Gilbert's, and it will be no good to try to avoid it; and I say you are much less capable a manager than Caroline, because I may use words like capable and manager by then; still, we shall always get away together, and talk in our own way?"

"You mean you will talk and I shall listen?" said Sarah.

"Yes, that is what I mean," said Julian.

"Julian, I believe you are all things to every one," said Sarah.

"Do you really think I am?" said Julian. "I have tried so hard lately to be that. It is as much as any one could be?"

"I mean to Dinah and Caroline and me," said Sarah.

"Well, that is every one," said Julian. "I see we shall always talk in our way."

"That is the best of not being capable of a real romance," said Sarah.

"Yes," said Julian. "We understand each other. How seldom that can be said of two human beings! If in the future I don't dare to say it, remember that I have said it."

Andrew shut the door after his guests.

"How did you feel when the news fell, Dinah?" he said.

"As you did," said Dinah. "For a moment as if I were unbelievably wronged. The next, as if I had always known it, what is involved in it. That Julian was anxious to settle down. He should not care about it, not Julian. I see he feels he should not, and that shows how he really does. Of course Gilbert has always openly and naturally wanted it. And that Sarah and Caroline did not care to be spinsters. I know

227

we are troubled about our own relation to the conventions; but we have an unassailable ground. Our courage at the moment will always be a thing to look back upon with heartache; and compassion for oneself is so real. We can't pass it on to Latimer, because now he is to live alone with Cousin Peter, it would be serious for him. How we miss Sophia! She would know how to sum things up."

"We are getting to exaggerate the virtues of Sophia," said Robin.

"Only her uses," said Dinah. "We must enhance something about her. People always do about the dead, and we could not deny a common office to Sophia."

"Shall we be able to bear the spectacle of all our best friends normal and prosperous and married to each other?" said Andrew. "Can we be so great?"

"We need not be quite," said Dinah. "We shall have some comfort. Cousin Peter will find a great difference here, now that he is not to be related to the Manor. And Tilly will simply have to be happy in her own way. And she did so want to be happy in other people's. She knew it was the only bearable way. Tilly found out so much. And Latimer will have to share our greatness, and no other of our advantages. And not even Latimer would make that choice. And Sophia lived and died, without ever finding out that her name meant Wisdom."

"We have much to be thankful for," said Andrew.

"We shall have to realise our position," said Robin.

"It is the only thing I have done for some time," said Andrew.

"Yes. Things like losing Sophia have been side issues," said Dinah. "Robin is even more fortunate than he generally is. He has managed what no one else in the neighbourhood has."

"I mean, we must learn how to deal with it," said Robin.

"I wish it could be dealt with," said Dinah. "It would have to be much better than it is."

"We never have any precedent to help us," said Andrew.

"Every one else would have hidden this," said Dinah. "We ought to have followed the only one there could be. But of course we did not."

"Shall we ever be able to marry?" said Robin.

"We could declare it, or else for ever hold our peace," said Andrew. "I think we have the right of choice."

"You would use yours to declare it," said Robin.

"You and I will be wedded to each other, Andrew," said Dinah. "That sounds dubiously in accordance with family traditions. But Robin will marry, and you and I will give our lives to keeping the family secret for his sake. Robin is the most like Sophia, and has the right to survive."

"I am not the survivor Sophia would have chosen," said Robin.

"No. Sophia never had her way in things that mattered," said Andrew.

"Her children take after her," said Robin. "Shall you mind leaving the Manor, Andrew?"

"Yes," said Andrew. "After seeing my youth wasted, and my life several times blasted in it, my parents cut off in their prime, and our family unspeakably besmirched in it, I can hardly tear myself from its walls. But of course I want to leave it."

"I feel all that," said Dinah. "The desire to leave as well. But we will take Grandfather's portrait with us, and carry our wasted youth and blasted lives, Father and Sophia, and everything, including the besmirching. It is all in him."

"People may ask who he is," said Andrew.

"Well, we can say he is our grandfather," said Dinah. "When they ask which grandfather, we cannot answer what is not the case."

"People will know us too well or too little, to ask," said Robin. "Well, Patty, come and decide the fate of Grandfather's portrait."

"Oh, I should leave it here, as you are leaving some of the things," said Patty, her tone not separating this object from any others. "Nobody will worry about it."

"Patty, how much more understanding of life you have than we have!" said Dinah. "Our views of Grandfather have got somehow warped. He has only twice his normal significance."

"Well, what do you say to all that is threatening, Patty?" said Robin.

"It does seem as if it ought not to happen, doesn't it?" said Patty, from a position of knowledge. "And as if we might have suspected it. I wonder what Mother would think. She would say it was absurd for the engagements to be double again. I am sure she would say that."

"Yes, let us push it into the shade of the ridiculous," said Dinah. "Sophia decides. We have put such absurdity behind us twice. We can feel in advance of it now."

"How has it all been to-night?" said Patty.

"Oh, a success, Patty," said Andrew. "That is, we have been the only people to endure anything worth mentioning; for I know you don't think Latimer's suffering calls for a word. And good hosts mind nothing but discomfort for their guests, nothing like consuming inner bitterness and self-pity."

"Cousin Peter was himself in the enhanced way he has been since Sophia died," said Robin. "Sophia's influence on him was all for good."

"We should have had to flee from him, anyhow," said Dinah. "On the ground alone of his escape from control, we could not remain here. Sophia should have left us directions about this menace on our orphanhood. Our parentage pales, as a slur, before this cousinship."

"I believe he treats us unconsciously as people under a cloud," said Robin.

"Consciously and openly," said Dinah. "I don't need to believe it. I observed it."

"The engaged people were enough not themselves, to show that their marriages may be a fair success," said Andrew. "Even from them I see that we were never engaged at heart. We have been the selves our experience has made us."

"They have," said Robin.

"Oh, well, things are over now," said Patty. "We shall be off to London, to start afresh. Well, anyhow it will be a change." Her voice betrayed the craving of years, and the young faces fell and brightened at the thought of it, and its being satisfied. "Well, there is one thing. Moreton Edge will find it very strange to have new people at the Manor." Patty seemed to end on a note of triumph; but Moreton Edge, what was left of it, as we know it, took the strangeness in its own way.

"Well, Latimer," said Peter, on the night of Tilly's wedding, "well, the next thing now will be this fresh family at the big house. Well, that is something to look forward to. That will be a lift-up, after all this flatness of losing everybody, and coming to the end of everything. That will be a thing to have in our eye, so to speak. Because it will make a difference. It will make a complete upheaval in the place, in its atmosphere, in its daily round. There have been Staces there for I don't know how many generations. It will quite mean a new life for us. People have to get to know their doctor."

"Yes. They will not be able to help it," said Latimer.

IVY WHEN YOUNG
The Early Life of Ivy Compton-Burnett 1884-1919
Hilary Spurling

Hilary Spurling's brilliant biography covers the first thirty-five years of Ivy Compton-Burnett's life, revealing a series of events almost stranger than fiction, and shows how she later used these experiences in her novels.

"One of the most distinguished biographies of our time" — *Sunday Telegraph*

"A definitive work" — C.P. Snow, *Financial Times*

"A story of extraordinary fascination and drama" — Anthony Powell

IVY AND STEVIE
Ivy Compton-Burnett and Stevie Smith
Conversations and reflections by Kay Dick

"We must be grateful for these two portraits, since they are so sharp, so well judged, and to my knowledge, so right" — Pamela Hansford Johnson, *The Sunday Times*

"What is delightful is the kind permission extended to the reader, in each case, to overhear Miss Dick and her legendary companions nonchalantly taking tea" — *The Times*

"Beyond their published and signed work, something of the essence of these two strange and gifted women has been conserved for the future" — Anthony Thwaite, *New Statesman*